LOVE AIN'T FOR KEEPING

JONATHAN CULLEN

LIQUIDMINDPUBLISHING

All rights reserved. No part of this book may be reproduced, distributed, or transmitted in any form or by any means, including photocopying, recording, or other electronic or mechanical methods, without the prior written permission of the author, except in the case of brief quotations embodied in critical reviews and certain other noncommercial uses permitted by copyright law.

Copyright © 2023 by Jonathan Cullen

www.jonathancullen.com

Liquid Mind Publishing

liquidmindpublishing.com

This is a work of fiction. Any resemblance to actual persons, living or dead, or actual events is purely coincidental.

ALSO BY JONATHAN CULLEN

The Days of War Series

The Last Happy Summer

Nighttime Passes, Morning Comes

Onward to Eden (Coming Soon)

Shadows of Our Time Collection

The Storm Beyond the Tides

Sunsets Never Wait

Bermuda Blue

The Jody Brae Mystery Series

Whiskey Point

City of Small Kingdoms

The Polish Triangle

Love Ain't For Keeping

Sign up for Jonathan's newsletter for updates on deals and new releases!

https://liquidmind.media/j-cullen-newsletter-sign-up-1/

CHAPTER 1

March 1972

In Boston, St. Patrick's Day never lasted just one day. It started weeks before, the anticipation of a holiday that, for a city dominated by the Irish for over a century, held an almost mystical significance. Most people didn't know what it meant, but everyone felt obligated to honor it. In the greenest neighborhoods, South Boston, Charlestown, and Mission Hill, the Irish tricolor hung from porches and doorways; shamrocks were taped to the windows of corner shops, delis, and social clubs.

It didn't become official until the infamous Mayor, James Michael Curley, made it one. In a snub at the Protestant establishment that controlled the banks and industry, he scoured the history books for any reason to make March 17th a public holiday. And he found one, a factually true but historically minor Revolutionary War event. On a cold night, George Washington's men dragged cannons to the highest point in South Boston, forcing the British to finally withdraw from the city. So it was no small irony that when a call came over the radio that night, it was to that very spot.

Any available detectives to Thomas Park. Possible homicide.

Waiting at the light, I felt the same dread all cops got when something happened right before their shift ended. I glanced at my watch, and it was ten to midnight. The only reason we were even working late was that the department was short-staffed.

"Shall I put on the siren?" Harrigan asked.

"You mean *hit the siren?*"

"I never hit anything without provocation."

When I looked over, he made a subtle grin. He sat with his hands in his pockets and his collar upturned. His dark skin glistened, a sign of the weariness we both now felt.

"I knew it was too quiet," I muttered.

"Never trust the silence."

"There you are, getting poetic again."

I flicked my cigarette and rolled up the window. The traffic light turned green, and I sped across the intersection of Andrew Square. Even on a Tuesday night, it was busy, people going in and out of dive bars, lingering on the slushy sidewalks.

After a long winter, much of the snow was gone, but the city still looked dreary. The roads were wrecked from the salt and plows. Turning onto Telegraph Street, we hit a pothole so big it felt like my stomach had gone into my throat.

"Have you gotten your springs checked, Lieutenant?"

"What do you know about cars?"

"Only when to have them repaired," he said. "Or when to get a new one."

I frowned, but he was right. The old Valiant was starting to show its age. The wheel wells were rusted, the seats torn at the seams. Captain Egersheim had suggested more than once that we use one of the department's newer unmarked cruisers. But I had owned the car for over a decade. It had been with me through every scrape, close call, and near-death experience. In a job that saw so much impermanence, even material things had sentimental importance.

As we came up the hill, I saw two cruisers in front of the park, their lights flashing. A small crowd had gathered, men in work jackets and women wearing coats over their nightgowns. In some parts of town, even a murder wasn't enough to get people out of their homes on a cold winter night. But South Boston was close-knit, the type of place where everyone was related and watched out for one another.

We pulled over and jumped out.

"Hey mister, did she get two in the hat?"

Stopping, I turned to see a boy about eleven or twelve with buck teeth and a trapper hat, his friend beside him on a beat-up Huffy.

"You see anything we should know about?" I asked.

They stiffened up and both shook their heads.

"Nuttin', mister."

After the Irish gang wars of the '60s, every child knew the slang of thugs and hoodlums. Many admired them too, a tragic consequence of poverty and tabloid news. When I was young, everyone feared criminals, but no one respected them. I hated to see kids so enthralled by violence.

A dozen people were standing by the entrance, two officers guarding the gate to the park.

"Is she dead?" an older woman asked.

"What makes you think it's a *she*?"

"A woman has a sense about these things."

We ran up the steps, coming out to a wide stretch of grass with walking paths and scattered lamps. As one of the highest points around, the park had an amazing view of the city and harbor. But we didn't have time to enjoy it.

"Lieutenant Brae?!"

A sergeant walked over, anxious and out of breath. He had a round head and thick mustache, his eyes bleary from the cold. I thought I recognized him—*Steve* or was it *Frank*?—but I wasn't sure. There was a time when I knew everyone on the force, but there were so many new officers now that I sometimes felt like an outsider.

"Whadda we got?" I asked.

He shook my hand and nodded at Harrigan, who never seemed to get the same reception as white cops.

"Not good."

"What's *not good*?"

"You better come see."

We followed him over to some trees. Three officers stood at the scene, talking and smoking as if they were in a locker room. One even made a wisecrack, which wasn't a surprise because they were young. Veteran cops, as cold as they could be, were never so disrespectful.

They parted as we approached, and in the overgrown weeds, I saw a dark shape. As I got closer, I realized it was a young woman. She wore blue jeans and a fur-lined suede coat, thick auburn hair pouring from the collar. With her back to us, she could have been asleep, but her posture was unnatural. Her legs were bent in different directions, one of her arms flopped behind her back.

I crouched and put my fingers to her neck, looking for a pulse although I had no doubt she was dead. Feeling something wet and sticky, I rolled her over. The sergeant shined his flashlight, and I gasped. Her throat was slit clear across, a sheet of dried blood on her neck and chest.

"Jesus Christ," I said, standing up.

"Tough place for a nap, eh detective?"

I wasn't sure which cop said it, but I gave them all a hard stare.

"Who reported this?" I asked the sergeant.

"No idea. Someone called the precinct. Said he was jogging by and thought he saw someone in the grass."

"Any ID?"

"We haven't checked. We just got here."

I glanced at Harrigan, who stood with his hands in his pockets, as still as a statue. Then I knelt and patted down the victim's coat. I had seen hundreds of dead bodies, maybe thousands if you included the war, and I always considered myself tough. But when I noticed her eyes, drooping and lifeless, my hands started to tremble.

I stood up. The sergeant had drifted over to his patrolmen like his job was over. And in many ways, it was. As a definite homicide, the death was now our responsibility.

"Was that a thorough examination?"

I turned to Harrigan.

"What?"

"It seemed rather perfunctory."

I didn't know the word, but I knew what he meant. I couldn't deny it had been a quick search, the kind of sloppy police work I would have scolded a rookie for. With a daughter at home, I got a particular dread when the victim was young and female.

"Shall I search her?" Harrigan asked.

It was clever. He knew I was too stubborn to let him.

I stooped again, my knees sinking in the damp ground. As I felt her jeans pockets, my fingers brushed her stomach, exposed by the shortness of her blouse. Her skin was cold, yet still soft enough that it felt alive.

"Don't get too friendly with her, Detective."

I got up and stormed over to the officers. This time I knew who to confront because the others looked away.

"What's your name, rookie?" I said, emphasizing *rookie*.

I stared at him, and he was cocky enough to stare back.

"Collins. I ain't no rookie, sir."

He had the beady eyes and permanent smirk of every street kid I had grown up with. With his olive complexion, I was surprised he had an Irish name. I would have expected *Santangelo* or *Papadopoulos*.

"How long have you been on the job, Collins?"

"Four years, sir."

He looked like a teenager, but I was at an age where every young person did.

"Did you have something to say?"

"It was just a joke."

His every word was tinged with sarcasm. Like any young hothead, he knew how to skirt that fine line between boldness and insubordination.

"Where's the stiff?"

Everyone turned to see Doctor Ansell coming toward us across the grass. Dressed in a long dark coat, he had a leather bag in one hand and a smoldering cigar in the other. I was glad to see him. It meant we could go home soon, and it also saved me the aggravation of having to berate the young officer.

"Doctor," I said.

"Don't *doctor* me. I should've been off at midnight."

"Join the club," one of the cops grumbled.

"At least you get overtime."

When the sergeant tried to point out the victim, Ansell waved him away and went straight to the body. After forty years as Chief Pathologist, he didn't need to be shown, informed, or directed to anything.

"Larynx laceration," I said.

"Some fancy words, Brae."

Short and stout, the doctor wore pince-nez glasses and spoke from the side of his mouth. I could have described him as old, but he had looked the same since I'd joined the force. Although he wasn't easy to get along with, when he liked you, he loved you. He was always a good guy to have on your side.

"Hold this, will ya?" he asked, handing me his cigar.

He squatted beside the victim and opened his bag. Taking out a stethoscope, he put it on her chest, a step that was unnecessary but required.

"When was this reported?"

"Call came in at 11:38," the sergeant said.

Sirens came up the hill. Lights flashed across the park. The ambulance had finally arrived.

"Brae?"

When I turned back to the doctor, he was holding something up.

"Back pocket," he said, handing me a blue wristlet.

Even in the darkness, I noticed Harrigan raise his eyes.

"I was gonna get to it," I said.

I unzipped the small bag to find a pack of Embassy Gold cigarettes, two keys on a ring, and some crumpled-up tissues. There were a few loose dollar bills and a pile of change mixed in with a nail clipper, a single stud earring, and what looked like a piece of a clasp. But there was no license or identification.

Two paramedics walked up with a stretcher.

"Nice of you two to show up," Ansell said.

One of the men was black, which in the past would have been unusual but was now more common. After the Civil Rights Act, government agencies everywhere were hiring more minorities. Some old-timers grumbled, but I had worked with Harrigan for so long that I never thought about his color.

"Let's get her suited up."

The paramedics got to work, taking out a body bag and placing the deceased inside it. Something about the darkness made it easier to watch. They loaded her onto the stretcher, her limbs bouncing with an eerie stiffness that reminded me of the dead frogs I used to see at summer camp as a boy.

"Let's do a last sweep," the sergeant said.

As his officers spread out to look for clues, he turned to me.

"Sorry about the kid," he said.

"Don't worry about it." I shrugged, pretending not to care. "He'll learn."

CHAPTER 2

We wouldn't know any more about the victim until Ansell did the autopsy. It was the tail end of winter, so I was sure he would only need a couple of days. The public morgue at Boston City Hospital was quieter in the cold months, with a lot of vagrants and elderly, but not as many murders.

We didn't expect any surprises. As gruesome as it was, a slit throat was no doubt a homicide. Other cases weren't so straightforward, such as strangulation or poisoning, and required more analysis. Still, we needed an autopsy. At the very least, it would show whether she had fought back or not, helping us to understand the nature of the attack. It might also give us clues as to the girl's identity. Without it, we would have a hard time finding the killer.

Harrigan and I drove down Blue Hill Avenue through Roxbury. The area I had grown up in was now a black ghetto. Stopped at a light, I saw some men outside a private club. They were dressed in tight jeans and platform boots, drinking from paper bags. One looked over and smiled, making me cringe. We used to be able to go everywhere undetected. Now, even in a civilian car, all the young hoods could spot us. As frustrating as it was, I admired their alertness, although I wished they had put it to better use.

"Lieutenant?"

Caught in a daydream, I didn't realize the light had turned green. The tires chirped as I hit the gas, and the men laughed and hooted, waving their arms.

I turned onto Seaver Street and stopped in front of Harrigan's building, the apartment he shared with his mother. After a long day, there wasn't much to say. We had worked together for so long that we could part without a word. Even so, I could tell something was bothering him from the extra tension around his eyes.

As he reached for the door handle, I said, "What is it?"

"Pardon?"

"You got that look."

"What look is that, Lieutenant?"

"You didn't like how I handled things."

He let go of the door.

"You seemed a bit off tonight."

"Just tired."

"We're all tired."

"I'm older than you."

In the headlights of a passing car, I noticed that his forehead was glistening.

"You feeling alright?"

"A bit of a cold, maybe."

"You gonna make it to Saturday?" I joked.

"I think I'll make it."

"Good. Tell your ma I say hello."

"She's asleep. But I'll pass it along in the morning."

"Now get outta here," I said.

With a faint smile, he opened the door and got out.

......

It was close to 2 a.m. by the time I got home. Pulling into the driveway, I turned off the engine and sat for a few minutes. The street was quiet, the houses all dark. Having spent most of my life in city apartments, I found the silence peaceful, if not a bit disturbing.

We had been living in West Roxbury for almost three years, a tidy neighborhood that bordered the suburbs. Although it was on the train and bus lines, most people drove to work. The only noise was the sound of kids playing; the only crime was an occasional car break-in.

I loved my new quiet life, but it was sometimes hard to reconcile with my job as a cop. I always felt guilty coming home late, mostly because my four-year-old daughter had gone to bed without seeing me. Beyond that, I knew I shouldn't have been working nights at this stage in my career. Most lieutenants didn't even leave headquarters. But I had never wanted to do paperwork. I only took the promotion after Captain Jackson said I could still work the streets.

After he died, Captain Egersheim let the practice continue. It was more out of necessity than to honor Jackson's promise. With a flood of retirements in the late sixties, and all the young men going to Vietnam, the department was understaffed. To get recruits, they overlooked things that only a decade before would have disqualified people. It might have explained how someone like Collins got on the force.

I walked in the door, quietly reaching for the light switch.

"Jody?"

Startled, I looked to see Ruth at the top of the stairs, her eyes sleepy and hair a mess. She had on a nightgown and cardigan sweater, her belly protruding.

"You're late," she said, but it wasn't an accusation.

"We got a call."

We used to argue about my hours. A cop's schedule was always hard on a family. But with another baby on the way, we needed the money, and the overtime helped.

"How're you feeling?" I asked.

Diagnosed with pre-eclampsia, she had been on bed rest for almost a month.

"A bit of a headache."

"How's Nessie?" I asked, taking off my coat and hanging it up.

"We played pattycakes and I read her *Make Way for Ducklings*."

I smiled, and she came down the stairs.

The kitchen light was already on when we walked inside. As safe as the neighborhood was, she still worried about burglars.

I got a box of *Hi Ho* crackers from the cabinet and milk from the refrigerator. I would have drunk it straight from the bottle, but with her there, I reached for a glass.

"There's chicken stew. I could heat it up if you'd like."

"Thanks. Why don't you get to bed?" I said gently.

"Are you coming?"

"In a little bit."

She smiled hesitantly, her arms crossed and eyes downcast. As Harrigan did with me, I could sense some uneasiness or concern. Everyone seemed to have something on their mind.

"Everything alright?"

"It's Nessie—"

When my eyes went wide, she said, "No, no, nothing's wrong. It's just that…I need some help."

"What about Nadia?"

The old Polish woman had been babysitting for us for over two years. Considering I was an orphan and Ruth's family lived three thousand miles away, she was the closest thing our daughter had to a relative. Nessie had even started calling her *babcia*, something we quickly stopped in case Ruth's mother ever came to visit.

"She's been great. But Nessie needs to be around other children. She's gonna start kindergarten next year."

I sipped the milk, wiping my mouth. Inside, I got tense, more out of fear than anger. I had always been overprotective.

"You're mad," she said.

"I'm not mad."

She followed me into the living room, and we sat down. I had a sleeve of crackers, but I didn't dare open it. Of all my sloppy habits, eating on the couch was the one she hated the most.

"What do you suggest?"

She leaned against my shoulder, tilting her head. The smell of her faded perfume was just enough to distract me. I even got aroused.

"Daycare. Just a couple of days a week. Nessie will meet friends. I'll get a break."

When she glanced at her stomach, I knew what she meant. The pregnancy had been hard, especially with pre-eclampsia. With my crazy schedule, her days were long. Having Nadia around helped, but she only came three days a week and couldn't stay past five o'clock.

Nessie had come into our lives through an investigation. The fact that she was the product of an affair between a prostitute and a priest was no shame, and it only made her more precious. For me, keeping her safe was more than an instinct, it was a mission. But I knew I couldn't hide her from the world forever.

"Okay."

Ruth beamed.

"Just until she comes," she said, rubbing her stomach.

"She?" I asked, and Ruth nodded. "What makes you think it's a girl?"

"A woman has a sense about these things."

Raising the glass, I slugged the last of my milk.

"So I've heard."

CHAPTER 3

When Harrigan and I walked into the captain's office, he was in the corner arranging his golf clubs. He had on a short-sleeved shirt and pleated pants. Golf in March *in Boston* seemed a stretch, but the weather had been getting better.

"Gentlemen," he said, so flustered he almost knocked the bag over.

Captain Egersheim was so clumsy it was funny. I had heard one official call him a dolt. Short and bald, he had a thick mustache that partially covered his tobacco-stained teeth. He walked with his head down and always seemed in a rush. And like most frantic people, he looked busy but never actually got anything done.

Watching him, I was sometimes repulsed. He was nothing like Captain Jackson, who had died four years earlier from cancer. But as incompetent as Egersheim was, he let me and Harrigan manage our own cases, which I appreciated. I realized I could only work with him after I stopped comparing him to our old boss.

"Have a seat," he said, and we did.

He sat behind his desk and reached for a folder from the stack.

"I just got the autopsy back for the *Jane Doe*."

"The girl from Southie?" I asked.

The captain squinted to read.

"Uh, yeah. Dorchester Heights, South Boston. Cause of death *massive blood loss*."

"Must have been the gash on her throat."

He looked up with a confused smile.

"I'd say so," he said, oblivious to my sarcasm.

"No other injuries?"

Egersheim shook his head.

"Blood alcohol zero. Slightly anemic." Looking at the report, he shook his head. "No ID? Any clues to her identity?"

"We were over there this morning, knocked on some doors. No one saw a thing."

He pretended to be thinking, but he had no patience for speculation or brainstorming. I was never convinced he even liked investigating murders. He had come over to Homicide from the Mounties, appointed after Jackson's death. I always suspected it was because his sister-in-law was married to the nephew of the chief, but I couldn't prove it. Like any bureaucrat, if he wasn't getting pressured about a case, he didn't put much effort into it.

"We're gonna run the prints," Egersheim said. "Check the missing persons' docket. Put your feelers out. If nothing turns up, she'll stay on ice for a while."

For all his flaws, being insensitive was not one of them. *Stay on ice* seemed harsh, so I was sure he had heard it from someone else, possibly on TV.

When he closed the file and reached for a cigarette, I knew the meeting was over.

"Yes, sir," Harrigan and I said in unison, moving to leave the room.

"Oh." He stopped us. "I need you two to work next weekend."

"You mean this weekend?"

The term had always been confusing. I never knew if *next weekend* meant the weekend coming up or the one after it.

"No. I mean *next* weekend. At the parade in South Boston."

When I glanced at Harrigan, he looked as relieved as I felt. He was getting married Saturday to his girlfriend Delilah, and Egersheim wasn't invited. Unlike Captain Jackson, who was a mentor and a friend, he was just a boss. We didn't socialize with him.

"Are we expecting a homicide?" I joked.

"The chief wants all available detectives. Everyone's gotta pitch in. We don't have the staff."

"What're we supposed to do?"

The captain gave me a sharp look —— he didn't like being questioned. Under Jackson, we never would have worked at a parade or other public event. It wasn't that it was beneath us, but it was a bad use of our time.

"Just keep an eye out. Help the beat cops if there's any trouble. With the situation in Northern Ireland, I think the chief wants to be extra cautious. Who knows? Someone might wanna make a political statement."

"And what better place than Boston?"

Egersheim made a tight smile. Although of Irish descent, he had grown up in suburban Newton and couldn't relate to the politics, prejudices, and peculiarities of the Boston Irish.

"I'll be out this afternoon," he said. "If you need me, leave a message at the front desk."

Harrigan and I left the office and went down the hallway. As we passed reception, a pretty secretary looked up smiling. In the back room, phones rang and typewriters clanked, the endless commotion of police operations.

We walked down the stairs and through the front doors.

"Who the hell plays golf in March?" I said.

"Apparently, he does."

"He can't be playing alone."

"I wouldn't be so sure."

I always envied Harrigan's understated humor, wishing I could emulate it. It would have gotten me out of a lot of trouble.

As we crossed the lot, the sun was out, the sky clear. Snow that only a month ago had covered every rooftop, awning, and overhang was starting to melt. After the winter gloom, the days were getting longer, but there was still a chill in the air.

"How's about lunch?"

When Harrigan looked at his watch, I knew it was too early. In all our years as partners, my only complaint was that we got hungry at different times.

"Could we stop by Delilah's work first?" he asked.

"She got a job?"

His girlfriend had come to Boston from Cleveland to get her Ph.D. in political science. After four years, she was finally graduating. I always thought students were slackers, so I was impressed that she was working already.

"She's running a daycare."

Surprised, I looked over.

"A daycare?"

......

When I pulled into the driveway, it was still light out, the earliest I had been home in days. Ruth met me at the door in a red apron, her belly round and full. With her hair in a bun, she looked like an ordinary housewife, but I still found her sexy.

"This is a surprise," she said.

I smiled and looked over to see Nessie on the couch.

"Daddy!" she exclaimed.

As I took off my coat, Ruth kissed me. Her parents never showed much emotion, something she blamed for her sister's depression. So she wanted Nessie to see natural displays of affection.

I walked into the living room and sat beside Nessie. Only a few months before, she would have dropped her doll and run over to greet me. Now she was more restrained with her emotions. Her babyish features were fading. She was starting to look like a little girl. When I was young, life felt eternal. I got a creeping sense that time was passing.

"How was your day?" I asked.

"Babcia made a pie."

I looked over to Ruth, who stood in the hallway with a horrified smile.

"No *babcia*," I said to Nessie. "It's Nadia."

With a pout, she repeated the word. It was hard telling a four-year-old she couldn't use nicknames.

I kissed her on the head and went into the kitchen where Ruth was stirring the pot. All winter, we ate stews. Nessie loved them and they lasted for days. Nevertheless, I was getting eager for a porkchop or steak.

"How was your day?"

I put my arm around her waist, leaning over to see what she was making.

"Quiet," I said.

"The calm before the storm?"

I frowned, but she was right. Crime always increased in the spring, including murders. Even the experts couldn't agree whether it was from the temperatures or the sunlight.

"I might've found a place for Ness," I said, and she turned. "Delilah is working at a daycare."

"Where?"

"The South End. Right near City Hospital."

"That's far."

"I could drive her."

"You sure you wouldn't mind?"

When I shook my head, she smiled, almost getting teary. Neither of us wanted to let Nessie go, but Ruth was exhausted, and I couldn't take off work.

"Thanks. Just until," she said, looking at her stomach.

"It's the right thing to do."

CHAPTER 4

THE ENTRANCE TO THE MORGUE WAS AT THE BACK OF CITY HOSPITAL, a windowless door between the loading dock and a dumpster. It once had a sign that had fallen off and was never replaced. Either way, anyone who needed to find it knew where it was.

For years, politicians had talked about updating, even relocating the facility. But no one cared about a city mortuary, so the place went overlooked while other public buildings were renovated.

There's a reason people called it *The Crypt*; even for a morgue, it was eerie. Harrigan and I went down the steps into the basement, following a corridor lined with old hospital equipment. There were wooden wheelchairs and crutches, gurneys that looked straight out of a Sherlock Holmes story. The air had a musty, oily smell. Giant boilers rumbled in the darkness beyond.

We turned at the end and came to a door. I knocked once, and moments later, it opened.

"Brae."

Doctor Ansell stood in a white smock.

"What's up, Doc?" I joked.

Frowning, he took a drag of his cigar and blew it out.

"This place is certainly Looney Tunes, but I ain't Bugs Bunny."

He waved us into his office, a large room with metal tables and filing cabinets, medical implements scattered around. There was a lab to the left, but the door was always closed.

"What can I do for you?" he asked.

"We had some questions on the *Jane Doe*."

"*Jane Doe?*"

"The murder in Southie on Tuesday night."

The fact that he had to think made the death even more tragic. But in a big city, she wasn't the only murder victim or the only unidentified body.

"Ah, right," he said, finally.

He put his cigar down in an ashtray and went toward the morgue, a large steel door that looked like the entrance to a torture chamber. When he opened it, we were hit by a rush of cold air. I blinked at the pungent stench of formaldehyde.

Inside, the plaster ceiling was cracked and covered in water stains; the walls were lined with corpse compartments. Squinting to read the labels, the doctor found the right one and opened it. As he rolled out the body, I felt a sudden dread. With a flick of his wrists, he lifted the sheet back, and I flinched.

As with all autopsies, her makeup had been removed. Still, her face was smooth white. Aside from some freckles on her forehead, there were no other blemishes, and her skin had the vague shine of plastic. To me, cadavers always looked more like mannequins than people.

"Sorry."

Ansell gave me a look of mild amusement.

"Don't worry, kid. It never gets any easier. We just learn to hide it better. Besides, he's the one sweating," he said.

I looked at Harrigan, whose forehead was glowing. He took out a handkerchief and wiped off the perspiration.

"This incision would've been a quick death," the doctor explained, pointing at the neck wound that had since been stitched up. "Right through the jugular. You couldn't stop that kind of bleeding with a vice grip."

"Any signs of a struggle?"

"Not that I could find. Doesn't mean she didn't. There just ain't no evidence for it."

"Someone surprised her," I said.

"With a damn sharp blade too."

He slid the bed back and slammed the door, the sound echoing like a tomb. We walked out, and he locked the main door. He grabbed his cigar and went over to a shelf, taking a small evidence envelope out of a box.

"She had some coins in her pants pocket," he said.

I felt Harrigan watching me, but I didn't look over. I had wavered while searching the body that night, something I was still embarrassed about.

"Thanks. We'll get them dusted."

"You might be interested in where they're from."

He held up a coin, and Harrigan and I stepped closer. On the front were the words *Fifty Pence* and a woman holding a trident and an olive branch. When I turned it over, I saw the head of Queen Elizabeth II.

"British," Harrigan muttered.

I wasn't surprised he immediately recognized it. He had spent his childhood on St. Kitts in the West Indies, which was a former British Colony.

"Maybe she was visiting relatives?"

"Perhaps she was an immigrant," Harrigan said.

The doctor took a long drag on his cigar and shrugged.

"She could be Anne Boleyn for all I know."

He handed me the coin and an envelope with the rest. Looking inside, I saw two and five-pence pieces mixed in with some nickels and dimes.

"Thanks, Doc."

"Anytime."

We walked to the door, and Ansell stopped, looking at Harrigan.

"Oh, I'm told you're tying the knot. Congratulations."

As dark as Harrigan's skin was, I could see him blushing. He had been trying to keep the wedding quiet, and I didn't blame him. Anytime a cop got married, it was an excuse for half the force to take him out and raise hell, even if they weren't invited.

"Thank you," he said. "How'd you hear?"
"Word gets around."

......

WE DROVE through the South End, a dense neighborhood of brick townhouses. In the 19th century, the area was a haven for the city's wealthy merchant class. Its cobblestone streets were still lined with gas lamps and maple trees, but now it was filled with flophouses, dive bars, and jazz joints. The buildings were mostly abandoned, and there were homeless people and junkies everywhere.

As Harrigan and I got out, I saw a sign above a doorway: *Sunnyside Nursery*. We went up the front steps, and I buttoned my coat to hide my holster. Harrigan opened the door, and we walked into a small lobby. One wall was covered with pictures of animals and cartoon characters; the other had a bookshelf.

"Hello, Trevor."

A young woman looked up, and for a second, I was stumped. No one ever called Harrigan by his first name.

"This is Jody," Harrigan said.

She had dark hair, a round face, and deep inset eyes. With her peasant dress and braids, I wouldn't have been surprised if she was a gypsy from Eastern Europe. But when she spoke, she had an Irish accent.

"Pleased to meet ya. Cecily," she said.

"Cecily doesn't sound Irish."

She smiled flirtatiously.

"No? T'was me great-auntie's name. We're not all Margaret's and Mary's ya know. Shall I fetch Delilah?"

"Please."

Moments later, Delilah walked out. Except for her beaded necklace and hoop earrings, she was dressed almost conservatively.

She and Harrigan kissed, and then she turned to me.

"Jody," she said.

She always shook my hand and had only stopped calling me *Mr. Brae* after I complained that it made me feel old. When we first met, she had a giant afro, which I always suspected was more about politics than fashion. A generation younger than me, she was a child of sixties idealism, and I was sure our views about the world were different. But she was friendly and polite, and the fact that she loved Harrigan was enough to gain my respect.

"Can I give you a tour?"

"Lead the way," I said.

She opened the door, and we walked down a long hallway, the floor creaking. The building was old, but the atmosphere was warm and vibrant. I peered into the classrooms to see children sleeping under colorful blankets while teachers sat quietly at their desks.

"It's naptime," Delilah whispered.

"How many kids?"

"We have twenty-four in daycare. Seventeen for preschool."

"You've got your hands full."

"We've got terrific staff. Most of our teachers are from the local colleges, Wheelock and Lesley."

"What are the drop-off and pickup times?" I asked.

"Any time, really. We close at six."

We reached the end of the hallway and stopped.

"Ernestine is four, right?" she asked.

It was funny to hear Nessie's full name, bestowed in honor of our captain, *Ernest* Jackson.

"Yes."

"Then she would be in here, the Kangaroo Room."

Through the glass, I could see seven or eight children lying on a shag rug. A young teacher with large glasses waved at us with a smile. I smiled back and then, like any good detective, searched around for dangers or vulnerabilities. There was a stairwell door beside the lavatory, a rear window with a grate over it.

"Do you take kids three days a week?" I asked.

"Of course, it's flexible.

I glanced at Harrigan, and he gave me an encouraging nod. I would never admit that I was afraid to put my daughter in daycare. But I knew he sensed it like he had sensed my hesitation the night of the murder. Having a close partner was similar to having a wife. They knew your every fear, worry, and dread.

"So, would you like to enroll?" Delilah asked.

She looked up, her lashes fluttering. She was the only black woman I had ever met with a blue tint to her eyes, or maybe it was the lighting. Either way, her kind face put me at ease. The daycare wasn't in the best neighborhood, but I trusted her enough to leave my daughter there.

"Yeah. I think so."

CHAPTER 5

WHEN I WENT TO PICK UP HARRIGAN THE NEXT MORNING, HIS MOTHER was waiting at the door to say he would be out sick. A *touch of the ague* was how she put it in her thick Caribbean accent. I wasn't concerned; he was as strong as an ox. In all our years working together, he had never been out with a common illness. More than likely, it was just nerves. His wedding was only two days away, and the anticipation of getting married was enough to make anyone sick.

Sitting at my desk, I was startled by a knock. No one came to my office, primarily because I never used it. When Harrigan and I weren't meeting with the captain, we were out on the streets. The room was cluttered with boxes that I still hadn't unpacked, old case notes and citations, the purple heart ribbon Ruth had framed for me.

"Come in."

The door opened, and I was surprised to see Collins, the sarcastic cop from the Southie murder.

"What do you want?" I snapped.

Looking back, he waved, and a young boy walked in. He wore a dirty plaid coat and bellbottom jeans with patches on the knees. As sloppy as he looked, he held his knit cap in his hands, some indication that he had been taught good manners.

"He saw something," Collins said. "At the murder on Telegraph Hill."

"Telegraph Hill?"

"Dorchester Heights. The monument."

I had never heard the term before, but it wasn't unusual. Every place in Boston had more than one name. To make matters worse, Dorchester Heights was in South Boston, not Dorchester, something that always confused transplants.

I got up and walked over.

"You were with your friend that night?" remembered, and he nodded. "What did you see?"

"Go 'head, tell him what you saw."

"A man," the boy said.

"What was this man doing?"

When he hesitated, Collins said, "C'mon, speak up," and I gave him a sharp look.

"He ran down the stairs and down Telegraph Street."

"Before the police showed up?"

The boy nodded.

"Remember what he looked like?"

"He had a leather jacket, a long one. He had a big mustache."

"What color was the coat?"

"Black," the boy said, and then blurted, "Brown!"

It was obvious he was nervous, so I didn't push him. Like most witnesses, what he told me first was the most reliable. Anything more would have been his imagination filling in the gaps.

I stood up and looked at Collins.

"Take him downstairs. Have them draw up a sketch. Be sure to get his name and address."

"That's easy," he said, and I squinted in confusion. "He's my little brother."

Collins had a proud grin, but I wasn't about to congratulate him. I turned to his brother instead. "Good work, kid. This is a big help."

The boy peered up with the timid smile of someone who never got much encouragement.

"Thank you."

I walked them out and then went in the other direction toward the bubbler. Even with steam heat, the office was always dry, and I got thirsty.

As I leaned over to drink, someone shouted, "Brae!"

I turned my head to see Egersheim scurrying toward me like a hyper dog. His tie was loose, his glasses tilted.

"I got a lead on the Southie case," I said before he could ask.

"Good. We're gonna need it."

I stood up, and our eyes locked. Stepping closer, he looked around and spoke in a whisper.

"We've got another dead girl."

My heart began to race, the warm rush of adrenaline. When I was younger, I loved the feeling, but now it just made me uneasy.

"Where?"

"Amrhein's in South Boston. The call just came in."

"I'll head over."

"Where's Harrigan?"

"He has the day off," I said.

He pursed his lips, but he couldn't accuse me of lying. He let us manage our own time, mainly because he didn't know how to submit the time sheets. Either way, except for some time out injured, Harrigan had a perfect attendance record, and I didn't want to jeopardize it.

"Let me get my jacket," the captain said.

"Your jacket?"

"We'll go together."

......

WE SPED over the Fort Point Channel bridge and into South Boston. West Broadway was a long stretch of barrooms, markets, pawn shops, and hair salons, punctuated by the occasional Catholic Church. Known for over a century as *Southie,* it was the place where the hordes of peasant Irish fleeing the Famine had settled and made it their own.

There were an equal number of cops and crooks, and many of them were related. While most other ethnic ghettoes had faded, South Boston endured. We had only gone a block before I saw a large mural on the side of a diner: *England Get Out of Ireland.*

"Why don't you use one of the department vehicles?" the captain asked.

"I like this one."

Conversations with him were awkward. The only things we had in common were that we smoked and liked the Dick Cavett Show.

"The new Monaco's drive like a charm. They've got V-8s," he said. "What's this?"

"Straight Six."

"Not as fast."

"But better on gas."

He frowned, but he couldn't argue. With all the trouble in the Middle East, there were rumors of an oil crisis. The government had been talking about building a pipeline from Alaska, but no one believed it was possible.

Ahead, I saw three cruisers parked next to Amrhein's. The restaurant had been around for eighty years. It claimed to have the oldest hand-carved bar in the country and the first draft beer pump in the city. While the elegant brick building was now rundown, it looked like a palace compared to all the tenements and empty lots around it.

We turned onto A Street and pulled over. As we got out, I saw cops in the alleyway and two ambulances parked nearby. With all the activity, I felt like we had arrived late to a party.

"Detective?"

I turned to see the same sergeant from the last murder.

"We meet again," he said.

"Yeah. What a pleasure."

"Captain," the officer then said, nodding to Egersheim.

Much like Harrigan, he never got the respect or attention I did. The difference was that I didn't mind when it was Egersheim.

We walked down the alleyway, officers parting to let us through. Between a dumpster and a doorway, I saw a woman lying on her side. Even from a distance, I could tell her neck was slashed. Men from

Forensics were taking photos and dusting for prints. In the midday sun, the image was gruesome.

"Looks like a murder."

I turned to see an overweight EMT. His expression was somewhere between wonder and amusement, and I would have guessed he was stoned.

"You don't say," I snickered, and I walked over to the body.

Like the last victim, she was young and pretty. She had short black hair and studded earrings. Her pink coat seemed to clash with her red flared pants, but as someone who only wore black, gray, and navy, I knew nothing about modern fashion.

Her eyes were open but looking sideways like she had sensed someone behind her the moment before she was killed.

"Ain't she a beaut?" an investigator said.

"A regular princess," his partner agreed.

If detectives were cold, men from *Forensics* were heartless. I couldn't blame them —— they worked long hours and saw the worst of humanity. They had every right to be cynical, while rookie cops like Collins only thought they did.

"Who found her?" I asked.

The investigator stood up, out of breath from crouching.

"Couple homeless guys, I guess."

"Who called it in?"

"They went into the restaurant. Luckily the manager got in early."

"Any witnesses?" Egersheim asked.

The agent ignored him and said to me, "Wanna give her a quick pat?"

"Sure."

I leaned down, careful not to let my coat touch the bloody water. Looking away, I reached into her jacket, overcome by the same dread I had felt last time. I searched her quickly, up her back and along her torso. Her body was stiff, but her skin was still soft.

"The responding officers found this over by the fence," the agent said.

His partner handed me a small plaid purse.

"No ID," he added and then turned to the paramedics. "Alright, boys. She can go."

The two men walked over with the stretcher and put her on it. With the war in Vietnam, they had to use a sheet because body bags were so scarce.

Egersheim and I escorted them out of the alley to the street where a small crowd had gathered, reporters and a few residents.

Chief McNamara had arrived, standing on the sidewalk in a long wool coat and gloves. With his wide shoulders and deep voice, he fit the role of a commander. He'd been drafted by the NY Giants in '43, right out of college, but he chose to join the Navy instead. Everyone respected him, and most officers liked him. The moment he saw us, he walked over.

"Brae," he said then he acknowledged the captain. "Paul."

"Two in one week," I said.

"A serial killer?" Egersheim speculated.

Whenever the age, sex, location, and method were the same, it was safe to assume a pattern. But the word made us all uneasy.

"Let's not get ahead of things," the chief said.

We hadn't had a psychopath on the loose since the Boston Strangler, who had been in jail since '67. Even then, most people knew they were safe —— anyone would have had better luck playing the lottery than becoming a victim. But for a few months, the city was gripped by panic. Random crime always fed into the deepest fears of the human psyche.

"Listen," the chief said, and we formed a small circle. "I need this wrapped up. I'm already getting pressure about the other girl…"

Egersheim and I nodded, knowing it was easier said than done.

"We'll get on it," the captain said.

"We got the parade next weekend. The pols are worried it might scare people off. We don't need any more bad press."

With its middle class in full flight to the suburbs, Boston had been struggling for years with a plunging tax base. Half the housing stock was subpar, and many of its historic buildings were beyond repair. For someone living in the richer neighborhoods, Back Bay or Beacon

Hill, it might have been obvious. I never could tell the difference. To me, the city had always been a dump.

After a short pause, the chief patted me on the shoulder. He shook the captain's hand too, which was a relief. Anytime a colleague treated me better than him, he took it personally.

Chief McNamara walked away. Reaching in his coat, Egersheim took out his cigarettes and offered me one.

"Welcome to spring," he said.

CHAPTER 6

RUTH AND I SAT IN THE FRONT PEW OF THE CHURCH. SHE HAD ON A long red dress, and I wore a double-breasted suit, dark gray with brass buttons. It was the best one I owned. I hadn't worn it since Captain Jackson's funeral four years earlier.

The African Baptist Church was on a narrow lane in Beacon Hill, surrounded by Georgian rowhouses and grander Colonial homes. The plain brick structure looked more like a stable than a church. It was built in the early 19th century when the north side of Beacon Hill had a vibrant community of freedmen and ex-slaves. Now it was in one of the poshest parts of the city, far from the ghettoes of Roxbury and Dorchester. Harrigan wasn't religious, so I assumed Delilah had chosen it.

Sitting behind us were Delilah's parents and two sisters. Next to them was Harrigan's mother, who looked dignified in her rose-topped hat and face net. Harrigan had invited some guys we had both worked with before making detective. Otherwise, the crowd was small, a couple of dozen people, and mostly black.

The inside of the church was simple, two rows of pews and a small altar with a lectern. The walls were bare, and a single chandelier hung from the ceiling. As with any old building, the air was stuffy, which made me squirm. I always got irritable in formal situations.

I was relieved when the minister walked out, a short black man in coattails. Holding up his arms, he began to sing. His deep baritone filled the room, and even I got a spiritual thrill. There were no bridesmaids and no organ music, none of the fanfare of Catholic weddings. Maybe the denomination preached modesty, or maybe Delilah had asked for it. Younger people always seemed to reject the traditions of the past.

Everyone turned, and Harrigan and Delilah came down the aisle arm in arm. She wore a long white dress that hugged her body, racier than anything I had seen on a bride. In his black tuxedo, Harrigan looked even more debonair than usual.

But even from a distance, I could tell something was wrong. His skin looked clammy, and even the worst wedding nerves couldn't produce the amount of sweat pouring off of him. As they passed, I glanced at Ruth, but she hadn't seemed to notice.

I turned back to the front as Harrigan and Delilah got to the altar. The minister greeted them first, then looked out at the congregation.

"My dear friends," he said. "Today we come together to celebrate the union of two of God's children…"

Suddenly, Harrigan started to sway. Then he fell backward. Women screamed while men ran to help. As the closest one to him, I leaped from the pew and got behind him, struggling against the momentum of his 6' 2" frame.

"Get him some water!" someone yelled.

Lowering him to the floor, I loosened his tie and felt his pulse, which was steady but elevated. The entire room rushed over and circled around us, the crowd small enough that everyone could see.

"Honey, honey, honey!" Delilah cried, leaning over him, her bouquet on the ground beside her.

"Call an ambulance!" I shouted.

……

. . .

"Jody?"

Ruth nudged me, and I was startled awake. Slumped on the bench, I looked over at the window. It was getting dark. We had been waiting at City Hospital all afternoon. An hour earlier, a nurse had come out to tell us Harrigan was stable, but we still didn't know what had happened.

"I'm Doctor Corbin."

I looked up to see a middle-aged man with white hair and thin lips. He had a folder in one hand, his glasses in the other. Delilah was the first one to stand.

"Delilah Reynolds," she said, and then she introduced us. "Ruth Brae and her husband Joseph."

The doctor smiled curtly, and we all shook hands.

"Come with me, please," he said.

Everyone looked over as we got up. With Delilah in her wedding gown, and Ruth and me dressed up, we had been a spectacle since the moment we arrived. Harrigan's mother and the minister had been there earlier, but they didn't stay long. A busy emergency room was no place for an eighty-year-old woman with arthritis.

We followed the doctor through the doors and into the hallway, where nurses and other staff were rushing around.

"Mr. Harrigan has been shot before," the doctor said, and it wasn't a question.

Delilah just nodded.

"There was…an incident," I said.

Thinking back to that night still made me shudder. I was surprised he had lived, but I was more surprised by what he did.

We had been investigating a house on a quiet beach road in Hull when the suspect opened fire. With Harrigan hit, I chased the guy into an abandoned Army tower. In the darkness, he almost snuck up behind me but was killed by Harrigan who had hobbled a hundred yards from the car with a gunshot wound.

The doctor stopped before we entered the room.

"The bullet is still lodged—"

"They said it was too close to the aorta," I blurted.

"That's correct," Corbin said. "From the x-rays, we're seeing a buildup of fluid around the pericardium. Our immunologist believes it might be an infection from the bullet."

"After fifteen months?" Delilah asked.

"Foreign objects often get encapsulated. Sometimes a little movement can release surface germs that had been dormant."

As technical as it was, it made sense. But I still didn't know what it meant.

"How is he?" I asked.

"Heavily sedated. We're administering a strong antibiotic."

"He'll be okay?"

We all stared at Corbin expectantly. I didn't envy his job, having to make predictions about health, the most unpredictable aspect of life. Like any physician, he could only go on statistics and his own experience.

"We expect him to recover," he said.

Delilah gasped out loud, and Ruth threw her arms about her. She had been strong all day, and I respected her for it. I knew what it was like to hold back emotion for long periods. The closest she had come to crying was when the paramedics said she couldn't ride in the ambulance.

"Shall I take you all in now?" the doctor asked, looking at Delilah.

"Yes."

CHAPTER 7

WHEN I PULLED OVER ON TREMONT STREET, I LOOKED AT MY WATCH. It was just after 8 a.m. I would have been earlier, but I'd lost track of time while installing the kid's seat Ruth bought after seeing a commercial. I hadn't ridden in a car until I was a teenager, so it seemed like overkill to me, but I never argued with her about safety.

"Daddy, is this the school?"

Nessie pointed at the front window, which was covered in stickers of reptiles, lizards, turtles, and crocodiles. I wanted to say *How'd you know?* but I knew to reserve sarcasm for adults.

"Yes, love," I said.

I got out, undid her belt, and handed her a Holly Hobbie lunchbox. We went up the steps, and I opened the door.

"Well, look at you!"

Cecily got up from the desk and came over. When she knelt, the back of her blouse lifted, and I looked away.

"What do you have there?"

"Holly Hobbie," Nessie said, sounding more like *Haw-wee Haw-wee.*

"She's beauuuuutiful."

Cecily had a sharp accent, different from the other Irish I had met. Before I could ask where she was from, the door opened. Nessie's teacher walked out, an older Italian woman who wore her hair in a tight bun and had several rings on her fingers.

"Hello, my dear," she said, holding out her hand.

I was barely able to kiss Nessie's forehead before she ran to her. The teacher smiled, and then they both gave me one last wave. I watched through the door as they walked down the corridor. That last second before they disappeared around the corner was always the hardest.

When I turned around, Cecily was kneeling at a table arranging some play blocks.

"Is Delilah here?"

"She's not due 'til later," she said.

I knew Delilah was at the hospital. Like me, she had been at Harrigan's side every hour that she wasn't at work or asleep. The night before, Ruth and I had given her a ride home. As a thirty-two-year-old graduate student, she still lived in a dorm, but I knew she was eager to finally move in with Harrigan.

"How is Trevor?" Cecily asked.

"Still unconscious. His fever is down."

"That's good news."

"As good as any, I suppose."

"He'll pull through," she said with a warm smile.

I appreciated the assurance but also resented the implication that the outcome could be anything otherwise.

"Where're you from anyway?" I asked.

"Ireland."

"Your accent…it's different."

"I'm from up North."

"Where's North?"

She looked up, a mysterious hesitation in her eyes.

"I'm from Belfast, Mr. Brae."

......

I SAT across from Egersheim in an uncomfortable silence. He wore a striped collared shirt with the sleeves rolled up, stains under the armpits. The light through the window illuminated the single wisp of hair at the top of his bald head that I often forgot was there. It looked like he had even tried to comb it back, something Harrigan and I would have joked about.

"I had no idea he was getting married."

With Harrigan in the hospital, it seemed the wrong thing to be worried about, but I understood why he was upset. It never felt good to be left out.

"It was just a small wedding. His mother's church friends, a few neighbors."

Leaning back, Egersheim nodded, but I knew he wasn't satisfied.

"I talked with the physician," he said. "Once Harrigan is released, he'll have to recuperate at home for a while."

The remark was optimistic enough that I smiled.

"It takes a lot out of the body."

"This *job* takes a lot out of the body."

"Don't I know."

In my twenty years on the force, I had been shot, stabbed, beaten, and knocked unconscious. Once I almost drowned when I tackled an assailant off a pier and my foot got caught in a lobster trap. I had crashed the Valiant a half-dozen times while on chases, breaking my wrist once or twice and even fracturing my skull. When I was younger, it was all part of the thrill, and after going to war, nothing seemed dangerous. Now at middle age, I felt the damage in those aches and pains that sometimes kept me up at night.

"We got some info on the *Jane Doe II*," Egersheim said, reaching for a case folder that was twice as thick as it had been the week before. "The purse—"

"Pocketbook," I said.

"Handbag, technically. It had traces of blood."

"Most likely hers."

When he glanced up, I could tell he didn't like my interruptions.

"No wallet, no ID."

"Our killer is meticulous," I said, a word I had stolen from Harrigan.

"It contained a lipstick case, a shot of rum," he continued, reading from the sheet. "Calfskin leather, nylon stitching, made in England—"

"England?"

"Catfields, Devonshire. Why?"

"Nothing," I said.

He closed the folder and leaned forward with his elbows on the desk.

"Jody." My eyes narrowed at the use of my first name. "I know you've got a lot on your mind."

I wasn't sure if he meant Harrigan or Ruth's pregnancy, but I appreciated the concern.

"Nothing I can't handle."

"I can get you some help, someone from patrol. Guys are itching to come up to *Homicide*."

I dismissed the offer with a frown.

"Harrigan will be back in a week," I said, and he gave me a skeptical look.

"We gotta get this guy."

"It's still early."

"Not as early as you think. I got another call from the chief this morning. He's panicking. We can keep two murders quiet for a week. But if there's a third, the press is gonna be on us like white on rice."

Coming from Egersheim, slang always sounded corny.

I wasn't surprised that the first victim didn't have a license on her —— lots of people left the house without one. But the fact that the second one had a purse and no ID was suspicious. All killers were aware that family members would report their loved ones missing, which made me wonder if this one somehow knew they would not. Either way, if he had been trying to hide their identities, there were better ways to do it.

"Anything in *Missing Persons*?" the captain asked.

"No matches."

The first place Harrigan and I had gone, even before the coroner, was the records room on the second floor. The files on missing people spanned decades, with some dating back to the late-19th century. We only went back a year, knowing that anyone reported before then had either intentionally disappeared or was half-decomposed.

"We're gonna have to hit the streets on this one."

"I'll see what I can find out."

"I've gotta head out," he said, and we got up. "If you hear anything, let me know. Immediately."

"Sure. When will you be back?"

It was too cold for golf, so I assumed it was lunch with the higher-ups or maybe a PR event.

"Early afternoon. I'm going to the hospital to see Harrigan."

CHAPTER 8

I COULD ADMIT THAT HARRIGAN WAS A CLOSE FRIEND, BUT I COULDN'T admit that I felt lost without him. I had only had one partner before him, an older Italian named Mike Gangemi from East Boston. As someone who never married and still lived with his mother, he was quirky. He wore his socks inside out to make them less itchy. In six months, he taught me everything he knew and then promptly retired. I always valued his mentorship, those bits of investigative wisdom that could be conveyed but not taught. Some of it I had passed on to Harrigan, but he always brought more to the department than he took.

I was shocked when he came up to *Homicide* —— so much so that I even complained to Captain Jackson. I had served with black guys in Korea, so that wasn't the problem. But law enforcement was like a microcosm of society, and society was rife with tension in the sixties. I didn't want race to be a distraction.

In the end, all my pleading was for nothing; Captain Jackson had made up his mind. As a Protestant from rural Maine, he viewed bigotry as just another form of weakness. I was glad he did because it only took a couple of cases and a few months for me to realize that Harrigan was the best partner I could ever ask for.

I felt his absence as I drove up to Dorchester Heights. In the narrow streets of South Boston, everyone could spot an outsider. Even from the confines of my car, I could sense their eyes on me.

When I got to the top of the hill, I parked right in front of the gate of the park. Knowing I couldn't sneak around undetected, I wasn't even going to try.

In a case with no leads, I sometimes found it helpful to go back to the original crime scene. Not because I thought the killer would return —— that only happened in movies —— but to get my thoughts in order. I didn't expect to find anything new. *Forensics* had already scoured the area for clues, and all they'd found were some bubblegum wrappers, a rusted Schlitz beer can, and the remains of a Playboy Magazine.

I lit a cigarette and went up the steps. When I got to the top, I braced myself against the brisk March wind. Over by the monument, a woman was walking her dog. Three kids were trying to launch a kite whose line kept getting tangled. On a bench, a young couple snuggled close together. I thought I smelled marijuana, but I wasn't there for a drug bust.

I walked over to the trees where the body had been found. There was no makeshift shrine to mark the spot's significance, no photographs or flowers, no notes from grieving loved ones. The only sign of what had happened was some matted grass. And even then, maybe my mind was filling in what I had seen that night. I was convinced that neither victim was local, or word would have gotten out.

"You a cop?"

I turned around, and the couple from the bench were walking toward me.

"Yeah," I said, stamping out my cigarette.

They wore faded jeans, and their hair was long and straggly. The guy had on a Woodstock t-shirt under his corduroy coat. Five years before, I would have called them hippies, but now every young person dressed like that.

"This about the dead girl?"

I gave them a hard stare —— I never liked being approached in public.

"Maybe."

The girl stepped forward, looking up at me with bug eyes.

"I work at the Blarney Stone in Dorchester," she said. "There's a waitress, an Irish girl. No one's seen her in a week."

"Whaddya mean *seen her?*" I asked, friendly but direct.

"Like, she ain't been to work."

I reached into my coat and took out a small writing pad. It was a miracle that I'd even remembered to bring one; Harrigan usually took all the notes.

"And what's this girl's name?" I asked.

"Cecily."

I struggled not to seem surprised. I had never known anyone with that name, and now I had heard it twice in one week.

"Cecily?"

"Yeah. I didn't know her too good. We only worked a few shifts together."

"Can you describe her?"

The girl shrugged her shoulders.

"Pretty, I guess. Dark hair. Tall. She couldn't carry trays over her head. She said she had broken her wrist and it didn't bend that way."

I don't know why I was so relieved —— I had seen Cecily from *Sunnyside* that morning, and the description didn't match. The wrist injury was interesting enough that I wrote it down and underlined it.

"Would you be willing to make an identification?" I asked.

She glanced at her boyfriend, who gave her a wary look.

"We ain't into seeing dead people, man," he joked.

"We could use a picture."

"Okay, I guess, sure," she said, nodding.

"Could I have your name?"

She hesitated.

"Anne Curley."

"A phone where we could reach you?"

"Who's *we?*"

Sensing her concern, I said, "It'll just be me."

"Okay. 269-5266."

After having her repeat it twice, I wrote down the number and closed the notepad. For the first time since Harrigan's hospitalization, I was feeling optimistic. I looked up at the scraggly couple and gave them both a sincere smile.

"Thank you."

......

I DROVE down Dorchester Avenue in midday traffic. As the largest neighborhood of Boston, it had every race and ethnic group in the city. I passed a Greek autobody shop, a Polish travel agency, an Italian market, and a Jamaican restaurant. The closer I got to Fields Corner, the more Irish it became. All the shop windows had shamrocks for St. Patrick's Day; businesses had names like O'Reilly's Bakery, Foley Contractors, and Connemara Cleaners.

I parked in front of the Blarney Stone, a corner bar with a stone façade and no windows. I hadn't been there since I was a rookie, but it looked the same. Inside, it was dark, and it took a moment for my eyes to adjust.

The place was busy for a Monday afternoon, the bar crowded with people dancing and playing around the two pool tables in the back. The walls were covered with posters of Irish sports legends; *The Dubliners* were playing on the jukebox.

I walked over to the bar, and a stocky bartender looked up.

"What can I get ye?"

Ye must have been an inherited quirk because there was no way the man was from Ireland. I took out my badge, which he acknowledged with a tentative nod.

"Got some questions about an employee," I said.

"What's his name?"

"It's a woman. A waitress."

"I only work days. The waitresses don't come in 'til evening. I'll have to ask the manager."

"If you don't mind."

Holding up his finger, he poured a drink for a customer and then went out back.

"Afternoon, mate," I heard.

I turned to the three men sitting beside me at the bar. They were all in their early thirties with long hair and scruffy chins. Their eyes were glassy from either too much booze or not enough sleep. The one closest to me wore a red turtleneck sweater under a leather bomber jacket while his friends had on wool coats. He was the size of a football player, with a large jaw and a big forehead.

"Looking for someone in particular?" he asked, so I knew they had seen the badge.

"Just someone who didn't pay his bar tab."

"That's probably Ian here," he said, elbowing the man next to him.

Having grown up around immigrants, I had always been attuned to accents. The way he said *here* reminded me of how Cecily spoke.

"You from Northern Ireland?" I asked.

They all looked at each other.

"Dublin," the big guy said, finally.

"The Big Smoke," the middle one said, and when I squinted, he added, "An old nickname. A term of endearment."

I smiled, but something about them made me uneasy. Even for three men drinking at a bar, they were a little too forward.

"How long you been here?"

"Since about nine this morning," the big guy said, and they all laughed.

"Over for St. Paddy's?"

"Aye. We hear it's a gas."

"That's one way to put it."

"And you, officer?" the middle guy asked. "Who are you after?"

It was the second time they had asked. Before I could respond, the bartender came out of the swinging doors.

"Manager must've just left," he said, flustered. "He's usually here in the morning to do the inventory. Give me your name and number. I'll have him call you."

As he waited, the other men went quiet. I knew they were listening. I was always hyperaware of my surroundings, something I got from two years in combat and two decades on the police force.

"I'll come back," I said.

"Pat," the big one said, "a pint for our American friend."

I glanced over, giving them a friendly wave.

"Thanks, but I gotta go."

"Sure, you only just arrived."

I looked at the clock behind the bar.

"I gotta get my kid."

It wasn't a lie: I had to pick up Nessie by five. I didn't like giving strangers explanations, but evasion caused more suspicion than the truth.

"Family first," the big guy said, raising his Guinness.

"Enjoy your stay." I tried to sound cordial.

"We will."

As I walked away, I felt them all watching.

CHAPTER 9

THE NEXT MORNING, I DROPPED NESSIE OFF AT 8 A.M. AND THEN RACED to City Hospital to see Harrigan before work.

When I walked into the hospital room, two doctors were standing beside the bed. The older one had glasses and a mustache and reminded me of a grandfather. The younger one was short with dark, thinning hair.

"Good morning," the older one said.

"I can come back."

"Are you a relation?"

Considering Harrigan was black, I almost laughed.

"We work together."

"Right," the younger one said. "Officer Brae?"

I nodded, and he looked at his colleague.

"The patient's mother has permitted Mr. Brae to be privy to all medical decisions."

The sentence was a mouthful, but I knew what it meant, and I felt honored.

"How is he?" I asked.

"Stable," the older one said.

Stable. While I hated the sterile language of medical jargon, it wasn't as bad as *serious* or *grave.*

"Good to meet you."

I walked over, and Harrigan lay stiff, his chest heaving up and down on a ventilator. With his eyes closed, he looked like a corpse.

"I'm Doctor Rosen," the younger physician said, "This is Doctor Petz, chief surgeon."

I was sure I had met them before, but with all the chaos, I couldn't recall.

"Surgeon?"

"Yes," Rosen said, then he looked at his colleague.

"We're pretty confident the contaminated bullet is what caused the infection. We also think it happened because the slug moved."

"Moved?"

As we spoke, a nurse walked into the room.

"Please, come with me," Petz said.

I followed them out and down the corridor. We turned into a small room with beds and X-ray equipment. Dr. Petz took a slide out of his folder and put it in the illuminator. He hit the switch and suddenly I was looking at Harrigan's chest cavity. His ribs were clear, but everything else was faint and blurry.

"See here," Petz said.

He pointed to a small black object that looked more like a smudge than a bullet.

"The slug is approximately two centimeters from the myocardium wall."

"Looking at Trevor's previous x-rays, we can tell it has migrated," Rosen said.

I couldn't help noticing that Petz always said *Mr. Harrigan* while the younger doctor used his first name. Generational distinctions were more obvious as I got older.

"They said they didn't want to try to take it out," I said.

"At the time, it was probably too big a risk," Petz went on. "In such a sensitive region, sometimes it's wiser to leave a foreign body alone, as long as there's a reasonable probability that it will remain stationary."

"So, how'd it move?" I asked.

"Maybe a fall? Maybe natural migration through the soft tissues? Our bodies are malleable."

"You have to operate?"

Petz looked at Rosen.

"That would be our advice," Rosen said.

"What if you don't?"

Petz's expression tensed up, not quite grim, but also not reassuring. I could tell he was a man used to giving difficult news.

"Assuming we contain the infection, he could recover. But if the bullet shifts, maybe hits the aorta, it could cause massive internal bleeding."

I didn't have to ask what that meant.

"Is the operation a risk?"

Our eyes all met. The room went quiet.

"There's always risk with surgery, Mr. Brae."

......

HARRIGAN'S SITUATION left me anxious and on edge, so I went straight to headquarters. Work was always a good distraction from the stresses of life. I got to the entrance just as it started to shower. There was nothing worse than cold winter rain. The forecast had said snow, but no one ever really knew. The weather in Boston was so unpredictable that even gamblers wouldn't bet on it.

I walked down the corridor with my head down. By now, everyone knew about Harrigan, and after Jackson's death, I didn't want any more sympathy.

Considering I was late, I would have welcomed a reprimand from Egersheim, if only to feel normal. But when I walked into his office, my jaw dropped.

"Brae," he said.

"Am I interrupting?"

Sitting across from him was the young cop, Officer Collins.

"Hardly," Egersheim said. "This is—"

"We've met."

"Juan Collins."

I didn't know what shocked me more, that he was in the room or that his first name was *Juan*.

"Hey ya, detective," he said, glancing back.

Somewhere behind his smile, I saw that sarcastic smirk. If I judged people too quickly, it was only because I had to.

"Take a seat," the captain said. "How's Harrigan?"

"He's been better."

"Since he'll be out a while, I've brought Officer Collins up from patrol."

I was beyond outraged. I had assumed he was there to discuss the Southie homicide, not to take my partner's job. Patrolmen were in short supply, and now almost anyone could get the job. But with the good pay and status, everyone wanted to make detective. If I ever decided to retire, I knew a dozen guys would be waiting to take my place. Still, I couldn't understand why someone so young would get it. I couldn't believe the captain hadn't consulted me first.

After a short, but uncomfortable silence, Egersheim cleared his throat.

"I got a call from the chief this morning about the Southie case," he said. "What's the update?"

"I've been asking around," Collins said. "No one ain't seen nothin'"

While the captain nodded, I ignored the kid, and not because I despised broken English. Only a rookie would brag about doing something that hadn't worked.

"A girl came up to me at Dorchester Heights yesterday—" I said.

"What were you doing up at the Heights?" Collins blurted.

"Flying a kite," I said, and Egersheim gave me a sharp look. "She said a waitress she works with hasn't shown up for work."

"You think that's a lead?" the captain asked.

"Don't know. But she thought it was important enough to approach me."

"She could've been playing you," Collins said.

Each time he spoke, I could feel my blood pressure rise.

"She said she'd make an ID," I continued. "I said we could use a picture."

Egersheim reached for the case folder, took out an autopsy photo, and slid it over. As I glanced down, Collins leaned over, invading my space.

"Ain't she a beaut?"

"She told me the girl was Irish," I said.

"Like everyone in this town."

Finally, I turned to Collins.

"Would you mind shutting the fuck up?"

"Brae!" Egersheim exclaimed.

......

WHEN I WALKED in the front door, Nadia was in the kitchen. She still came by to help Ruth on the days when Nessie wasn't in daycare.

Short and stout, Nadia was the stereotype of a Polish *babcia*, although she wasn't that old. She wore loose dresses and had swollen ankles. As dowdy as she was, I imagined that she might have been pretty when she was young.

"Soup and bread," she grunted, looking over with a spoon in her hand.

"Thanks, Nadia," I said, hanging up my coat. "Maybe in a bit."

"Daddy!"

I looked up, and Nessie walked down the stairs. Her pink zip-up was tight, a sign that she was growing. Ruth had talked about getting her two-piece pajamas, but I still liked her in baby clothes.

"Hi, love," I said, picking her up.

I brought her into the living room where Ruth lay on the couch in slippers and a nightgown.

"Sorry, I'm late," I said, and she moved her legs so I could sit.

"I figured you would be."

LOVE AIN'T FOR KEEPING

"Yeah? Why?"

When Nadia called, I put Nessie down, and she ran into the kitchen.

"I heard about the murders in South Boston," she explained, and when I frowned, she added, "It was on the morning news."

I felt a simmering dread, but I had known the deaths wouldn't stay quiet for long. Not every homicide made the local news, which was a sad commentary on the times. But the murder of two women, especially ones so young and pretty, was always a good story.

"It's too bad," I said.

"Do they know who did it?"

Like every other housewife in the city, Ruth had been particularly paranoid about crime since the Boston Strangler murders of the early '60s. I thought about lying to her but knew she wouldn't buy it.

"Not yet."

Nessie came running back into the room. Her face beamed, and she had something in her hand.

"Taffy!" she said, jumping up and down.

"Just lick it. Don't bite."

With a mischievous grin, she pretended to bite it. I reached to take it, and she giggled and ran away.

"Dishes clean."

We looked over, and Nadia was in the foyer, putting on her coat.

"Thanks, Nadia," Ruth said.

She leaned up and gave me a pointed look. I didn't understand what she meant until she mouthed the word *money*. Like any old immigrant, Nadia was too proud to ask. Standing up, I reached for my wallet, walked over, and handed her a twenty.

Moments later, her ride pulled up, and Nessie ran over to hug her goodbye. Once she left, Ruth said, "Honey, go wash up for bed."

Nessie looked down with a pout, but she never gave us trouble. She walked up the stairs, and I listened until I could hear the water from the sink.

"How's Harrigan?" Ruth asked.

"Not great. They wanna operate to take the bullet out."

"And you're worried?"

"How're you feeling?" I said, changing the subject.

"Not great," she said with a hint of sarcasm. "I've had a dreadful headache."

"Did you call the doctor?"

When I looked at her, she pursed her lips and shook her head.

"Let's go somewhere this weekend," she said softly, rubbing my back.

"This weekend?"

"Like New Hampshire or Maine."

"I can't."

I got distracted when the nightly news came on.

...It's been ten days and protests continue in Belfast, Northern Ireland after the Abercorn Restaurant bombing..."

My eyes grew fixated on the screen, images of people marching through the streets with banners, their fists raised, shouting.

"I...have to work," I said.

"This weekend?"

The camera flashed to another scene, young men throwing bottles and rocks at British soldiers, who responded with water hoses.

"Jody, are you even listening?"

Snapping out of it, I turned to her, and she looked worried.

"Are you okay?" she asked.

"Sorry. I have to work at the St. Patrick's Day parade on Sunday."

CHAPTER 10

WHILE METEOROLOGISTS HAD BEEN RIGHT ABOUT THE SNOW, THEY didn't say there would be rain too. The result was a slushy mix that left road conditions bad and visibility even worse.

Traffic was backed up everywhere, cars sliding around. I saw two accidents before I even got to Forest Hills Station. Only a week before, it had been almost sixty degrees, and now it felt like January. I understood why people moved to Florida.

When I finally got to the daycare, I couldn't find a space, so I double-parked and left the car running. Cars beeped, and one guy rolled down his window until I gave him a cold stare, and he sped away.

Inside was just as busy with Cecily frantically manning the phone. One of the teachers walked out, a bubbly young blonde I had never met before. Nessie ran to her, and I watched as they went down the corridor, knowing she would look back. When she did, I waved, and she smiled.

Cecily hung up and looked at me. Her braids were out, her dark hair following.

"Madness out there, isn't it, Mr. Brae?"

"Please, it's Jody."

"Maybe to you. Not with the Missus."

I tilted my head, curious.

"You mean Delilah?"

"A lovely woman, but a stickler for formalities."

"Can I still call you Cecily?" I joked.

"Of course. It's fine the other way around."

I turned to go and then stopped.

"Are there many *Cecilys* around?"

When the phone rang again, she picked it up and said *hold, please*.

"I haven't met any here in the States. But there weren't many back home."

"Did you ever work at Blarney Stone?"

I knew the question was bizarre. An unusual name was no connection between a dead girl and a living one. But it was coincidental enough that I had to ask. Something must have struck her too because her expression changed.

"No," she said. "Why do you ask?—"

Delilah burst through the front door carrying two bags filled with kids' snacks.

"Jody," she said, out of breath. "It's like a blizzard out there."

"A wet one."

Cecily and I rushed over to help, each taking a bag.

Delilah wore a snug red blouse and flared pants, turquoise earrings that matched her eyeliner.

"How's our little princess?" she asked.

"She was up at 5 a.m."

"I'll put these in the kitchen," Cecily said.

She took the bags and walked down the hall, leaving Delilah and me alone.

"Were you at the hospital?" I asked.

"I'm going over at lunch. You?"

"Heading over now. Any news?"

"His fever has been down for over 48 hours," she said.

"And the surgery?"

"Maybe the end of next week."

She peered up with a confident smile. But behind it, I sensed a deeper worry, a quiet dread. I only recognized it because I had it too.

For two people from such different backgrounds, we were now bound by love and friendship. It was hard to look at her without feeling anguished about Harrigan's condition. If someone so strong and steady, almost invincible, could be struck down by illness, what did that mean for the rest of us?

We were spared any more emotional tension when a parent walked in with her son. Instantly, Delilah composed herself and turned to greet them.

I ran out and got back into the car. There was no need to rush to headquarters; the lot wouldn't be plowed for a while. Instead, I made a U-turn in traffic and headed for City Hospital only a few blocks away.

When I pulled in the front gates, the staff was shoveling the sidewalks, clearing the entrance area for ambulances and drop-offs.

I drove around back and parked beside the dumpster. The mortuary wasn't open yet, something I could tell by the undisturbed snow. When I saw Doctor Ansell getting out of his blue Oldsmobile 98, I ran over to meet him.

"Brae," he said, wincing in the flurries. "I thought you were my intern."

"Do I look that young?"

"You look that ugly."

"You're late," I said.

"Who wants to drive in this mess?"

He took out his keys and unlocked the door. I followed him down the basement stairs and along the dark corridor. I had gone there hundreds of times, and it still gave me the creeps.

"You're lucky I'm in a good mood."

"Must be the weather," I joked.

"I cleaned up last night."

I didn't have to ask what he meant. I had known Ansell long enough that I knew all his quirks and habits. Every Tuesday night for over thirty years, he and his friends from childhood had a card game. The only way you could get out was through death or bankruptcy.

Opening the door, he hit the lights, and we walked inside. He took off his coat and hat, hung them up, and then reached for a half-smoked cigar in the ashtray.

"Now," he said, turning around. "What can I do for you?"

"The *Jane Doe* from Southie. I need to know if she had a broken wrist."

"Like a broken wrist or a break that had healed?"

"An older break."

"Probably wouldn't be in the report. I can take a look."

"If you don't mind."

Walking over, he opened the door to the morgue, and I was relieved he didn't ask me to come in. As I waited, I could smell the cold dankness of the room. I always tried not to pity victims, especially dead ones, but it never worked. It was sad to think she had been lying in there unclaimed for a week.

Moments later, Ansell returned.

"You got me, Brae," he said like it had been a bet.

"A break?"

"A *broke*," he said sarcastically. "I'd have to cut some tissue to know for certain. But it looks like she had a distal radius fracture at some point, mostly likely in adulthood."

"Would that cause problems?"

"Decreased range of motion, maybe some chronic pain."

"Enough to make it hard to hold a tray?"

"Sure," he said, getting matches out of his desk drawer. "Why? You think you got a lead?"

"Possibly."

He lit his cigar and nodded, but I knew he wasn't interested. Like a lot of people who saw death every day, he wasn't intrigued by it. So, I wasn't surprised when he moved onto another topic, one concerned with life.

"How's Harrigan?"

"He goes in for surgery Monday."

"That's a tough break," he said.

"Yeah."

He walked over to the filing cabinet and opened the top drawer.

Taking out an autopsy report, he tossed it over, and I caught it just in time.

"The lady from behind Amrhein's," he said before I could ask.

"*Jane Doe II*."

"Could be *Jane Doe* one thousand. I don't keep track."

"Anything interesting?"

"Naw. Pretty straight. *Forensics* find any hairs? Blood?"

"A lot of hairs and a lot of blood. The trouble is they were all hers." He smirked.

"I can tell you one thing, Brae," he said, tapping his cigar on the ashtray. "Whoever this freak is has an extraordinarily sharp knife."

"I figured so."

"No. This is different. Just the way the epidermis was splayed. It's hard to keep a blade that sharp."

"I'll take that under consideration," I said, half-joking.

"I ain't here to do your job or to tell you how to do it. But I wouldn't be looking for a guy with a kitchen knife or switch blade."

The door opened, and a young guy in an overcoat walked in, his boots wet. While I knew he was an intern, the doctor had so many I could never keep track of their names. They all looked the same, gawky medical students with thick glasses and pimples. Ansell even had a woman intern, but she was out on maternity leave.

"How's Harrigan?" he asked.

"I'm going up to see him now."

"That's not what I asked."

When our eyes locked, I grinned, but his expression stayed firm. Bluntness was a part of his character and only meant he was concerned.

"His fever's down," I said. "They're thinking of doing surgery next week.

"He's in good hands."

"I know."

CHAPTER 11

"This is NOT your decision!" Egersheim barked. "It's not even my decision."

I never liked getting the captain upset, but it was amusing to watch. He couldn't sit at his desk, instead standing by the window, rubbing his hand over his bald head.

"I just think that with Harrigan coming back—"

"We don't know when he's coming back!" he said, and it stung. "I spoke with the department physician yesterday. The infection still isn't gone. Now they wanna operate."

Harrigan had been on antibiotics for five days. He was so big the doctors had given him the strongest possible dose and yet he still wavered. His temperature was down, but his blood pressure was up, a sign that he was still fighting off the infection. That morning was the first time I had had a full conversation with him since he collapsed at the wedding. While he knew what had happened, he spoke slowly and was at times confused.

"He looks like he's twenty-two years old," I said.

"Maybe he is, but he's been on the force for four years. He took the detective exam in January. Got a 96, by the way. He's on the list. I don't make the rules."

"Couldn't we give it a couple of weeks? If Harrigan isn't back, we'll bring him on."

"Brae, normally, I'd agree. But we've got two dead girls. The chief is breathing down my neck. It's been a week and you've still got no leads."

"We have a witness."

"A twelve-year-old kid who saw a guy with a beard."

"A mustache."

"That's not a description."

"We've got the girl who said a waitress from her work was missing."

"Great. And did she see the body to ID it?"

He stared at me, and I looked down. The number Ann Curley had given me was for a hair salon in Southie, and they didn't recognize the name. I hadn't expected her to lie, but no one wanted to get involved in a murder case.

"It was a fake number," I said.

Every misstep seemed to give Egersheim more satisfaction.

"Then that doesn't give much credibility to her story."

"Not true. She said the waitress couldn't hold trays because she had broken her wrist. I went to see Ansel this morning. He checked the body and one of the wrists had signs of a previous break."

"Lots of people break wrists, Lieutenant."

The captain didn't usually like to argue, so I knew he was under a lot of stress.

"Seems like a connection to me," I said.

"Did you go back to the bar to see if she worked there?"

"Not yet."

"What are you waiting for? That was two days ago? If you're too busy, you can send Collins—"

"The kid won't help."

"He's not a kid for chrissakes!"

The captain's expression changed. When I looked back, Collins was standing at the door. He had on a dark blazer and chinos. It wasn't a suit, but it was better than what most of his generation wore.

"I can come back," he said.

Egersheim shook his head and waved him in. Collins walked over, and when he sat down in Harrigan's chair, it felt like sacrilege. But I knew I couldn't blame him, even if I didn't like him. He hadn't made the decision to bring himself to *Homicide*.

"Hey, Detective," he said with a nervous excitement.

I glanced over and gave him a hard stare.

……

FOR THE FIRST HOUR, Collins and I didn't talk. Or at least, I didn't. Like any young guy, he couldn't shut up or sit still. As we drove, he commented on everything from the size of women's breasts to the best place to get barbecue. While none of it interested me, I let him go on, responding with an occasional raised eyebrow or nod. But then he reached for the radio.

"Don't touch that!"

He looked at me, a smile creeping from the corner of his mouth.

"It looks old."

"It is old."

"How come you don't drive one of the new Monaco's?"

"I don't like Dodges," I said.

"Why not?"

"They overheat and the turn ratio is too wide."

The technical details seemed to stump him, something I noted for the next time I wanted to shut him up.

"You don't say," he said, gazing out the window.

When we got to Fields Corner, it was early enough that shopkeepers were just pulling up their grates. We parked in front of a Caribbean Market and walked across to the Blarney Stone. As I reached for the door, I heard, "Can I help you?"

I turned and saw a man holding a two-wheeler stacked with crates of beer. Anheuser, Molson, and Pabst Blue Ribbon. He wore a collared shirt and had on glasses.

"I need to talk to the manager."

"You're looking at him," he said. "Mind gettin' the door?"

I opened it, and Collins and I followed him. Inside was dark, and the air stank of stale beer and cigarettes. The man hit the lights, but it didn't make much difference.

"Now," he said, standing the dolly up next to the bar. "What can I do for you?"

When I flashed my badge, Collins did too, which seemed too much. Even if he was only temporary, I didn't want a partner that mimicked my every move.

"Is this about the bodies in the ice chest?"

Making light of crime to a cop was always a risk, but he was friendly enough that I laughed.

"You think it's that easy?" I joked.

He walked over, dusting off his hands, and we shook.

"Richie Devan," he said.

"Jody Brae. Do you have a waitress named Cecily?"

"*Had*. Haven't seen her in over a week."

"Any information on her? Last name, where she lives?"

"Sure," he said. "If you can trust it."

"Why?"

"These Colleens come and go—"

"She was Irish?"

"Right off the boat. We're supposed to verify visas, but it's impossible. They just use fake names anyway."

"Welcome to America," I said.

"They all know the game, especially the ones from up North."

"She was from Northern Ireland?"

As we spoke, I watched Collins' eyes flit back and forth. He hadn't interrupted yet, so I was sure he was confused.

"Belfast, I think," Devan said. "I'll give you what I got."

We walked through the flap door into the back. On one side of the room was a big walk-in cooler; on the other side, beer cartons were stacked against the wall.

Devan went over to a desk in the corner and sat down. Opening the side drawer, he adjusted his glasses before flipping through the folders.

"This is her," he muttered.

He took out a wrinkled job application, and I quickly got my notepad.

"Cecily Madden," he went on. "Date of Birth, 2/12/48, Belfast, Northern Ireland. Current residence, 199 W Sixth St."

"That's Southie?" Collins said.

"Could I show you a photo?" I asked Devan.

He gave me a hesitant look, but I knew he wouldn't say no. He didn't seem like the queasy type.

"Sure."

I reached into my coat for the autopsy photo, showing it discreetly even though no one else was around. The manager took a quick look and then nodded.

"That's her," he said with a faint sigh of sadness or regret. "Such a shame. I hope you get the bastard who did it."

"We will."

"Let me know if there's anything else I can do."

I smiled. Cooperation from the public was expected, but respect was a bonus. With the war, riots, and student protests, the past ten years had been tough for anybody in law enforcement.

"Just one more question," I said as we walked back out to the bar. "Last week, there were three guys in here. They said they were from Dublin but..."

Before I could finish, Devan was shaking his head.

"That's like describing a short skirt in a whorehouse," he said, and Collins and I chuckled. "The city is loaded with Irish now, especially with all the trouble up in the North."

"Okay, thanks."

"My pleasure."

......

WE DROVE down Dorchester Avenue toward South Boston. Traffic was so heavy that, between lights, we never got faster than 10 MPH. I was tempted to use the sirens, but I didn't want any more attention than necessary. Collins was already making a scene, his window down and arm hanging out. I could have told him to roll it up, but I didn't want him to know that I was cold.

"What's the hell's the difference between North and South Ireland anyway?" he asked.

"One's in the north. One's in the south."

Collins laughed. If there was anything I liked about him, it was that he didn't get offended by sarcasm.

"Seriously."

"First, it's *Northern Ireland,* not North. It's a separate country, like Canada."

"And the South?"

I thought for a moment.

"That's regular Ireland, I guess."

It was strange that, as someone who had grown up in the most Irish city in America, I knew so little about the country. Ruth and I had gone there once after our wedding, mainly because she had seen an *Aer Lingus* travel poster. But when we weren't in the hotel bedroom, we were roaming the countryside in our rented Vauxhall Viva, stopping at small postcard villages. A honeymoon was no time to learn about the politics and history of a place.

"They said there was British money on that Irish girl who was killed up the Heights."

I glanced over.

"Who said that?"

"It was in the case report."

"You read it?"

He nodded, and I was impressed he had done his homework.

"Don't they use British money up there?"

"Up where? The Heights?" I joked.

"In Northern Ireland."

"Yeah. I mean, I think so," I said, which was about as much as I knew about foreign currency.

"Then maybe she's from Northern Ireland, not *regular* Ireland."

"And how's that help us?"

"It narrows it down."

It was a good observation, but I wasn't about to brainstorm with him. I would only do that with Harrigan.

We turned down W Sixth Street, a narrow lane of shabby wooden rowhouses. Some had alleyways between them, but most were side by side.

Growing up in Roxbury, I always considered South Boston a step up because it had a beach. But even the flower boxes and lace curtains couldn't hide the poverty. After living for a few years in the leafier parts of the city, I realized they were both slums.

We stopped at the address, a gray three-story house with a flat roof. The paint was faded, the sills all splintered. If I didn't know better, I'd think it was abandoned.

The doorbell looked broken, so I knocked. Seconds later, an elderly woman in a nightgown opened the door.

"Yeah?" she said, her voice raspy.

She leaned out, squinting in the daylight. Her face and neck were covered in spots, either freckles or something worse. If she had any teeth, I couldn't see them.

"Afternoon, Madam. Does Cecily Madden live here?"

"Maybe," she said.

Collins and I looked at each other, the first time we'd had the same reaction.

"Pardon?"

"I rent rooms. Five dollars a week. Wanna stay?"

She let out a loud cackle.

"She's an Irish girl. Auburn hair."

"Sorry, honey. Half the girls here are Paddies."

The slur was harsh, especially in South Boston. But the Irish had a reputation for disparaging their own.

"Could I show you a photo?"

"Photo? Like her prom picture?"

I frowned.

"Ma'am—"

"It's Charlotte," she said, a name that was strangely elegant for such an old hag.

"Charlotte. A young woman was killed last week. We're trying to identify her."

"The girl behind Amrhein's?"

"No. Another girl, in Thomas Park."

She hesitated, one eye squinting.

"Okay, let's see the picture."

Showing an autopsy photo was always a risk. Not everyone could handle seeing a dead body. But I took the chance, glancing around first before taking it out.

"Ha! I know her," she said without the slightest shock or revulsion. "She ain't no Cecily."

"No?"

"Trudy was her name, like my mother. The little hussy still owes me money."

Collins chuckled, but I held back.

"She was staying here?" I asked.

"For a bit."

"When was the last time you saw her?"

"Maybe a week ago."

"Did she associate with anyone?"

"Couldn't say. I don't keep track. This ain't no convent."

With each question, her responses got snippier. I wasn't sure if she was crazy or just eccentric, but I knew she wouldn't be much more help. Being a good detective meant knowing what was a lead and what was a waste of time.

I looked at Collins, and he nodded back.

"Thanks, Ma'am," I said, forcing a smile.

"The name's Charlotte."

CHAPTER 12

ALL AFTERNOON, WE SCOURED THE DRINKING ESTABLISHMENTS OF Boston's Irish corridor. We started at the Eire in Dorchester and ended at Flanagan's in South Boston where I learned the difference between a bar and a pub was that a pub served food. We only went to places frequented by Irish immigrants because if we had expanded our search, it could have taken a month. Boston had a bar on every corner.

While some people were helpful, most had no interest in talking —— and not because we were cops. St. Patrick's Day was tomorrow, and the celebrating had begun. By midday, the bars and social clubs were packed, making me wonder if anyone had jobs. In Southie, the city had already started putting up barricades and no parking signs for the parade.

Everyone we asked had heard about the two murders. Some even gave us their own drunken theories about who did it and why. But no one had any idea who the girls were.

By six o'clock, the sun was beginning to set, casting shadows through the gray and slushy city. It was past rush hour, but the streets were still gridlocked. I hit my horn half-heartedly. Nessie didn't go to daycare on Thursdays, so I wasn't in a rush. But I still wanted to get home before she went to bed.

"Can you drop me at North Station?" Collins asked.

We were so close to headquarters that I could see it in the distance. "The train?"

"The subway."

"You don't have a car?"

"Not yet," he said.

For such a pompous kid, it was strange to hear the embarrassment in his voice.

"I thought you live in Southie?"

"Charlestown."

"What about your brother?"

"He ain't really my brother. He's my *step*-stepbrother. My uncle's brother is married to his father's second wife. They live in Southie."

Sometimes it took a genealogy chart to understand the layout of Boston's fractured blue-collar families. In such a tribal city, if people weren't related through marriage, they were usually related by divorce.

I cut the wheel and went down Bowdoin Street, a straight shot that would have taken three minutes without traffic. When we approached North Station, the bars along Causeway Street were crowded with people waiting to get inside. I pulled over but changed my mind as he reached for the door. "Hey, I'll drive you."

"You don't mind?"

"We're already halfway there."

I couldn't let him take the subway home. He had paid for lunch at Joe & Nemo's, something that surprised me, and he hadn't made a wisecrack all day. Even if I was bitter, I couldn't hold a grudge forever.

We turned onto N. Washington Street and went over the Charlestown Bridge, under the giant overpasses that lay half-complete in the mud flats along the Charles River. Construction on the Central Artery had started in '59 and still wasn't finished. The highway cut the city in two like a giant wall. While it made life easier for suburban commuters, it broke up communities and looked like hell.

We came into Charlestown, a one-square-mile neighborhood of narrow and winding streets, situated on a small hill. If South Boston was the Irish capital of America, Charlestown was its second city, equally as gritty and clannish to a fault. Surrounded by highways and water, there was only one way in and one way out. All the windows had shamrocks, and Irish flags hung from the flagpoles.

We came down the far side of the hill and turned into the Bunker Hill projects, a sprawling brick complex on the edge of the Mystic River. Built after the war, its first residents were veterans who were probably just amazed to have running water and heat. As they moved out or died off, it turned into a white slum. Even the snow couldn't hide the litter in the courtyards; the walls were covered in graffiti, mostly shamrocks and slurs. Every space for grass or vegetation had been paved over, giving it the look of a prison yard.

Most residents were decent people, but they couldn't stop the drug dealing and violence. Like some twisted department quota, we relied on it every year for about a dozen murders, most of which were never solved because of a *code of silence*.

"Where'd you get a name like Juan?" I asked.

Collins looked over.

"My mother is Puerto Rican."

It explained his complexion, but not the underlying scandal of being mixed. In the order of Boston's racial taboos, marrying a Hispanic was only second to marrying a black person.

"How'd that go over around here?" I asked, looking around.

"Sometimes I got called a spic. I had to crack a few heads," he said, hitting his hand with his fist. "But my pops said I'm mostly Irish."

I grinned. I liked his spunk.

"Brae. Ain't that Irish?" he asked.

"I think…I don't know," I muttered. I always got flustered when someone asked about my background. "I was adopted."

He pointed out his address, a small corner unit in the shadow of the expressway.

"See you tomorrow," he said, extending his hand.

I hesitated before shaking it, not wanting him to think we were now buddies.

"Sure. See you tomorrow."

......

I WAS HALFWAY home when the call came over the radio: *Any available homicide detectives*. If the dispatcher had just said *detectives*, I could have ignored it. But with Harrigan out and a shortage of officers, I had to go.

Reaching for the receiver, I asked for the location and wasn't surprised it was Dorchester, which always had more crime. I raced across the city, and it was late enough that the streets were quieter. As I drove down Dorchester Avenue, I didn't have to search for the address because sirens were everywhere. The entire street was blocked off; residents were standing out on the sidewalks. I parked in front of a hydrant, jumped out, and ran toward the scene.

"Detective," I heard.

A sergeant walked over, but I didn't ask what had happened. I already knew.

"Where is she?"

He waved, and I followed him. In the narrow space between two parked cars, I saw a sheet over a body. Underneath was another young woman, about the same age as the others. She had thick eyebrows and rosy cheeks, her brown hair feathered back. There was a patch of blood on her sweater, just over her chest, but her throat wasn't cut. I held my fingers to the side of her neck but didn't feel a pulse.

"She's gone," a cop said.

As I stood up, his partner nodded with a grim look. No one wanted to say what we were all thinking —— three was a pattern. It was either a serial killer or someone out for vengeance.

"Outta the way!"

Looking back, I saw Doctor Ansell charging toward us in a long coat and hat.

"Brae," he said. "Twice in one day. To what do I owe the pleasure?"

I wanted to say *ask her*, but sarcasm didn't seem appropriate. Even the beat cops looked disturbed by what had happened.

Ansell put his bag down on the curb and crawled between the cars.

"Goddammit!" he shouted as his elbow hit a bumper.

Taking out his stethoscope, he listened for a heartbeat and then lifted the victim's eyelids one at a time. With a grunt, he turned her on her side, feeling around with his hands.

"She got it in the back," he said, and the two officers looked over.

"The back?"

"Yeah. Wanna see?" he asked, and I couldn't tell if he was being serious.

"I'll take your word for it."

Ansell was out of breath when he stood up. He wiped his hands on his coat and then fixed his hat.

"Went right through. Must've been a long blade."

"Came up from behind you think?"

"Maybe. She didn't go easy. She struggled. She's got abrasions on her hands. Even lost a shoe."

I followed his gaze to a single bare foot hanging out of the sheet.

"Detective?!"

A young officer walked up, an excited look on his face.

"That lady found this," he said, handing me a leather purse. "In the yard."

I looked over and saw an elderly woman leaning against the fence of her yard. When I nodded in thanks, she gave me a sour smile and looked away. Older people weren't used to the street violence of the modern world.

I opened the purse, groping through the usual assortment of makeup and lipstick cases, a pack of Kotex tampons. When I felt a small booklet, I froze like I had hit gold. Opening it, I saw it was a foreign driver's license. Across the top, it said *United Kingdom*, then beneath it was a photo of a pretty young woman and the name *Doris Hearn*. Unless it was a forgery or fake, we finally had an identification.

"Brae!"

Hearing Egersheim's voice sent a shiver up my spine. He never showed up to calls, especially at night. As I saw him scurrying toward me, I knew the case had reached a breaking point.

"We might have a lead," I blurted.

He glanced at the body and then at me. I showed him the license.

"Is it her?"

In the dark, I couldn't confirm, but there was no time for hesitation or uncertainty.

"Yes."

CHAPTER 13

I GOT HOME JUST BEFORE ELEVEN AND DIDN'T TRY TO SNEAK IN, knowing Ruth would be up anyway. The natural ups and downs of her pregnancy were worsened by the pre-eclampsia, which disrupted her bodily rhythms. At night, she couldn't sleep, and in the daytime, she sometimes got so tired she would collapse onto the nearest chair. For a woman who was always so vibrant and energetic, it was hard to watch.

The light was on in the kitchen, soft music playing on the radio.

"Jody?" she called, coming into the hall.

She still had an apron on from making dinner, but I didn't press it. We kissed on the lips, and I took off my coat.

"How's Nessie?"

"Out like a light. I took her to Billings Field today. She met a little girl named Ruth. She thought it was so funny that we had the same name."

I smiled, thinking about the waitress. The same names seemed a common thing.

We walked into the living room, and I turned on the news, keeping the volume low for Nessie's sake.

"Delilah called. Harrigan's fever broke."

"No more fever?"

She nodded, biting her lip with a smile.

"They think the infection is gone."

I sank back into the couch, tilting my head back, overcome by relief. It was the best news in weeks.

"I made some fried potatoes and sausages," she said.

"A little late for dinner, isn't it?" I joked.

"I was hungry. Can I get you some?"

"Thanks. I had a late lunch," I said.

Collins and I had eaten at two o'clock. Before, the wait would have been agonizing. More and more, working homicide struck me with a queasiness I never used to feel. Sensing my discomfort, Ruth changed the subject. "How was work?"

"I got a call on the way home—"

Our eyes both went to the TV.

...BREAKING NEWS THIS EVENING. A local woman was found suffering from stab wounds outside McSorley's Pub on Dorchester Avenue. She was taken to the hospital where she was pronounced dead...

STARING AT THE SCREEN, I just cringed. In the old days, the press would give us at least a few hours before reporting a murder. They didn't even have the facts straight. She wasn't a *local woman*, she only had a single stab wound, it was a half block from McSorley's, and she was pronounced dead at the scene, not at the hospital.

Either way, I knew it was a tipping point. A third murder would send the city into a panic. There could be no more stealth, no more careful investigating. Now it was a race to find the killer.

Ruth didn't have to ask because she could see my expression.

"Again," she said, and I nodded. "Is it the same—?"

"We don't know," I said, but my instincts told me otherwise. "Her neck wasn't cut. She was stabbed in the back."

Even as I said it, I knew I was making excuses. I didn't want to believe there was a serial killer on the streets. But unlike the public, my concern was more technical than emotional. With motives that were twisted, and often psychotic, psychopaths were less predictable and harder to catch.

Ruth moved closer and put her head on my shoulder. Her warmth was a comfort, her slow, steady breathing like a chant. As we sat in silence, another story followed that, for some strange reason, made me more anxious than the first.

IN WORLD NEWS TONIGHT, *two British soldiers were killed while trying to defuse a car bomb on Grosvenor Road in Belfast. The heavy sniper fire that followed hampered efforts to retrieve the bodies...*

RUTH PEERED up like she could sense my apprehension. I knew she wanted an answer or an explanation. The troubles in Northern Ireland had been in the news for months, not always the leading story but frequent enough to notice.

Like most Americans, I didn't understand the conflict. Fighting over religion seemed like something from Biblical times or the Middle Ages. Everyone I grew up with was either Jewish, Catholic, or, in the case of blacks, Baptist. There were too many other reasons for groups to hate one another.

Compared to three murders in Boston, the unrest in Ireland was as vague and distant as the coup in the Congo or the Rhodesian Bush War. Violence and strife only felt real when they were close to home.

"How fitting," I mumbled.

Ruth looked at me with a curious smile.

"Pardon?"

"The victim was from Belfast."

......

For all our complaining about insomnia, Ruth and I had fallen asleep together on the couch. We woke up late, frantic but touched to find that Nessie had dressed herself.

When I pulled up to *Sunnyside Nursery*, my hair was a mess, and one of my shoes was untied. I had been in such a rush I didn't put on my holster, and my pistol lay exposed on the passenger's seat.

I got Nessie out and fixed her coat. Walking in, I was surprised to see Delilah at the desk on the phone. She was usually running around helping the teachers and getting supplies. Her afro was combed out, but she wore a conservative red suit, a blouse with a Chelsea collar. She always rode that delicate line between hip and traditional.

"Good morning," she said, hanging up.

"Phone duty?"

She stood up and came around.

"Cecily didn't show up."

"Is she sick?"

"If she is, she didn't tell us. She didn't show up yesterday either."

Delilah crouched down to Nessie.

"Can I take your lunchbox?" she asked.

"Yes, please," Nessie said with a lisp.

It was the answer she gave every adult, the politeness she had learned from her mother. While manners were important, I couldn't wait to teach her judgment. Not everyone deserved respect; it had to be earned. In a world full of liars, cheats, and manipulators, I didn't want my daughter to be too trusting.

A teacher walked out, the older Italian lady who always smiled but seldom spoke. She took Nessie's hand, and I watched them as they went down the hallway.

"She's quite a little lady," Delilah said.

"Like her mother," I said, but there was no time for small talk. "I heard the fever's gone."

"Did you go by the hospital last night?"

"No," I said, feeling a twinge of guilt. "Something came up at work."

Something came up. I don't know why I tried to lie or downplay it.

Whenever there was a major murder or death, everyone knew I was involved.

"Was it that girl in Dorchester?"

I hesitated.

"Yeah."

She sighed, her eyes burning with shock and grief.

After a moment of silence, she said, "The doctors want to operate on Monday."

"This Monday?"

She nodded.

"They're afraid whatever pathogen caused the infection might still be dormant on the bullet."

I understood what she meant, but I would have phrased it differently.

"Then I guess they better get it out," I said.

Our eyes met in a moment of shared hope and fear. She even got teary. But when a teacher came out looking for drawing paper, she quickly collected herself.

"We'll see you at 3 p.m., Mr. Brac," she said with a formal smile.

"3 p.m.?"

"Didn't you know? We close early today for the holiday."

......

When I walked into the office, Collins was leaning over Egersheim's shoulder. I wasn't jealous, but it was too close for a rookie detective. The captain seemed to like him, probably because Collins didn't intimidate him.

I had to admit that, after only two days of working together, I was starting to warm up to the kid. I respected that he had read the case notes. A lot of patrolmen struggled just to get through the sports pages. He also had enthusiasm, a rare quality when most cops and officials, especially the older ones, had been jaded by the job. After dealing with hippies and radicals, it was a relief to meet a young person who appreciated law enforcement enough to make a career of it.

"Brae," Egersheim said.

"Hey, Lieutenant," Collins said.

"Sorry I'm late."

"I hear Harrigan is doing better."

He got updates from the department doctor who was in contact with the hospital, and not just out of concern. Anytime an officer was out sick or injured, he was watched by human resources in case of a permanent disability or death.

"Fever's gone," I said.

"Have they scheduled the operation?"

"Monday."

"Monday?"

It was sooner than anyone had expected, especially for such major surgery. The fact that it seemed rushed made everyone worry that his condition was worse than the physicians were saying.

I sat down and Collins took Harrigan's seat beside me. He was in the same suit he'd worn the last three days, a coffee stain on the lapel giving him away.

I was impressed that he even wore one. Detectives in other departments now wore street clothes, jeans and polyester shirts. Even when they were undercover, it was still sloppy. Egersheim didn't mind, but Captain Jackson would have been horrified. Above all, he valued professionalism. If there was any benefit to losing someone, it was knowing they didn't have to live through the changes in the world that would have disappointed them.

"A message came over the telecopier this morning," the captain said. "From the RUC."

"Royal Ulster Constabulary," Collins added. "The police in North Ireland,"

"*Northern* Ireland," I corrected.

"They've confirmed the identity of Doris Hearn. She left Ireland at the beginning of the month."

"Any idea why?"

"No. Her mother's deceased. Her father has been living in London for twenty years. She told her sister she was going to Boston with some friends for St. Patrick's Day. *Forensics* mailed the autopsy photos. It'll take a week to get a definite ID."

"That's one down," I said.

"Not enough, I'm afraid. The chief is giving a press conference on Tuesday. If we don't have a profile of the suspect, there's gonna be mass hysteria."

While *mass hysteria* was an exaggeration, I understood his fear. Spree killers had the advantage of speed. They weren't always the hardest to catch, but they were the hardest to stop.

The phone rang, and the captain picked up. I heard squeaking but couldn't distinguish a voice, the result of artillery blasts in the war. His expression went from indifferent, to curious, to surprised in a matter of seconds. With a nod, he thanked the caller and hung up.

"Well boys," he said. "Looks like we might have another lead."

CHAPTER 14

COLLINS AND I WALKED UP TO THE PORCH OF A RUNDOWN TRIP-DECKER on Dorchester Avenue. It was next to a liquor store and across from a baseball park, only two blocks from the Blarney Stone. Like all the houses in the area, it had worn shingles and a flat roof. Rusted gutters sent snowmelt trickling into the driveway.

Fields Corner was busy for St. Patrick's Day, the curbs so jammed with cars we had to park in front of a hydrant. The revelry would last all night and into the weekend, a holiday that was, ironically, celebrated for being celebrated. Except for that fading generation of elderly who still saw its religious significance, it was just an excuse to take the day off and get drunk.

We walked into a musty vestibule, and I scanned the directory, all Irish names. My eyes landed on Murphy/Devin and I pressed the button. Seconds later, the door buzzed open.

We walked up a narrow staircase to find a young woman waiting at the top. She wore bell-bottom jeans, a baggy sweater, and socks with no shoes. Her eyes were hollow, but the rest of her face was obscured by her long, dark hair.

"Deirdre?" I asked, and she nodded.

"I'm Detective Brae. This is Collins," I said, unwilling to call him *detective*.

"Did anyone see you come in?"

She had a strong Irish accent and smelled of alcohol.

"No."

She brought us into a living room with a coffee table, couch, and shag rug. It was as plain as a college dormitory, except with a woman's touch. There were plants on the windowsills and some cheap prints on the walls, landscapes of mountains and streams. In the corner was a makeshift bar with an assortment of hard liquor.

Collins and I sat on the couch, and she took the sofa chair, curling her legs beneath her. She was anxious and jittery and couldn't look us in the eye. I didn't know if she was manic or on drugs, but the drinking had done nothing to calm her down.

"You have information about the woman who was found behind Amrhein's?"

She lit a cigarette and blew out the smoke, finally looking at us.

"I know who she is," she said.

I took out my notepad and pen.

"I'm listening."

"Her name was Janice O'Brien. She was staying here."

"What do you mean *staying here*?"

"She's only been over a couple weeks—"

"From Ireland?"

"Belfast," she said.

I could tell she was too by the way she said it, Bel-FAST.

"What makes you think the victim was Janice O'Brien?"

She flicked her cigarette into an empty beer can, her fingers shaking.

"Last Monday, she got a phone call. It was a man. An hour later, she left. She never came home."

"Any idea who he was?"

"She didn't say. None of us are friends, really. We're just flatmates."

"Who else lives here?"

"Three other girls, although one is moving to Quincy with her guy this weekend."

"All Irish?"

She nodded.

"Do you recall what Janice was wearing that night?"

"A pink coat," she said.

"Anything else?"

She took another drag, shifting in the chair, thinking.

"Like flared pants, I believe. Red."

As I expected, the description matched. Still, I had to ask. Some people would do anything for attention, and I needed to weed out the nutjobs.

"Would you be willing to identify her?" I asked.

She looked up, her eyes suspicious.

"What? Like, see the body?"

"We could use a photo," I said gently.

"I suppose. I prefer not to get involved."

I wanted to say *You already are*, but there was no use threatening someone who had contacted us voluntarily.

"My immigration situation isn't square," she added, which I knew meant she didn't have a visa or a green card.

"Not our concern," I said, giving her a reassuring smile.

Before she got spooked or changed her mind, I reached into my coat and took out the photo of *Jane Doe II*. When I held it up, Deirdre put her hands to her mouth. Strangely, she seemed more shocked than devastated.

"Oh my God, it's her," she said.

I shoved the picture back in my coat.

"Thank you," I said.

At some point, we would need an affidavit. I wasn't going to ask her yet. For someone who was in the country illegally, she had been cooperative enough. I didn't want to scare her away in case we needed to ask her more questions.

I looked over at Collins, signaling it was time to go. So far, he hadn't said much during interviews. I knew he wasn't afraid to talk or speak his mind, so I took it as a sign of respect.

We walked over to the door, and I turned to Deirdre before leaving.

"Curious, why'd it take you a week to report this?"

She smiled, so I knew she wasn't offended.

"Like I said, we're all just flatmates. The girls come and go. We don't get into each other's business. Katie went to New York for a week and didn't tell anybody."

It was a good explanation, and one I could relate to from experience. In the hustle of young adulthood, no one paid much attention to what other people did.

The moment Collins and I walked out, we heard Irish music. Traffic in Fields Corner was at a standstill. A group of men walked by us wearing Leprechaun hats and shamrock buttons. They carried cases of beer and had open bottles in their hands. It was the one time of year that we overlooked public drinking.

"Things are heating up," I said.

"Ain't even three o'clock."

I looked suddenly at my watch.

"I gotta get my kid!"

We jumped in the Valiant and sped off.

It took almost forty minutes to drop Collins at headquarters and get back to *Sunnyside Nursery*. When I pulled up, my heart dropped when I saw Delilah on the stoop holding Nessie's hand.

I jumped out and ran over.

"Daddy!"

I smiled at Nessie and then looked up at Delilah.

"I'm sorry."

Her face was tense, but she seemed more worried than frustrated.

"It's okay, really. I had work to do."

I took Nessie's lunchbox and then grabbed her hand. As we turned to go, Delilah said, "I got a call today from a friend of Cecily's…"

Before she went on, she looked down at Nessie. I could tell she was trying to be careful with her words.

"She said she hasn't been home in two days."

When she raised her eyes, I understood the implication.

"Do you have an address?"

She reached into her purse, took out a scrap of paper, and handed it to me. I shoved it in my pocket without looking, too focused on the quiet dread in her eyes. Although I understood her concern, everyone was feeling paranoid, and young people weren't known for their reliability. She'd probably found something better and moved on.

"I'll check it out," I said.

"Please do."

......

NESSIE and I sang together the whole ride home, which after a day of investigating murders felt almost surreal. By the time we got to West Roxbury, the problems of work seemed far away. But all the tranquility faded when I turned onto our street and saw an ambulance.

I pulled over and got out, leaving Nessie in her car seat. As I ran toward the door, two paramedics came out with Ruth on a stretcher. She had a blanket over her and an ice pack on her head. My panic lessened, but only slightly, when I realized she was conscious.

"What's wrong?!" I shouted.

Our neighbor Esther walked out behind them, her husband Jim standing on the lawn in his bowtie and sweater vest.

"She just bumped her head," Esther said.

"I'm fine," Ruth said, but her voice was strained. "I just fainted."

"Her blood pressure is seriously elevated," one of the paramedics said.

I froze on the walkway, feeling helpless.

"Jody, where's Ness?" Ruth asked.

Snapping out of it, I ran over to the car and got her. As we walked back, she gripped my hand, and I knew she was confused.

"Momma?"

"Honey, everything's alright. Momma has to go to the hospital."

When Nessie looked up, my heart sank. After everything I'd been through with the war and work, all it took was a child's look to crush me.

"We'll meet you there," I said.

"Not Nessie," Ruth insisted.

"We'll watch her," Jim offered. "She can play with the girls."

When I looked at Ruth, she nodded. I kissed Nessie on the head and told her we would be gone for a little while. Like most kids, she didn't understand enough to complain or argue. I was relieved when Esther knelt with her arms out, and Nessie ran to her.

Ruth blew me a kiss, and the paramedics shut the doors. I got back into the Valiant, turned around, and followed the ambulance as it pulled away.

CHAPTER 15

"She may have a concussion."

Sitting across from the two doctors, I felt like it was reverse interrogation. I was used to being on the authoritative side of the table. They had brought me into an office, a special courtesy because they talked to most people in the waiting room. But physicians respected cops who, in some ways, were working toward the same goal.

"How's the baby?"

It should have been my first question, but I had been afraid to ask. As someone who couldn't even protect his own body from harm, I couldn't imagine doing it for two.

"The child is fine," one of them assured me. "The pre-eclampsia is our main concern. She's four weeks from term. If we can't get her blood pressure down, she'll have to stay."

I nodded reluctantly, knowing how Ruth hated to be confined.

"When can I see her?"

"Now."

We all got up and went out to the hallway, passing a nurse's station decorated with Shamrocks and leprechauns. We turned into a small room, where she was reclining with a bandage on her head.

"Jody," she said.

I walked over and leaned down for a quick kiss. Her lips were dry and chapped.

"How're you feeling?"

"The headache's gone."

"From the fall or pre-eclampsia?" I joked.

"It's all the same at this point."

She sounded bright, almost cheery. I was sure whatever drug she was on helped.

"Tell me what happened."

"I was cleaning the oven. I know I shouldn't have been. I wasn't feeling great anyway. When I stood up, I got dizzy. That's all I remember."

The image of her collapsing alone filled me with a quiet rage. I knew I wouldn't always be able to protect her and Nessie, but I was going to try.

"Luckily," she went on, "Esther came by to borrow baking soda. I had left the front door open to air out the smell. She saw me on the floor. Ugh! I don't know how long I was there."

She spoke like she was retelling a mishap from a lady's luncheon. For all my hesitation about moving to a suburban part of the city, I was glad to have neighbors who cared.

We talked for another twenty minutes, mostly about Nessie. If Ruth asked about the investigation, I was prepared to change the subject or even lie. After such a traumatic fall, she didn't need any more worry. I was saved when an older nurse came in with dinner. I looked at Ruth and then at the woman, stepping aside so she could put down the tray.

"You go," Ruth said. "You have to relieve Esther."

Like everything, she made it easy for me.

"I'll come by in the morning," I promised.

I leaned over, and we kissed again.

"Don't forget to tell Nessie to brush," she said as I walked away.

I waved with a smile and left. I took the elevator down and followed the corridor to the next building. I didn't know if Harrigan could see visitors, but I couldn't be at the hospital and not try.

The light was on when I got to the room, the door wide open.

"Lieutenant."

I stopped in shock.

On the chair beside the bed was Captain Egersheim. Harrigan was awake and sitting up. He had tubes and wires in his arms, but otherwise, he looked alert, almost normal.

"Gentlemen," I greeted them.

"You working tonight?"

It seemed a strange question for a boss to ask, but we made our own schedules.

"Ruth had a fall."

"Is she alright?" they asked at the same time.

"She just bumped her head. She's fine. She got lightheaded."

I walked over and stood next to the bed.

"You ready for Monday?" I asked.

Harrigan peered up, his eyes bright but slightly bloodshot.

"As ready as can be."

I patted his shoulder, overcome with emotion that I couldn't show. In some ways, I was more worried about him than Ruth, if only because I knew the risks were greater.

Tired from the day, I looked around for a chair but didn't see one. To my surprise, the captain got up and said, "Here. Take this one."

"You sure?"

"I've gotta get home."

"Thanks."

He extended his hand to Harrigan, and they shook.

"Get well," he said, then he looked at me. "Jody, any chance you could—?"

"I'll be in first thing in the morning."

He didn't have to ask, but I appreciated the courtesy. Whenever an investigation reached a crisis point, there were no breaks, and weekends were like any other day. Department policy required eight hours of sleep for every sixteen hours worked, but no one ever followed it.

Egersheim put on his hat and walked out, and the room went silent. I was glad he was gone. He wasn't a nuisance, but I could never relax around him. Harrigan and I needed to discuss the case —— something that, ironically, we couldn't do around him.

"You look anxious, Lieutenant," Harrigan said.

"Good. That means my outside matches my inside."

He grinned.

"The murders were the headline story again tonight."

Following his gaze, I saw a small TV in the corner. It made me wonder why Ruth's room didn't have one.

"I wish I could say I was surprised. Did they say *serial killer*?"

"It was too low. I couldn't hear."

The local media loved to sensationalize. After the Boston Strangler, they had been more careful. They had done more to cause panic than to allay it at the time. Still, I was sure every news station in town was waiting to write about the next murder.

"Has there been any progress?" Harrigan asked, a polite way of saying *Have YOU made any progress?*

"We got a lead today."

"The captain told me. A woman who knew the Amrhein's victim?"

"A roommate. She said the girl's name was Janice O'Brien. She's Irish."

The fact that I called them *the girls* and he always said *the victims* was somehow significant.

"So, we have two Irish victims and one British?"

"We don't know that."

"The young woman from Thomas Park had UK money."

"A few coins."

"The one killed on Dorchester Ave. was from Belfast."

"Doris Hearn," I said.

"Do they not use British currency in Northern Ireland?"

"That's right," I said, although I knew he knew the answer.

"So she could be Irish too."

It was the same thing Collins had said, which made me think they had been talking.

"Maybe it's a coincidence."

"Maybe it's a pattern. If they're all foreigners, it would explain why people aren't coming forward to report them missing."

"Yet," I said.

"Yet."

Maybe I was getting old. I used to be more creative with the evidence, more daring in my theories and speculations. Now I was cautious about everything.

"So, what? You think it's a lone wolf? A sociopath?"

"Or someone with a vendetta."

"Now you sound like Columbo."

Harrigan chuckled. Despite the tension, his heart monitor hadn't increased a blip, some indication of his steadiness and calm.

"I'd be looking for an Irish man."

"On St. Patrick's Day weekend? Good luck."

"With the parade Sunday, what better time? Every Irish person in the city will be there."

"We have no witnesses, no profile."

"The boy from South Boston saw him."

"Yeah, a guy in a long leather coat with a mustache," I snickered. "It's a needle in a haystack."

"Then bring a magnet, Lieutenant."

I appreciated the encouragement, but we had gotten as far as we could. At some point, brainstorming just became gossip and banter.

"How's my replacement doing?" he asked, and I gave him a sharp look.

"Collins ain't your replacement. He's a stand-in."

"Is that not the same thing?"

I frowned, but he had a point. He always got me on the technicalities.

"He's just a hotheaded kid," I said.

"Weren't we all once?"

Too tired to philosophize, I didn't answer. I was saved when someone knocked.

"Hello, love," Delilah greeted Harrigan. "Hi, Joseph."

She had changed since I saw her earlier, now wearing a long blue dress and tall boots. In her arms was a bouquet, which she promptly put down on the table. Only a woman would be thoughtful enough to brighten up a hospital room with flowers.

"You're here late," she said as I got up.

"I had to—"

"Ruth is here," Harrigan said.

She stopped.

"Here? Like in the hospital?"

"She had a little fall today," I said. "But she's fine."

"I'm so sorry, Jody."

She was the only person I ever knew who switched between my full name and nickname.

"She gets dizzy sometimes."

"She has pre-eclampsia, right?" she asked.

I wasn't surprised she knew what it was.

"Yeah. She's on bed rest."

"Well, if you need to drop Nessie off at daycare some extra days, just let me know."

"Thanks, maybe," I said, stumbling because I hadn't thought that far ahead. "We've got a babysitter."

When I stood to offer her my seat, she was too busy to notice. She was propping up the flowers and throwing out the paper plate and milk carton from Harrigan's dinner. After checking his cardiac monitor, she moved the IV line, which had gotten twisted around the bed rail. Her assertiveness reminded me a lot of Ruth.

"I'm gonna go," I said.

Looking up, Harrigan lifted his arm. When we shook, his grip wasn't as firm as usual, and I noticed his eyes were starting to sag.

"Find our friend," he said, a veiled reference to the assailant.

"What time's surgery Monday?"

"3 p.m.," Delilah said.

"I'll be by before then."

"Don't feel obligated, Lieutenant."

"I never do."

Our eyes locked, and he smiled faintly.

"Get some rest," I said.

I turned around and walked out.

CHAPTER 16

WHEN I GOT TO HEADQUARTERS THE NEXT MORNING, COLLINS WAS standing outside the captain's office. He had on a different suit, navy blue with a black tie, which somehow brought out his darker complexion. I never doubted he wanted to be a detective – a lot of cops did. He just seemed too young and reckless. Considering punctuality was one of the qualities Captain Jackson valued the most, I had to respect Collins for it.

"Hey, Lieutenant," he said, raising his cup of coffee like a toast.

It was barely eight o'clock, so early for a Saturday that the hallways were empty. Above I could hear footsteps in the operations room, which was open around the clock. Otherwise, the only person I saw was an elderly black janitor buffing the floor.

"How long have you been here?" I asked.

He shrugged.

"Aw, maybe a half hour."

I could have been earlier too. I hadn't slept the night before. But Nadia needed a lift, so I had to pick her up in Dorchester. I was going to visit Ruth until she called and said she was getting out. Her blood pressure was down, and her heart rate was back to normal. I was equal parts grateful and relieved. It couldn't have come at a better time. With the investigation and Harrigan's surgery, I felt ready to crack up.

"Any signs of Eger—?" I said, before changing to *the captain*.

Calling a superior by his last name was a bad example for any new detective.

"Naw. I didn't see his car in the lot."

Aw and *Naw*. Everything Collins said had a tinge of street slang, a habit I had been trying to break for years.

"I got someone who might know something," he added.

If I had made a nickel for every *someone who might know something* in my career, I would have retired as a millionaire already.

"Let's hear it."

"I was at a bar in Southie last night. A guy I know told me he met a girl there two weeks ago who looked like the one from Thomas Park."

"How'd he know what she looks like?"

"He read it in the paper."

I acted skeptical, but I was interested. It was the first witness since Collins' stepbrother to have possibly seen the killer.

I reached into my pocket for my keys. I was the only other person with access to the captain's office, something he insisted upon after he went on vacation and left evidence for a trial in his filing cabinet.

"You think he's reliable?"

"He's a little wacko but he's straight enough. He said she was Irish. She got into an argument with a guy, and he ran out after her."

"The night she was found?"

Collins tilted his head, thinking.

"He wasn't sure. He's there every night."

When we walked in, we were hit by the stench of Egersheim's cigarettes.

"Long hair, mustache," he went on. "Maybe mid-thirties. Same thing my brother said."

The description was vague, but I couldn't blame the witness. All young guys dressed the same.

"You know where he lives?"

"I got the address."

"We'll check it out. Good work—"

Egersheim burst in, scrambling over to his desk with his head down. For some reason, he had an umbrella, although it wasn't raining. He took off his coat, hung it on the chair, and sat down.

"Now," he said, and I could feel his anxiety. "What's the latest on the triple homicide?"

Considering the murders were on different days and at different locations, it was the wrong classification, but I wasn't about to correct him. He was obviously frustrated. I was surprised he even asked for an update since I'd just seen him at the hospital the night before.

"We've got someone who might have seen someone with one of them," I said.

The captain squinted.

"What?"

I looked over at Collins, who deserved any credit if the witness turned out to be valuable.

"A guy I know. He saw the girl from Thomas Park."

Egersheim slapped his hands on the desk.

"Look. If this investigation was about finding people who thought that they knew the victims or a ten-year-old—"

"Twelve," Collins said.

"A *twelve-year-old* kid who saw a guy in a leather coat, we would've had an arrest a week ago. We've got no prints, no blood matches, no motive, no suspects!"

In all our time working together, he had never lost his temper. I used to think it was because he was meek. Now I attributed it to Harrigan, who had a calming effect on everyone.

"The Chief wants answers. He's already threatening to bring in the State Police to help!"

I wanted to argue back, but I bit my tongue. With an understaffed department and scant evidence, we couldn't be expected to move any faster. And while I could always take a scolding, it was embarrassing in front of Collins.

"Give me until Monday," I said.

Collins and I stood up. As we turned to leave, Egersheim said, "I still need you both to work at the parade tomorrow."

......

THE D STREET Projects were on the west side of South Boston —— a neighborhood of wooden tenements, vacant lots, and corner stores that sold everything from bourbon to baby formula. Just on the other side of Fort Point Channel, it was worlds away from the sleekness of downtown, whose buildings loomed a mile in the distance. While other housing projects had turned black in the sixties, this one had not. It was defended by its residents like a proud but besieged outpost of white urban despair.

As we pulled in, I felt the excitement of the coming celebration. People lingered in doorways drinking from paper bags; music blared from the hallways. Many of the apartments had tacky Irish decorations, big shamrocks and cartoonish leprechauns, a tribute to the fading heritage of people whose ancestors had arrived generations ago.

Collins pointed, and I pulled into a lot where half the cars looked abandoned. As we got out, I saw some kids huddled around a barrel fire in a litter-strewn playground, the jungle gym rusted and tilting. I fought the urge to yell at them; we weren't there for petty crimes or delinquency.

I followed Collins down an alleyway. Every courtyard we came to looked the same, a nightmarish land of identical three-story brick buildings.

"You know this area good," I said.

"I lived here as a kid. Before my folks got divorced."

I knew it too, but mostly as a crime scene. It was easier to navigate when it was nighttime and there were half a dozen cruisers with their lights on.

Despite all the problems in the Southie projects, Harrigan and I never went there much. If there was a homicide, it was usually something simple, a dispute between neighbors, or a botched robbery. Everything else was handled by the local precinct.

LOVE AIN'T FOR KEEPING

Finally, we turned toward a doorway. If we had gone any farther, I would have asked why we just didn't drive.

"How do people get their groceries in around here?" I joked.

"We could've parked out front. I figured we'd draw less attention this way."

"Less than walking a half mile through the projects?"

He shrugged his shoulders with a boyish grin. Either way, it was impossible to go unnoticed in a place where everyone knew each other, and most were related. As we walked, I saw housewives peering out their shades, men watching us from alcoves and breezeways.

We opened a rusted door and walked down a hallway, the smell of mold and cigarettes overwhelming. At the end, Collins stopped.

"This is it."

He knocked hard, and we waited. Moments later, the door opened, and a man looked out. Short and thin, he wore a collared shirt with a ragged sweater over it. His tan and grizzled face seemed more the consequence of hard living than of age. I knew he couldn't have been older than thirty.

"What's up, Billy?" Collins said.

The man waved, and we walked into a small living room. The couch was old and stained. The coffee table was covered with cards, an overfilled ashtray, and a six-pack of Schlitz. The Celtics game was playing on a small black & white TV. I noticed an Army jacket hanging over one of the chairs, which steered my revulsion more toward sympathy.

"This is my partner," Collins said.

For now, the term was accurate, but it still made me cringe.

"Hey," the man mumbled.

"You think you saw the girl who was killed up the Heights?" I asked.

He peered up, his eyes red.

"Maybe. I was drunk."

Considering what he had told Colling, it was an answer I didn't expect. I assumed he had misgivings, not wanting to be a snitch. Or maybe he had lied all along. But if he knew or saw anything, we had to find out, and everyone had their price. Not interested in playing games, I reached into my pocket and took out a twenty-dollar bill.

"Will this refresh your memory?"

At first, he just stared at it, almost like he was insulted. Then he snatched it from my hand.

"I wasn't looking for money. I told Juan that," he said, looking at Collins. "But I'll take it."

"What did you see?"

He cleared his throat.

"There was a girl in the Quiet Man Pub a couple weeks ago. A young chick—"

"What'd she look like?"

"Pretty thing. Red hair."

The autopsy report had said *auburn*, but it was close enough.

"She was at the bar," he went on, "just smoking."

At the mention of a cigarette, he reached for one on the table and lit it.

"She was alone. I offered to buy her a drink and she said no thanks. She had an Irish accent, so I asked her where she was from. My grandparents were from Galway—"

"Did she say?"

"Up North," he said, taking a drag. "Maybe an hour or so later, I can't remember. The place was packed. I was drunk by now. I see her talking to some guy."

"Can you describe him?"

The way he hesitated, I thought he wanted more money.

"Regular looking dude. Long hair, dark mustache."

"Tall, short?"

"Not big. Maybe my size," he said, which I guessed was about 5' 8".

"Anything distinctive? A scar, missing teeth?"

"Nothing I could see. He had on a leather coat, shiny leather."

"Long?"

He stopped.

"Yeah, it was long. Like a trench coat. It seemed like they were arguing."

"Seemed like or were?"

"It was hard to tell at first. But then he grabbed her arms. Now, this ain't the Taj Mahal…"

I was impressed by the reference, but the metaphor wasn't right.

"You can't hit a woman," he continued. "Two guys ran over, grabbed him. The girl took off in a huff-"

"She left the bar?"

"Out the door. A minute or so later, the guy goes running after her."

"What makes you think he was *running after her*?"

"First, I ain't never seen neither these people in Southie. I mean, she was Irish. There's lots of Irish, but they don't really mingle with locals. But this guy looked dead serious. I saw it in his eyes."

I looked over at Collins who, for the first time, wasn't grinning. So far, we had a few leads, none of which were conclusive. The only victim we had identified was Doris Hearn, but it brought us no closer to a motive or a suspect. Somehow, this felt like our first break.

"Could I show you a picture? You can tell me if it's the same girl?"

"Sure."

I reached carefully into my coat, making sure I had the right one. He pursed his lips and took a breath. In the photo, her eyes were closed, her face pasty but unblemished. As good as she looked, it was never easy to see a dead person, especially a girl so young.

"A spittin' image," he said, looking away.

As I put the picture away, my eyes caught his combat jacket.

"You a vet?" I asked.

He arched his back, raised his chin.

"11th Infantry Brigade. United States Army. You?"

"Korea. Marines."

I didn't say it to brag, but out of comradery. Anyone who had been to war shared a bond that went far beyond age, heritage, or social class. I didn't know the guy, but I respected him.

"Thanks for your help," I said.

"Anytime."

As we turned to go, I stopped.

"Curious. What made you come forward?"

"I didn't really come forward. I was up at the Quiet Man, and I seen him," he said. "I knew a girl was killed. We don't put up with that shit around here. Get the bastard!"

"We will."

Collins and I left and went down the hallway.

"You know everybody," I said as we walked out the door.

"I get around."

I smiled, remembering what it was like to be a young cop. Boston then felt like one big extended family. When I wasn't working, I was out with colleagues, hopping between the bars and nightclubs like we owned the town. And we did. After the war, everyone loved the police, craving safety and security in a world that had almost destroyed itself.

For me, those days were long gone, and I missed the thrill of being cool. With a wife and daughter at home and another child on the way, I didn't socialize much. All the places I frequented had changed names or closed; all the hotshots and wise guys I knew were either dead or in the suburbs. I always thought only crooners and film stars faded out. But everyone lost those friends, places, and connections that once made them feel important.

Even if I was getting old, I still had a job to do. Collins had a lot to learn, but it didn't hurt to have someone younger and more in tune around.

"Want me to drive, Lieutenant?"

As I opened the car door, I looked at him across the hood.

"Not on your life."

CHAPTER 17

I SPED UP TO THE ENTRANCE OF CITY HOSPITAL AND PARKED OUT front. If anyone complained, I would just flash my badge. I ran inside and across the lobby. As I turned the corner to the elevators, Ruth was coming out in a wheelchair, a young woman in scrubs pushing her.

"Jody!"

I leaned over and kissed her on the cheek.

"You ready?"

She patted the bag on her lap, the few personal items she had brought. She was wearing the clothes she'd arrived in, no doubt desperate to change after two days in a hospital gown.

I looked at the orderly and said, "I can take it from here."

Ruth smiled and blew the girl a kiss. I pushed her back through the lobby and out the front doors.

"Chilly," she said.

When I opened the door, she got up and waddled toward the car. I tried to help, but she shooed me away.

"Monday is the first day of spring," I said.

"You'd never know it."

I got in, started the engine, and turned around. As we came to the gate, we hit a pool of slushy water before pulling out into the street.

"Did you visit Harrigan?"

"Yesterday," I said. "I'll go by Monday before the operation."

"Was Nessie good?"

"Good," I said, distracted.

At the intersection of Tremont Street, I blew a red light and almost hit a milk van. Ruth didn't say anything, but her sharp look was enough to make me slow down. Considering that she was pregnant, I should have been more careful anyway.

Before we were married, she loved excitement, fast cars and late nights. She drank more than I liked, but it added to her mystique. Now she had settled into the quiet routine of motherhood. Her youthful spunk was gone, but I wouldn't trade the stability in our lives for those reckless days.

"How is the investigation?" she asked.

I glanced over.

"We've got a few leads."

"A few?"

"How're you feeling?"

She smiled like she knew I didn't want to talk about it.

"Better."

We got to the house in less than fifteen minutes, which was good even for a Saturday. When we pulled into the driveway, Nadia was standing in the doorway with Nessie, who had on a pink dress with a bow in her hair. I grabbed Ruth's bag and we walked up to meet them.

"My girl," Ruth said, bending down to hug Nessie.

When we walked inside, I smelled something delicious. Nadia was always cooking. If it hadn't been for her, I would never have had Pierogis or Pyzys. She didn't just make Polish food. Even with our old Westinghouse oven, she made a perfect meatloaf and a cottage pie Nessie loved.

While Ruth walked upstairs to shower and get changed, I went into the living room to spend some time with Nessie. She had laid out a blanket with her dolls and their accessories alongside a miniature table and two chairs.

"Looks like a picnic."

"They have dinner," she said, kneeling and putting the dolls in their seats. "This one for Delilah."

She handed me a tiny fork, and I smiled.

"She has the same name as Delilah from school?" I asked, and she nodded.

Sitting on the couch, I leaned over to play with her when something on the TV caught my eye. It was the St. Patrick's Day parade in New York City, one of the largest in the country. A line of children marched holding crosses, one for each of the thirteen people killed in 'Bloody Sunday' in Derry two months before.

I never cared much for the holiday, mainly because I gave up drinking before I joined the force. But seeing the somber faces of the children made me realize it was about more than just green beer and rebel songs. I didn't know much about the politics of Northern Ireland, but with at least two of the victims from Belfast, I felt like I was going to learn fast.

"Jody?"

I looked over, and Ruth was on the stairs in a bathrobe. One leg was showing, which gave me a sudden arousal. With so much going on, I hadn't thought about sex in days.

"Can you get a towel from the dryer?"

As I went to stand, the phone rang, sending a shiver up my spine. We hardly ever got calls, especially at dinnertime. Nessie must have noticed my reaction because she gazed up with her mouth open.

I ran into the kitchen and grabbed the receiver off the wall, hoping it was a neighbor or the wrong number.

"Brae?" I heard, and it was Egersheim.

"What's up?"

"Did you get a call from headquarters?"

"We just got home."

When he paused, I knew it was serious.

"We've got another dead girl," he said.

As we spoke, Ruth was standing in the doorway, Nadia over by the pantry holding a broom. It was hard to talk with both of them watching.

"Is that so," I said, vaguely.

"Did you hear what I said?"

"Where?"

"Hibernian Hall."

"I'll leave now."

When I hung up, Ruth and Nadia were staring at me.

"Who was that?" Ruth asked.

"Um, just the captain. There's been an, um, incident. They need me on the scene."

As much as I tried to downplay it, she knew. Ruth could read me like a book.

I went back into the den where Nessie was holding a toy cup to the mouth of one of her dolls.

"You feed her," she said.

She pointed at the doll Ruth's sister had sent the Christmas before, the first time we had heard from her in three years.

"Honey, Daddy has to go out for a bit."

Her lips curled down in a pout.

"Why?" she moaned.

I leaned over to kiss her and then stopped, worried she would sense my anxiety. I hated that kids were so aware.

When I walked over to get my coat, Ruth was standing in the foyer. With her bathrobe loose, I could see the tops of her breasts. It was a struggle not to gawk.

"When will you be home?" she asked softly.

"A couple of hours."

"Is it—?"

"Yes, maybe, I think," I said, distracted. "I'll know soon."

Stepping forward, she put one arm around my back and pressed her lips to mine. Pulling away, she gave me a seductive look that was at once a promise and a threat, some guarantee that I would come home safe.

"Then I'll see you later."

CHAPTER 18

UNLIKE OTHER NEIGHBORHOODS, ROXBURY WAS QUIET ON THE NIGHT before the parade, which was no surprise. In less than a decade, it had gone from Jewish and Irish to entirely black. St. Patrick's Day didn't mean much to Southern transplants who'd come looking for work after the war.

The area had been poor when I'd lived there as a kid, but now it was a ghetto. The crime was high, the roads were bad, and there were lots of abandoned buildings. After several racial incidents in the sixties, the department had a delicate truce with the community. Having Harrigan as a partner always gave me more credibility, but most people still didn't trust the cops.

I could see police lights flashing and hear sirens as I turned onto Dudley Street. The road was blocked off by two cruisers, so I didn't have to look for a parking spot. I stopped and jumped out, nodding to the officers as I ran toward the scene.

Ahead, I saw cops and other officials standing by an alley next to Hibernian Hall, a large brick building that had once been the center of Irish music and dance. Now, it was the last Irish holdout in the changing neighborhood.

People had spilled out from an event, men and women who, as white people, now looked out of place in the area. Some locals were peering out from the jazz club next door.

"Brae?"

I turned to see Egersheim rushing over in a baggy trench coat, hands in his pockets.

"You just get here?" he asked.

It felt like an accusation, or maybe I was oversensitive. Before moving out to the farthest edge of the city, I always lived in places where I could get anywhere fast. Even Captain Jackson used to compliment me on how quickly I responded to calls after hours.

We walked down the alley, and I saw officers and other personnel lingering in the darkness. As chaotic as the scene on the street was, no one here seemed in a rush.

"What happened?" I demanded.

While my tone was blunt, it was the only way to get the attention of a dozen cops and paramedics.

"Stabbed," a young black officer said. "A bunch of times."

"In the chest," another said.

Over by the wall, I saw a dark shape on the pavement. One of the cops shined a flashlight, and I froze. It was a young woman in her early twenties. She had on a wool coat and a nice skirt. Although her blouse was dark, it couldn't hide the blood stains on her chest.

"Who reported this?" Egersheim asked.

"A passerby," a cop said.

"We got a witness," someone added.

My body was still as I stared at the corpse, but inside I felt ready to burst. I could have blamed it on coffee or not having eaten. But the fact was that I was shaken.

"Detective?" an officer said, and I blinked as if coming out of a daze. "Did you hear what I said?"

"Yeah, a witness. Where?"

As I asked, a cop was walking over with a middle-aged black man in a scaly cap and dress coat. I rushed toward them away from the body.

"Lieutenant," the officer said. "This guy thinks he saw the assailant."

"I ain't think I seen him. I seen him."

I heard a faint Southern accent, which wasn't unusual. Most black people in Boston hadn't even been there for a generation.

"What did you see?" I asked.

"I was smoking out front of Jake's," he said, pointing at the club. "All sudden, I hear a scream. It weren't no regular scream. It was the kind 'o scream that makes your hair stand up…"

It sounded dramatic, but I knew exactly what he meant.

"So, I run over, and I see this dude on top of that there girl. I shout, 'Hey, man,' and he takes off running…"

We followed his gaze to the end of the alley where a dumpster sat in front of a rusted fence. Turning, I made eye contact with the nearest sergeant.

"We've got all available units canvasing the area," he assured me.

"Can you describe him?" Egersheim asked.

The man thought for a moment, puffing on his cigarette. He was calm for a murder witness as if he had seen violence before.

"Regular-looking white dude, I'd say," he said. "Maybe thirty-five."

"Anything specific?"

"I only seen him a split second. When I came running down, he looked back. Then he took off."

"Did he have a thick mustache?"

The man stopped like he was stunned I knew.

"As thick as a donkey's tail," he said.

When I laughed, Egersheim and the officer laughed too. Even at the most tragic times, humor made things a little easier.

"He hopped that fence?" I asked.

"Faster than a scalded cat."

Again, we all laughed, although I didn't think the guy was trying to be funny.

"Thanks," I said.

"Get all his information," Egersheim said to the cop.

He should have asked the man first as a courtesy. In rougher neighborhoods, being a witness sometimes meant being a snitch, which was why so many people didn't come forward about crimes.

Hearing a gruff voice, I turned to see Doctor Ansell charging toward us. He had an assistant with him, a young man in a plaid coat, tie, and glasses. They were out late for a Saturday night, but the doctor always worked. There were rumors he even slept at the office.

"Brae," he said. "Another one of yours?"

I watched with an amused smirk as he passed by.

"What'd he mean by that?" Egersheim asked.

"My case."

"It's everyone's case now."

For once, I couldn't disagree with the captain.

When we walked out of the alleyway, the sidewalk was mobbed with people. The chief had arrived, talking to reporters who had their cameras and mics lined up. As the fourth murder in two weeks, the press would no longer sit back to see what the department did. I had watched enough crimes and scandals unfold to know this was a tipping point. Despite Vietnam and all the other problems in the world, Boston had a serial murderer on its hands. The public would be looking for answers.

"Hey, Lieutenant."

Officer Collins came through the crowd, fully dressed but not wearing a tie. His suits always looked slightly too big, as if he had inherited them.

"Is she dead?" he asked.

I held out my hand, urging him to lower his voice. While I knew he was excited, he spoke too loudly for such a crowded scene.

"Knife wound."

Egersheim acknowledged Collins with a nod and then walked over to the chief and his staff. He never sought attention, but he also never lost an opportunity to get it.

"How'd you get here?" I asked.

"My uncle drove me."

"Same one that gave you that suit?"

Looking down, Collins smoothed out his jacket like he was offended.

"Actually, yeah," he said.

I chuckled at his reaction, but it was a bad time for sarcasm. A woman had just been murdered.

"C'mon," I said. "Let's get outta here."

......

AS WE PULLED AWAY from the scene, the paramedics were carrying the body to the ambulance. A line of officers stood holding back the crowd which, almost an hour after the incident was reported, was still growing.

I took out my cigarettes and gave one to Collins.

"You ever think of getting a car?" I asked.

He nodded, taking a drag.

"With detectives pay, hopefully soon."

I didn't reply because I didn't want to disappoint him. He had come up from the ranks as a temp, something I knew the captain had already explained to him. The politics of promotions were complicated, and favoritism was only a part of it.

I didn't know if Collins had connections in administration or if he had just gotten lucky. Either way, I admired his work ethic. Egersheim would never have called him at home, so I was sure he had been listening to the police radio and came out on his own. I wouldn't let him take Harrigan's place, but I also didn't want to see him go back down to patrol.

Only a quarter mile down Dudley Street we started to see white faces again. At Upham's Corner, the Dublin House bar was packed with people standing on the sidewalk holding drinks.

We turned onto Columbia Road toward the expressway, the quickest way to Charlestown. For a highway that had done so much damage to the soul of the city, it was the easiest way to get around.

"Have you heard anything else on the street?" I asked.

I told myself the question was to encourage him, but the truth was, I needed the help.

"Not since talking to Billy."

"You think his story checks out?"

"I know it does. He wouldn't lie to me."

I glanced over.

"Yeah? What makes you so sure? He came up to you in a bar."

"It ain't like that. I know him," he said, something I either missed or that he hadn't mentioned.

"Know him? Like how? Like you played Little League together?"

Collins grinned.

"Kinda. He's actually my stepfather's stepbrother."

Even doing the quick math, it seemed impossible he had an uncle so close in age. But I didn't bother asking him to explain.

"Hey!" he exclaimed.

When he glanced back, I looked in the rearview mirror. The sidewalk was dark, but the streetlamps gave off enough light that I could see a man walking alone.

"What is it?"

"Can you slow down?" Collins said.

"Hang on."

If it was someone suspicious, slowing or stopping would only alert him. I continued to the next light and made a U-turn in front of St. Margaret's Church. By the time I got to the next light and swung back around, the guy had gone another thirty yards but was still in our sights.

Luckily, a half dozen other cars were passing too, giving us cover as we approached. The man had on a long leather coat and dark hat. He walked with a wide swagger, his hands in his pockets. Although he could have simply been going home after a night of drinking, something about the deliberate way he walked made me uneasy.

"Got your gun?" I asked, and Collins patted his coat. "Open your window."

He rolled it down, and we pulled alongside the man. At first, he didn't notice, which in itself was some indication of innocence.

"Hey, buddy?!"

Stopping, he turned to us squinting. In that split second, I saw his face and his mustache. Then he broke into a full sprint.

"Get him!" I shouted, and Collins jumped out the door.

I punched the gas, hoping to cut him off at Dorchester Avenue the next block over. Skidding to a stop, I got out and ran back up the sidewalk. But they were both gone.

I looked between the houses, massive triple-deckers with narrow driveways and no yards. I walked down one but gave up because I couldn't see. Harrigan was always the one who carried the flashlight.

"Lieutenant!" I heard.

I ran toward the voice, and Collins came out of the shadows.

"Where is he?"

He shook his head, struggling to speak.

"You alright?" asked.

He walked over and leaned against a parked car, his chest heaving as he tried to catch his breath.

"Asthma," he said with a nervous laugh.

"The department know?"

He looked up, and when our eyes met, his were watery.

"No."

"That son of a bitch," I said looking around.

"I...I chased him down that driveway. He hopped a fence. Sorry, I couldn't see a thing."

"You got better eyesight than me."

"Should we call it in?"

At this point, any progress was good, but I also had to be careful. If word got out that we chased someone for no reason, the newspapers could say the department is incompetent, accuse cops of being bullies. The public was sensitive. Until the killer was found, we would be the target of everyone's fear and frustration.

"Naw," I said. "You get a good look at him?"

"Yep. You think he might be the guy?"

"Maybe."

"If not, why would he run?"

We walked toward the car, which sat parked with the lights on and the engine running. As we got closer, I realized I left the door open too. With all the bars along Dorchester Avenue, I was lucky a drunk didn't get in it and drive off. It wouldn't have been the first time the Valiant was stolen during an investigation.

"Let's keep this between us," I said.

"Sure," he agreed, still panting.

We got in and closed the doors.

"You think you should be smoking with asthma?"

"Probably not."

CHAPTER 19

GETTING ANYWHERE IN SOUTH BOSTON ON THE DAY OF THE ST. Patrick's Day parade was almost impossible. I drove up and down the narrow streets of the West Side and couldn't find a spot. The curbs were lined with cars jammed together bumper to bumper. Many had out-of-state plates, including New Hampshire, Rhode Island, and even one from Ohio. Some were parked in front of fire hydrants and handicap ramps, which could have been a boon for the department. But no one was giving out tickets because every available officer was on duty.

Chief McNamara wasn't one to overreact; he must have had good intelligence to justify his concerns. Big events were always a risk to public safety and security. With the war in Vietnam, the troubles in Ireland, and the general state of American society, there were plenty of reasons to worry about agitators.

I hadn't been to the parade in almost a decade. I had lost the desire for excitement early in life, and crowds made me anxious. If I couldn't trust people as individuals, I certainly couldn't trust them in groups. Outside of Korea, some of the worst violence I had ever seen involved mobs, including the time I watched a dozen youths beat a black guy to death after a football game at Roxbury Memorial High School. The police made no arrests, mainly because most of the witnesses were white, and no one would talk. Such was the state of race relations in the early fifties.

When I finally found a space, it was in the lot of the housing project where we had interviewed the man Collins knew. I turned off the engine and then checked my gun, making sure the safety was on. I didn't want an accidental misfire at an event with thousands of children.

As I got out, two boys on bikes stood glaring at me in front of a stoop. They had dirty faces and piercing eyes. I never liked the suspicious looks of strangers, but on kids, it inspired more pity than anger.

Forcing a smile, I walked off. I continued up D Street with a procession of people carrying foldable chairs, blankets and coolers, and drinking beer despite the cold. Many wore green hats and Irish knit sweaters, their faces painted with shamrocks and rainbows. Some were already drunk, and it was only 10 a.m.

When I came out to West Broadway Street, the sidewalks were packed. The parade had begun, floats and dancers going by. Hearing cheers, I looked over to see a giant banner that read ENGLAND GET OUT OF IRELAND! With all the political violence in Belfast, people were fired up.

Aside from an occasional insult, threat, or catcall, it was mostly peaceful. The real trouble wouldn't start until later. With drunken youths roaming the streets, many of them from the suburbs, there were always fights, sometimes a stabbing or two.

I weaved through the crowd and got to the next corner where a line had formed in front of a mom-and-pop liquor store.

"Brae?!"

Startled, I turned to see Collins leaning against a lamppost. In his long coat and hat, he was too dressed up. Even I had worn a casual jacket and sweater.

"Brae?" I questioned.

"I wasn't gonna shout *detective*."

"Good point."

As we walked, I smiled at kids and nodded to adults. The sky was

LOVE AIN'T FOR KEEPING

overcast, but I wished I had worn sunglasses to observe people more freely. I got the feeling that everyone knew anyway, probably because I could always spot a cop. I liked going undercover, but surveilling in public felt like grunt work.

Many people looked familiar, including a custodian from headquarters and a guy who worked behind the counter at Sam LaGrassa's deli. I even saw Charlotte, the crazy owner of the rooming house on W Sixth Street.

"What, exactly, are we looking for?" Collins asked.

"Anything suspicious."

It was the same vague phrase that frustrated me when the captain or chief said it. I wished I had a better answer.

"Like that?"

I looked to see some men passing around a joint outside a closed laundromat. They were all in their early twenties, with scruffy beards and boots. One wore an Army jacket, and there was nothing more telling about the consequences of war than a young veteran who looked down and out. I could have harassed them about the pot, but they weren't causing any trouble. We weren't there to enforce the drug laws.

I heard arguing and looked over to see two officers restraining a drunk teenager who had stumbled into the parade path. I was about to go help when Collins tapped my shoulder without speaking, something that immediately got my attention.

When I turned, he nodded. It was strange that, in the crowd of thousands of people, I knew exactly who he was looking at. In the doorway of a dingy bar, I saw a man smoking. He wore a long leather coat and had a thick mustache that twitched each time he took a drag.

As Collins and I stared, a tingle went up my back. Even if he was the man we chased the night before, it didn't mean he was the killer or even a suspect. A coat and a mustache wasn't a description —— it was a fashion style.

Of all the tough cases in my career, the flimsy evidence and unreliable witnesses, this was the worst. At a time when logic and reason weren't getting me anywhere, I had to rely on the one thing that never let me down —— my instinct. And something told me this guy wasn't right.

I started down the sidewalk while Collins took the street. Even in the confusion of the moment, I realized he'd made the better choice. The man hadn't noticed us approaching, but something he saw up ahead must have startled him. Instantly, he dropped his cigarette and ran.

"Get him!"

Collins and I chased after him, down a side street which was practically an obstacle course with all the double and triple-parked cars. I was winded after only a few yards. Collins flew by me, but I didn't know how long he would last with his asthma.

Soon I lost sight of the man, so I kept my eye on Collins instead. He turned right, and I followed him, but I was losing steam. I hadn't run that fast or that long in years. Most of our foot chases were short.

In seconds, I went from a sprint to a jog and then finally, to a walk, heaving from exertion. Ahead I saw a small city park between the rowhouses. Hearing shouts, I reached for my pistol, my heart pounding. When I came around the corner, I stopped.

Standing in the middle of a basketball court was Collins, his gun out and pointed. His clothes were ruffled, and he was missing a shoe. In front of him were three men, all with their hands up. Instantly, I recognized them as the guys I had talked to at the Blarney Stone two weeks before.

As I approached, I held up my badge so everyone could see, including some mothers who stood panicked with their children beside a jungle gym. In any confrontation, it was always wise to make it clear who the authorities were.

"Interfering with police work," Collins yelled.

He sounded nervous, which made me think he had never been in a tense situation before. I walked over and put my hand on his arm, gently urging him to lower the gun. Not knowing who the men were, we had to be cautious, but I also didn't want a shootout.

"Where's the suspect?"

"Gone," Collins said, breathing heavily. "They got in my way. We all tripped over each other."

When I looked at the men, they looked disheveled too. The tallest one had scuffs on his leather jacket. Seeing Collins' shoe, I walked over and grabbed it, handing it to him. Then I went straight up to the guy in the middle. He didn't flinch, but the fact that they still had their hands in the air told me they wouldn't try anything stupid.

"We meet again," he said.

"What the hell were you doing?!"

"We thought your man was a burglar," he snickered. "We're Good Samaritans."

Even at the bar, they had given me an eerie feeling, with their forced chumminess and probing questions. I ignored it at the time. If I looked into everyone that I thought was suspicious, I would have spent a lifetime investigating.

Someone must have called the police because a cruiser sped up and stopped. Two cops got out and ran over.

"What's going on, Lieutenant?"

They were young enough that I didn't know them, so it was nice to be recognized.

"Check them," I said.

"What?" the men said, getting suddenly defensive.

"We ain't done nothin' wrong!" the tall one snapped.

The cops looked at them and then at me. The rules around *probable cause* were murky. After all the conflict between the police and the public in the sixties, the department was strict about being heavy-handed. It would have been one thing to frisk them in a dark alleyway. But in broad daylight with dozens of witnesses, I needed proof of wrongdoing. Chasing after the same suspect wasn't good enough.

I held out my hand, signaling for the cops to hold back.

"You wanna tell me why you were after that guy?" I asked.

The tallest one shrugged his shoulders. With his cold eyes and steady stare, I knew he was the most defiant.

"Just trying to help out, Officer."

"Have we broken a law?" his friend asked.

"Are we free to go?" the third man said.

They were fair questions, even if I didn't like them. Everyone waited for my response, including some locals who stood watching from the fence.

In the past, I might have threatened the men, berating them out of frustration. But suspicion without facts was just a hunch, and instincts weren't evidence. I had to admit I had nothing to hold them on.

"Go on," I said. "Get outta here."

CHAPTER 20

"You don't pull out a gun in public!"

"They interfered with the apprehension of a suspect!" I said.

Egersheim ran his hand over his dome like he still had hair.

"And what suspect is that, Lieutenant?" he asked, his tone smug.

"I'm telling you, that guy fit the description—"

"A long coat and mustache? For chrissakes Brae, that's the whole city. They weren't breaking any laws. We've got a dozen witnesses to prove it."

"They had accents. Maybe they're here illegally."

"Now you're grasping at straws," he said, and I knew he was right. "You don't pull out a gun unless there's an imminent threat. Collins should have known better."

It sounded like a line from a police training manual, but nothing about theory worked on the streets.

"The kid was nervous."

I couldn't believe I was defending someone I'd despised only a week ago. Collins had proved better than I expected, and I owed him my support.

"Look, Brae. The chief is giving a press conference tomorrow at noon…"

"But—"

"Don't interrupt me!" he barked. "That means he's gonna be coming to me first for an update."

I stared at the floor, more let down than defeated. It was hard to explain an instinct to someone who didn't have it. I didn't resent Egersheim for not coming up through the detective ranks, but I resented that he acted like he was as skilled as those who did. If his sister-in-law wasn't married to the nephew of the chief, he would have still been with the Boston Police Mounted Unit.

"I need a full report by tomorrow morning," he went on, "including who you've interviewed, where, when, and why. Typed and double-spaced. You understand?"

"Yes."

When our eyes met, he gave me a look that was at once firm and timid. It wasn't that he didn't like conflict —— no one did. But he was the type of person who worried most about his reputation. He didn't want people not to like him. That quality might have been good for politics, but it was awful for a senior police official.

The meeting ended with an abrupt silence. As I got up to leave, Egersheim stood too.

"What time's Harrigan's surgery?" he asked.

"Um, three o'clock, I think."

He rubbed his chin, looking down.

"Let's pray for the best."

For once, we had something that we both agreed on.

"Amen."

I walked out and headed down to my office. When I entered, Collins was sitting on the chair beside my desk, right where I had left him. I had told the captain he was at lunch, which technically wasn't a lie because he had a sandwich and potato chips while he was waiting.

I wouldn't let him come to the meeting. While Egersheim always had limits on how hard he came down on me, I worried Collins would get berated. Joining Homicide during this investigation would have been a baptism by fire for any officer.

"How'd it go?" he asked.

"Not good."

"Am I screwed?"

It was a funny question, the kind I would have asked at his age.

"Naw," I said, and he looked up. "We're both screwed."

He grinned nervously.

"What're you doing tonight?" I asked.

"I was gonna take my girl to see *The Godfather*."

"I was thinking of doing some overtime. See if we can spot our psychopathic friend."

"You think we will?"

"It's obvious he's on the move. Now we know what he looks like."

Collins stood up.

"I can take her out tomorrow night," he said.

I was tempted to refuse, to tell him to go out and have a good time. But I didn't want him to think I expected anything less. I was already impressed, so I wanted to keep pushing him. What he lacked in experience, he made up for in enthusiasm. Beyond that, he agreed the guy we had chased twice was suspicious. We would either both be right or both be wrong.

"Good. I got some business to take care of. Meet me in the lot at six."

......

I GOT to City Hospital an hour before Harrigan's surgery, and he was already being prepped. I begged the staff to see him, but they all said no. It was only after I flashed my badge that the lead nurse agreed, saying she did so because her State Trooper uncle had been killed on the job.

Using police influence for a civilian matter was against department policy, and probably a Civil Rights violation. But the bigger risk was letting Harrigan go into the operating room without seeing him. All my life, I had had to make tough ethical decisions in the moment.

When they brought me into the room, he was standing on a scale in the corner. The hospital gown was hilariously small for his size, looking more like a miniskirt. I had to struggle to keep from laughing. But I was glad to see him upright. I had been injured before and knew what it was like to sit in bed for days.

"Lieutenant," he said, glancing over his shoulder.

The nurse made a note on the chart, and he stepped off.

"You look good," I said.

"You've always been a terrible liar."

I smiled and walked over.

"How're you feeling?"

"Each day, a little better."

"Where's Delilah?"

"She left ten minutes ago. She had to get back to the nursery."

Nursery sounded funny, a word I remembered from childhood but that had been replaced by *daycare* and *preschool*.

"Feel free to talk for a few minutes," the nurse said, and I had forgotten she was still there. "But he needs to lie down."

I walked with Harrigan to the bed, and he was unsteady. When he got to the mattress, I tried to help, but he wouldn't let me.

"She's concerned about an employee," he said.

"Who?" I asked, distracted.

"Delilah. One of her employees hasn't been to work in over a week."

"Right. The Irish girl. She probably found another job."

"No," Harrigan said, firmly enough that I listened. "It's not her character. Would you please look into it?"

Our eyes met, and I nodded.

"Of course."

"Her name is Cecily."

"I know. I've got her address," I said, reaching for my wallet.

I took out the slip of paper Delilah had given me. I only wanted to show Harrigan that I had it, but when I opened it, I froze.

"What's wrong, Lieutenant?"

After two frantic weeks, the names and places were all starting to sound the same. So, it took me a moment to realize why I was so confused.

"Cecily Madden," I said. "This can't be right."

"Why not?"

Sometimes I forgot he had been unconscious for a week and sedated for another. Except for what he saw on TV or what I told him, he had none of the details of the case.

"The girl from Telegraph Hill."

"Telegraph Hill?"

"The Heights."

"Which *Heights*?"

"Thomas Park!" I said.

The case was frustrating enough without a crime location that had three names.

"The first murder," I went on. "I went back to the scene. A girl came up to me. She said a waitress she knew hadn't shown up for work."

"Much like Cecily?"

I ignored the question, already feeling guilty I hadn't followed up with Delilah.

"Her name was Cecily. We went to the Blarney Stone where she worked. The manager pulled her file. It said Cecily Madden."

"Then it's obvious someone used her name."

"But why?"

"Why is it obvious or why did someone use her name?"

I smirked.

"There's only one person who might know," he said.

I looked down at the note, an address in Brighton.

Two orderlies walked in with a nurse, and I knew he had to go. I put my hand on his forearm, the closest we were going to get to a sentimental farewell.

"Good luck," I said.

"Fate. I don't believe in luck."

"Now you sound like Ruth."

He smiled, but in his eyes, I could see his apprehension.

"That's a compliment."

"You don't have to live with her," I joked.

We both laughed. In the gritty world we grew up in, sarcasm was often the only way to show emotion.

"See you tomorrow."

I nodded and walked toward the door.

"Lieutenant," he called, and I turned around. "How's the lad?"

"Collins? He ain't you."

I meant it as a wisecrack, but it was poignant enough that the nurse looked up with a warm smile.

"He doesn't have to be. He just needs to be good."

CHAPTER 21

SOUTH BOSTON WAS QUIET AFTER THE PARADE, THE SYMBOLIC END TO the St Patrick's Day season. We drove down West Broadway, the street littered with beer cans and cigarette butts, discarded clothing and broken chairs. On the corner, men from the Department of Public Works were shoveling piles of frozen trash into the back of a pickup.

Despite some poverty, the area had always been clean. I had to admire the pride of its residents who kept up their houses, sweeping the sidewalks and re-painting shingles. The housing projects had curtains and window boxes. Even the abandoned buildings were boarded-up and tidy. In an era when neighborhoods changed overnight, Southie was stable, and I understood why people fought to keep it that way. Only a mile from downtown and with a beach and a boardwalk, it had more charm than some bland South Shore suburb.

Collins flicked his cigarette out the window. I wanted to scold him for smoking with asthma, but I wasn't his father, and he was an adult. As someone who went through almost a pack a day, I was in no position to criticize him.

We drove without a plan or a strategy. With the chief's press conference the next morning, I knew heads were going to roll, including my own. If I wasn't going to get any credit, I at least wanted the overtime.

Leaving Andrew Square, we drove over the expressway. As we entered Dorchester, the landscape wasn't much different, an endless repetition of triple-deckers, churches, family-owned shops, and bars. Everything on this side of town was just an extension of the Irish ghetto.

"So, tell me about this girl," I said.

As I groped for a lighter, he held out a lit match before I could find it.

"She's *fine*," he said with a flair.

Youth slang changed so fast that I was still getting used to *groovy* and *far-out*.

"Fine? What, like fine & dandy?"

He didn't seem to get the joke.

"I met her at a Badfinger concert," he said. "She's from Cambridge, half-Greek."

Only in Boston would the first things that mattered about someone be where they were from and what their background was.

"You been out with her yet?"

"A couple times."

"You like her?"

He hesitated.

"She's cool."

I could have pressed him, but I no longer got a thrill from hearing about the romantic exploits of a twenty-five-year-old.

As we rolled up to a red light, I saw some people coming out of the Bulldog Tavern, one of the many dive bars along the avenue. My eyesight was bad, especially at night, but something about them caught my attention. When Collins noticed me staring, he looked over at the group.

"Is that who I think it is?" he asked.

I didn't have to answer —— his reaction was enough to confirm my hunch. There was enough traffic that I could pull over and park without raising suspicion.

"Open that," I said, so distracted I couldn't say *glove compartment*. "Quick! The binoculars."

He handed them over and I adjusted the focus. A second later, the group came into view. On the corner were the three men we ran into at the Southie Parade. They stood in a circle, smoking and talking. Suddenly, Collins grabbed my arm.

"Hey, they're moving!"

I reached for the shifter and then stopped. We were both eager to find any link to the murders, and the men were suspicious. But until we had evidence or a clearer picture of who they were and why they were sniffing around, I had to let them go. Egersheim had already scolded us for cornering them in the park. I didn't want to get accused of harassment. I would probably only get one chance to question them, so I wanted to make it count.

"We can't do anything, can we?" he asked.

I watched as the men piled into a black car. Squinting, I read the license plate and quickly got out my notepad to write it down.

"Not yet."

……

THERE WERE three types of bars in Boston. The first were those that were friendly to cops; the second were those that weren't. Then there was the third kind that occupied a murky middle ground. These were usually places frequented by both criminals and locals alike, and their level of hostility depended on the state of society in general.

During the Irish gang wars, many bars around the city were off-limits. But after the social unrest of the late 60s, tensions between the department and the underworld had settled into a fragile peace, probably because they were united in their hatred of student protesters and black radicals. Both organizations wanted security, they just sought it in different ways.

When we walked into the Bull Dog Tavern, I didn't know what to expect. I hadn't been there in twenty years. The last time was in those few crazy months between coming home from Korea and entering the police academy.

The place was small but loud; the sounds of raspy laughter and pool cues cracking echoed off the walls. The bar was filled with working-class guys, but there were a few women too: young bimbos in skimpy blouses, older women with beer guts and caked-on makeup. Through the thick smoke, I felt dozens of eyes watching us. It was the one time I wished we hadn't worn suits, which in this type of place indicated that you were either a cop or a tax collector.

"Juan!" I heard, and Collins stopped to shake someone's hand.

Immediately, I felt some tension leave me. In any setting, it always helped to know at least one person. Everywhere we went, Collins ran into some friend or acquaintance, reminding me of when I was young. If I got jealous, it was only of his youth and enthusiasm. I was long past the age of wanting to be popular.

We approached the bar, and the bartender came over, a skinny guy with a white collared shirt and crew cut. While the crowd seemed tame, flashing a badge was always a risk, but we didn't have time to hope for friendliness and cooperation. So I took it out and showed it to him.

"What can I do for you?" he asked.

"I wanted to ask about three guys who just left."

He raised his eyes. I knew it was too vague.

"Mid-thirties, leather coats."

His expression changed.

"Yeah," he said. "I think they were just here."

"Any idea who they were?"

"Don't know. I was downstairs. Let me check with the owner."

When he waved, an older man in a sweater and scaly cap hobbled over. He had thick white hair, and his face was round and ruddy.

"Damn cigarette machine is out again," he grumbled.

"Sean," the bartender said. "Did you serve those three Micks who just left?"

The man gave me and Collins a wary look.

"I'd say it depends on who's asking?"

I showed him my badge, but his attitude didn't change.

"They didn't get any drinks."
"Did you talk to them?" I asked.
"Briefly. They were only in here a few minutes."
"What did they want?"

With each question, he seemed to get more and more annoyed. I couldn't tell if he didn't like cops or if he was just crabby by nature.

"They were looking for someone," he said.
"Who?"

The man shrugged his shoulder.

"Just some guy."
"Did they describe him?"
"A mustache, dark hair. Irish."

CHAPTER 22

EVEN WITH DROPPING COLLINS OFF, I GOT HOME BEFORE ELEVEN. I PUT us both in for a full shift, which meant we would get paid until midnight. It was a minor abuse of overtime, but I didn't care. Throughout my career, I had worked plenty of extra hours for nothing.

In some ways, it seemed like the case was following us, rather than the other way around. I woke up every day waiting to see what would happen next, which was fine for a television series, but agonizing when it meant murder. Police patrols around Southie and Dorchester had been increased, but with no solid leads on the suspect, the best the department could do was create the illusion of safety.

When I walked in the front door, Ruth was on the couch in a nightgown, a copy of *Vogue* magazine in her hands. There was a glass of wine on the table, which explained why the room was chilly. She always got warm when she drank and had probably turned down the thermostat.

"You supposed to have that?" I asked, hanging up my coat.

"The doctor said a glass here and there is okay."

I raised my eyes but didn't argue. *A glass here and there* was about as specific as *maybe* or *someday*.

"How was Ness?"

"Out like a light. Nadia made her those dumplings she likes."

I smiled and walked over. With the TV on low, I knew she wasn't watching it, just using it for background noise.

"Pierogis," I said, leaning over to look at the bump on her head.

"Don't," she said as I touched it.

"How is it?"

"Still a little sore."

I sat down, and we kissed.

"How's this little girl," I said, looking at her stomach.

"Who says it's a girl?"

"I thought women had a sense about these things?"

Ruth frowned.

"Which reminds me. Delilah called. She's really worried about that woman—"

"Cecily?"

"Yes."

The eleven o'clock news came on, and I saw a special alert. Staring at the screen, my heart pounded. I felt a sick sense of relief when I realized it was just a building fire in Mattapan.

"Any update on—"

"Nothing," I said before she could finish.

I didn't want the sanctity of my home tainted by the word *murder* or *killings*. She knew I was frustrated. I couldn't hide it from her.

For all our trust and shared intimacy, she stayed out of my work, although she didn't like it. In some ways, it wasn't fair because she felt the stress too. That was probably why she always fantasized about me retiring.

A couple of days before, she told me about a story she read. A former police captain from Worchester now operated a bed & breakfast in Vermont. It sounded romantic, and I understood the appeal of dropping everything and escaping the hustle of the city. But dreams were often better than reality. The last thing I wanted to do was change bed sheets and make omelets for strangers.

As she reached for her wine, I leaned against her shoulder, overcome by deep exhaustion. I had the urge to go upstairs and take off my suit, but she was easy to fall asleep on. So I closed my eyes and sank into a comfortable oblivion.

......

SOMEHOW THAT NIGHT I had made it up to the bedroom, although I couldn't remember how. In the throes of a tough investigation, the days were a blur, and the moments often indistinguishable. More than ever, I needed Harrigan's insight or at least his support. While I was good at the tactics, he was good with the details and strategy. He knew how criminals thought, and I knew how they behaved, which was why we worked so well together. When it came to arrests, he could run faster, mainly because he was younger, taller, and didn't smoke. But I was always a better shot, the one skill that hadn't diminished with age. I trusted that Collins would have my back but not that he would be successful. In any tense situation, experience often meant the difference between life and death.

When I came downstairs, Ruth was on the couch with her feet up, just like the doctor ordered. Nadia had arrived and was cooking pancakes on the stove.

I walked into the kitchen to find Nessie in her highchair, showing her doll how to use a fork. Nadia glanced at my shoulder holster, something I wore so much that Nessie no longer noticed. But as a woman who had lived in Poland through the war, Nadia had a different experience with weapons. I was sure it brought back terrible memories.

"Daddy, are you going?"

Leaning over, I kissed Nessie.

"Yes."

"Why?" she moaned.

"Honey, Daddy has to work," Ruth called over from the living room.

"I'll be home later, love," I said.

She looked down with a pout, her bottom lip protruding. Nadia was clever enough to bring over her breakfast to distract her.

I walked out to the foyer, looking over at Ruth as I put on my coat.

"Your tie is uneven," she said, grinning.

"Thanks."

I fixed the knot and went over, kissing her on the lips.

"How're you feeling?" I asked.

"Tired."

"What time does Nadia leave?"

"Around four."

"Esther is always around."

"Why? What time will you be home?" she asked, lowering her voice.

"Hopefully for dinner."

She grabbed my hand, pulling me down for a second kiss. It was more sensual than the first, more passionate. With only a month until her due date, even I was getting uncomfortable with the idea of sex.

"Be safe."

"I will."

Traffic over the Charlestown Bridge was at a standstill. With all the construction on the expressway loop, I couldn't see beyond the cranes and cement trucks to know if it was an accident or road work. I could have put on the sirens, but it wouldn't have gotten us anywhere. So I sat still with my hands gripped to the wheel. The cigarettes didn't help, and the coffee I'd had an hour before just swashed around in my stomach, adding a tinge of nausea to my agitation.

When I glanced at Collins, he was leaning back in the seat, tapping his hand to a Led Zeppelin song, or was it King Crimson? I didn't know. I hated rock & roll, preferring the smooth sounds of the big bands I had grown up with.

Either way, he was more relaxed than me. In his sunglasses, he even looked cool. If I missed anything about being his age, it was that feeling of invincibility, even if it was just an illusion. I used to despise young people, but I was starting to pity them, knowing that, despite all the bluster and confidence, they were facing years of mistakes, setbacks, and heartbreaks.

"How'd the date go?" I asked.

"Great. I fucked her."

I cringed.

"Jesus. Don't go around telling everyone that!"

"I ain't. I'm just telling you."

"Well, I'm honored," I snickered. "Is it gonna go anywhere?"

"It already did."

I frowned but didn't respond. At least for men, once a conversation was tainted by the insinuation of sex, it couldn't go back to seriousness.

When we finally approached Brighton, I could see the giant cross of St. Elizabeth's hospital at the top of the hill. We drove through Oak Square and turned down a side street, following the directions I had memorized from a city map that morning. Raised in Roxbury, I didn't know much about the area other than that it was filled with bars and college students from nearby BU and Boston College.

We stopped at the address, 11 Hardwick St, a small colonial in a neighborhood of modest single-family homes. I had expected a triple-decker or apartment building.

When we walked up the steps, I pressed the doorbell, and moments later, it opened. A fortysomething woman in a skirt and cardigan sweater peered out. With her small lips and dark hair, she made me think of how Ruth might look in a few years.

I held out my badge with a smile, knowing that any woman would be wary of two men coming to the door.

"Yes?" she said, and I detected an Irish accent.

"Does Cecily Madden live here?"

"No."

"Did she ever?"

"What's this about?"

"Ma'am," I said, although she was still at an age where I could have used *Miss*. "We're investigating the deaths of four girls—"

"I know about them. Who doesn't?"

"Cecily's gone missing we think. We're... concerned."

With no evidence that she was a victim, I wasn't about to imply it. But mentioning the murders was enough to change the lady's attitude. She looked up and down the street and then opened the door.

"Please. Come in," she said.

She brought us into a living room with two couches and a console TV. There were oil paintings on the walls; the side tables had glass lamps with beaded shades. I smelled cigarettes but didn't see ashtrays, so I assumed she didn't smoke in there.

She invited us to sit and then asked, "Can I get you some tea?"

"No thanks. We won't be long."

"Cecily had been renting a room from me—"

"You sure that's her real name?"

She winced in confusion.

"I never considered it wasn't. A lovely girl, really. I'm from Ireland, so of course we got along. But she's from up North. Lots of trouble there at the moment."

I reached into my coat for my writing pad. I still wasn't used to taking notes.

"When was the last time you saw her?"

"Well, last Wednesday, I'd say. In the morning. She works at a kindergarten in the South End. Sometimes she goes out with friends after, but she has a key. I waitress most nights, so our paths don't cross very often."

"When did you realize she was missing?"

She shifted on the sofa. The word *missing* seemed to make her uneasy.

"Saturday, I'd say. A man came by looking for her."

"Looking for her? Who?"

"Don't know. He was Irish. Definitely from the North."

"Can you describe him?"

"Blondish hair. Combed back. A big fella. Six foot or more."

"And what was he wearing?"

"A leather coat—"

"Long?" I interrupted, looking up.

"No. More like the ones pilots wear."

"A bomber jacket?"

"Right. He wore blue jeans too."

"Are Cecily's things still here?"

"She didn't have much. I checked her room. It looks like she didn't take anything."

I glanced at Collins, and then asked her, "Mind if we have a look?"

"Not at all."

We stood up and followed her over to the stairs, which were covered in wall-to-wall carpet. With its white walls and heat vents, the house was newer, much like my own, probably built in the fifties.

At the top, we went down a hallway with a modern bathroom and a couple of bedrooms. As we passed, I looked in. She must have noticed because she said, "I've got two other girls who stay here."

"Tenants?"

She glanced back with a mischievous smile.

"Acquaintances," she said.

I smiled back, realizing the insinuation. To help with the bills, a lot of homeowners rented rooms, usually to students or people from whatever ethnic group they belonged to. While it wasn't legal, it was also hard to prove.

She opened the last door, and we walked into a small room. It had a single bed and a dresser with a mirror, a clutter of makeup and spray bottles on top. On the floor, a large suitcase was open to reveal stacks of folded clothes. A coat was tossed in the corner, some shoes lined up against the wall. Beside the bed, a side table was covered with things, cigarette boxes and empty packs of chewing gum. Although clean, the place looked like a hovel, reminding me how unsettled the lives of young immigrants were.

"Hey," Collins said, holding up a 45 record. "Good band."

Squinting, I saw *The Who* on the label but couldn't make out the rest.

I nodded but didn't agree. Rock and roll was all noise and outrage to me.

"Looks like she left everything behind," I said to the woman.

She stood leaning in the doorway, her arms crossed. I realized then

I didn't even know her name. Investigations were impersonal, and unless someone was a witness or victim, it wasn't always necessary to know.

"Thank you," I said.

"I wish I could be more help."

CHAPTER 23

WHEN EGERSHEIM SAID HE DIDN'T WANT US AT THE PRESS CONFERENCE, I couldn't tell if it was to protect or punish us. So Collins and I went down to the cafeteria to watch it.

We got a table by the television, a small Zenith someone had donated to watch the *Red Sox* and other sporting events. As people walked by, it was obvious that Collins knew more cops than me.

I wasn't jealous, but it made me think about retirement. I was far from the end of my career; few officers retired in their forties. But I was getting older, something I realized when Collins flew by me in the foot chase at the parade. I knew more than him, and wisdom always trumped youth or fitness, especially in crime-solving. But age was something that no one could ignore.

We sat through the last ten minutes of *Hollywood Squares* until finally the midday news came on. As expected, the first story was the press conference about the murders.

People gathered around the TV holding trays of food and coffee. On the screen, I saw Chief McNamara walk out in a brown blazer, his tie tight around his thick neck. His thin hair was slicked back, more from sweat than from Brylcreem or pomade. He was a strong leader, but he didn't like public speaking and wasn't good at it.

Standing behind the podium, he looked at the men on either side of him. One was a deputy superintendent, and the other was the head of the State Police. He adjusted the mic and began to speak:

GOOD AFTERNOON. *As many of you are aware, there've been four homicides in the city in the last week and a half. All the victims are young women in their early twenties. So far, two have been tentatively identified. While we are working diligently to make an arrest, we're asking the public for help. If anyone believes they might know the identities of the other two victims, please call the hotline on your screen...*

I ADMIRED HIS TACT, not using words like *psychopath*, *spree*, or *random*. With the public on the verge of panic, he had to be careful about what he said.

I'VE BEEN *in close contact with Mayor White in terms of security and keeping the public abreast of any developments. In light of the severity of this case, I've asked Colonel Murgia of the Massachusetts State Police to assist with the investigation...*

I GOT tense but kept a straight face. If we hadn't made any progress, it was because we had no evidence. We were detectives, not psychics. And we weren't the only ones to blame. The street cops, *Forensics*, and even the records department had a part to play. We were only as good as the information we got. But when it came down to it, the responsibility was ours alone. Or, as Captain Jackson used to say, *it may not be our fault, but it's our problem.*

Having the State Police involved was embarrassing, and no small sign that the chief had lost confidence in *Homicide*. I didn't know if they would take over or just help us —— jurisdictional roles were always messy in a mixed investigation.

"Does that mean we're out?" Collins asked, leaning on the table, an anxious expression in his eyes.

"Don't know. Let's get outta here."

The press conference wasn't over, but I had heard enough. With a small crowd around the television, I didn't want to get bombarded with questions. Every employee knew investigations were confidential. But that wouldn't stop them from asking.

Somehow, we made it out of the cafeteria without anyone noticing. I turned into the first stairwell, and Collins followed. He always did what I said and never argued. When I first met him, I thought he was just an impudent kid. In the past week and a half, he had proven to be so much more.

"Back to your office?"

"Hell no," I said, pushing out a side door.

The air was cold, but the sun was out, a fair compromise for any March afternoon. We walked around to the front lot where two news vans were parked. Sneaking between the cars, we got to the Valiant and jumped in.

"What now?" Collins asked.

I started the engine and turned to him.

"Now, we're on our own."

......

IN ANY INVESTIGATION with few clues and a lot of urgency, there is a risk of getting sloppy. We could have cruised around Southie and Dorchester again, stopping at every bar, diner, and convenience store, showing the autopsy photos to anyone who would look at them. The chief had already asked the public for tips, so it wouldn't have seemed that desperate.

The case was a strange contradiction. While people wanted the suspect caught, no one seemed particularly interested in the victims, as if they didn't matter. Had they been local girls, there would have been an uproar. Two years before, a college student raped the daughter of a building contractor after a party in Back Bay. The case had only been open for a week before the suspect was found dead in a dumpster in the Combat Zone. Such was the swiftness of vigilante justice in Boston.

Over the years, I had seen a lot of unclaimed deaths. In the records room alone, there was a whole row of cabinets dedicated to cold cases. But they were usually drifters or drug addicts —— people who had, either deliberately or because of their circumstances, decided to retreat from society. Pauper graveyards had been around for centuries for just those types.

None of these girls fit that profile. They were all young and pretty, with hip clothes and coiffed hair. At first, the killings had seemed random, the work of a psychopath. But with two victims from Belfast, it was clear there was a connection to Northern Ireland. While it made the case more complicated, it wasn't unusual. America had a long history of importing violence from other countries.

As we drove down Boylston Street, two cruisers sped by in the other direction. I panicked until I turned up the radio and realized it was just a stabbing between two homeless men on the Boston Common.

"Gimme a cigarette," I said.

There was nothing worse than running out when I needed it the most. Collins seemed flattered that I asked, quickly taking one out and lighting it for me. Cracking the window, I took a drag and blew out the smoke.

"You hungry?" I asked.

"I'm always hungry."

I could have joked that it was from too much sex but didn't. At his age, once that topic was raised, there was no going back to casual conversation.

We pulled into Victoria's Diner, a small brick building on an isolated stretch of Massachusetts Avenue, or *Mass Ave* as it was known. The food was good, but the place also held a sentimental significance. I had been going there for over twenty years, from my days as a rookie to one of my first dates with Ruth. In the shadow of the expressway, it was far from the hustle of downtown. Everyone from cops to criminals came there to eat and mingle.

We walked in and were greeted by a spunky blonde waitress. I asked for a table near the back, and she waved for us to follow. When we sat down, she gave us menus, but I already knew what I wanted, and Collins did too. The fact that I ordered a Reuben, and he had a cheeseburger and fries seemed to symbolize our generational differences. But he drank his coffee black, which was enough of a commonality for me.

As we waited for our food, I asked him for another cigarette.

"What the hell are these?"

He grinned.

"Lucky Strikes."

"They taste like shit," I said.

"They're cheap."

"Aren't you getting detective pay now?"

"It hasn't kicked in yet."

When the waitress came over with more coffee, I asked her for change for a dollar. I got up and walked to the front where a cigarette machine stood beside a big potted plant. As I dropped in the dimes, the door opened, and I felt a breeze.

"Brae," I heard, and I glanced back to see Doctor Ansell.

With him was a pretty young brunette, her hair in curls. It wasn't his wife, so I assumed it was a new intern. He took off his hat and gloves, his glasses fogged from the cold.

"You must be celebrating?"

"How do you mean?" I asked, pulling the knob for the cigarettes.

"Harrigan," he said, and my heart started to race. "He came through alright."

The doctor always had a strange smile, somewhere between a grin and a smirk. I tried to stay composed, but the news was overwhelming. When the intern gave me a sympathetic look, I knew it showed.

"I...I didn't hear that," I said, my voice cracking.

"Well, kid. I just did."

I had known Ansell for years, and while we had never gone out socially, he knew more about my life than most of my colleagues.

When Ruth had depression a few years back, he gave me advice on what to do; when Captain Jackson got cancer, he consoled me like a father.

As we faced each other, a waitress walked over. She must have sensed the poignancy of the conversation because she didn't interrupt.

"Go ahead, Brae. Eat your lunch."

I smiled.

"Right."

Leaning in, he whispered in my ear.

"Then go out and find that bastard."

He held out his hand, and we shook.

The food had arrived by the time I walked back to the booth. I dropped the cigarettes on the table and sat down to eat.

"Marlboro," Collins said, picking up the pack. "Can I try one?"

"No."

He had already given me half a dozen, but I wanted to test him a bit.

"Really?"

I snickered and gave him one. In any partnership, the ability to take a taunt was as important as loyalty.

"What's your schedule look like for the rest of the week?" I asked, biting into my sandwich.

"Like with work?"

"Like with everything."

"I dunno. Nothing planned," he said.

"Good. You're gonna be doing some overtime."

CHAPTER 24

"THIS IS A COLOSSAL DISAPPOINTMENT."

Seated across from Egersheim, Collins and I looked at each other. I didn't know if the captain meant he was disappointed in himself, us, or humanity in general. News of the State Police involvement with the murder case was on the front page of the *Globe*, right beneath a story about a 100-pound bomb that exploded in Belfast, killing six and wounding hundreds.

"This doesn't make us look good," he went on.

While I was getting tired of listening to him complain, it was true. If even one of the murders had happened outside the city, it would have justified the need for outside help. But bringing in another police agency was an insult to the whole department.

I didn't know if the chief had requested it, but I wouldn't have been surprised. Above all, senior officials had to worry about public perception. Before, I might have felt humiliated, but I no longer cared. With a wife and child at home, my only concern was getting a paycheck and getting home safely.

"I pulled the plate on that car," I said.

It was important enough that I should have told the captain when I walked in. I kept it as a wildcard, knowing it would be a good distraction if he continued to harp about the State Police. And I was right.

"And?"

"It's a rental car from the airport," I said.

He raised his eyes, and I knew why. Rental car records were notoriously unreliable, something the Attorney General had been complaining about for years.

"You think these men are somehow connected to the murders?" he asked, his skepticism clear.

"I think they know something."

"Why? Because they were running through Southie on parade day?"

"They weren't just running. They deliberately got in our way."

I looked at Collins for support, but he just sat quietly.

"For what?" the captain said. "A man you saw on the street?—"

"Look, I don't know if he's the killer, but he was definitely the guy we chased the night of the Dudley Square murder."

Egersheim looked down, tapping his pencil on the desk. As much as I hated to draw any similarities, Captain Jackson used to do the same thing.

"You think they're protecting him?"

"I think they're after him too," Collins blurted.

The captain and I both turned. I was more proud than stunned, maybe even a little ashamed. It took a twenty-five-year-old kid to say what I had been thinking. In the annals of urban crime, killers chasing killers wasn't unusual. But it was almost always gang-related, people who had been fighting with each other anyway.

After a short pause, Egersheim cleared his throat.

"I have a meeting with the chief this afternoon. See what you can find out about these men."

I didn't know if he accepted the theory, but he didn't scoff at it, which was a good start. As inept as the captain was, he was our boss. We needed him on our side.

......

. . .

WE DROVE through the Sumner Tunnel, a one-mile passage that went beneath the harbor. It felt like an underground raceway, cars overtaking each other on two narrow and treacherous lanes. With the thick brick walls, the noise was deafening, and diesel exhaust from all the trucks created a sickly haze. By the time we breached into the afternoon sunlight at Maverick Square, I rolled down the window to clear the air.

"He ain't a bad sort," Collins said.

I coughed into my fist.

"Who?"

"The captain."

We continued towards the airport, turning down an access road before the terminals. We pulled into the lot of National Car Rental and parked in front of a small brick building. Getting out, we walked in, and an older man with glasses and a company shirt was on the phone behind the desk. When he saw us, he hung up and came over.

"Can I help you?" he asked.

Collins and I both flashed our badges, which was some indication of our urgency.

"I need to know who rented this car," I said, taking out my notepad.

He looked at the plate number and then up to us.

"With all due respect, officers. I can't release customer information without—"

Before he could finish, I was holding out two twenty-dollar bills. I didn't have time to go to court for a search warrant.

He stared at the money, that moment of internal ethical debate. We would get the information eventually, which was probably why he snatched the bills and shoved them in his pocket.

"Hang on," he said.

He opened a drawer and flipped through the files, taking out a folder.

"1970 Buick Skylark. Black," he said, and I nodded. "Registered to a *Martin Rowe*."

I wrote it down.

"What's his home address?"

"It just says Sheffield, UK."

"UK?" I asked.

"That's what it says."

"How long is the rental?"

He squinted to read the fine print.

"It was reserved from March 4th to April 4th," he said, looking up. "They have it for exactly a month."

"They?"

"Yeah, three guys. I remember them. They asked me if I knew any decent hotels."

I tensed up, looking him straight in the eye.

"And what did you tell them?"

"I said there were lots. I gave them a coupon I had to the Howard Johnson's Motor Lodge in Dorchester."

"Thanks."

I looked at Collins, and we ran out. We got back into the Valiant and circled the airport road, which was a giant one-way loop. At midday, traffic was starting to pick up, and it took a half hour just to get through the tunnel.

We got off the expressway and turned into Howard Johnson's, a midrise building at the end of the exit ramp. I drove around the lot looking for the car. There were enough black Skylarks that I had to read the plates.

When we didn't see it, I parked, and we went inside. The lobby was sleek and modern, with white chairs and abstract art on the walls. We walked over to the front desk, and a woman looked up. With a navy blazer and her hair in a ponytail, she looked professional, but I could tell she was very young.

"Good afternoon," she said.

"Can you tell me if a *Martin Rowe* is staying here?"

She put her hand to her chest.

"Oh, I'm sorry. We can't divulge the names of our guests."

It sounded like something she had been taught to say at a training seminar.

I leaned against the counter. With a curt smile, I took out my badge, and she got flustered.

"It's urgent."

"I...I'd have to check with my manager," she said.

"Is he here—?"

"It's a *she*."

"Of course."

She scurried through an office door and moments later, returned.

"I'm sorry, the name again?" she asked.

"Martin Rowe."

She opened the ledger, and I watched as she scanned the list. I wasn't surprised the manager had said yes. The line between personal privacy and public safety was always hazy, and most companies preferred to side with the police.

She looked up, nodding quickly.

"Yes. He's here."

I could tell she was hoping I didn't ask which room number. But knowing they were staying there was enough, and now wasn't the time to question them.

"Thank you."

CHAPTER 25

As I approached the hospital room, I felt a paralyzing sense of dread. Then I peered in to see Harrigan upright in the bed, Delilah on the chair beside him. They didn't notice me, which gave me a chance to watch them unawares. They smiled as they spoke, interacting with the delicate tenderness of a couple very much in love.

When I first met Delilah, I didn't hate her —— she was a hard person not to like. But I never thought we would get along. With her big afro and bohemian jewelry, she seemed like just another self-righteous graduate student. Only after I got to know her did I realize she was so much more. Like a lot of younger people, she had radical ideas, but that didn't mean she was a radical. Ruth, who had no opinions on politics or society, loved her, and that was enough of an endorsement for me.

"Lieutenant?"

I walked over and held out the tin of the *Victoria* biscuits he loved, some nostalgic comfort from his childhood on St. Kitts. Because they were British, they were hard to find. I had to go to a Caribbean market in the South End.

With Harrigan still immobilized, Delilah took the box and put it on the table beside several bouquets.

"How're you feeling?" I asked.

"A bit lightheaded. All in all, well."

Aside from looking tired, his eyes were clear and alert. Beneath his gown, I saw several inches of gauze wrapped around his chest, making me wonder if the surgeons had gone in through the front or the back.

"They got it all?"

He glanced at Delilah, and she smiled back, her lashes fluttering.

"They got it all. Would you like to see it, Lieutenant?"

I thought he was being sarcastic until Delilah took out a plastic specimen bag. She held it up and I saw a small slug, slightly tarnished but otherwise in perfect shape. With no shell casing, it was hard to tell the caliber. But I knew it had been a rifle, so I assumed it was a Winchester 30-30.

The thought of the searing metal penetrating his body made me shudder. Even war was an abstraction until you had been shredded or pulverized. In Korea, the only injury I got was when a two-inch piece of shrapnel from an explosion a half-mile away bounced off my shoulder. While it only left a bruise, some staff sergeant had seen it, so I got a purple heart.

"How's the new detective?"

I snapped out of a daydream.

"Actually..." I said, looking back.

I called out for Collins, and he appeared in the doorway. When I waved, he walked in, his arms tight to his side like he was entering a wake.

"Hey," he said.

"This is Harrigan."

Harrigan lifted his arm to shake, the most he had moved since I arrived.

"And Delilah," I said.

He nodded to her with a nervous smile.

"How's it working with this renegade?" Harrigan asked.

His humor calmed any awkward tension.

"Aw, he's alright."

"Better than alright," I snickered. "Can you believe this kid don't have a car?"

"Could he not take one of the cruisers?"

"Now you sound like Egersheim," I said, and we all laughed.

"Any news on the case?"

"What case?"

I smiled, but Harrigan wasn't amused.

"Nothing really. We're getting some help," I said.

"So I heard."

A nurse came in pushing a cart filled with tubes and dials. I was glad for the interruption. I didn't want to discuss the investigation out in the open and, more importantly, I didn't want to upset Harrigan. The last thing he needed was to worry about work.

"Pardon," the woman said. "I have to drain his wound. If you could all just wait outside."

Delilah stood up and got her coat.

"I have to go close up the daycare," she said. "I'll be back in an hour."

Harrigan glanced up with pleading eyes.

"You really don't have to."

"If that ain't self-pity masked as nobility, I don't know what is."

Collins and I smiled, although I didn't think he understood what she meant.

"But if you do," Harrigan said. "I wouldn't mind if you brought me a small butter pecan."

"The only man I know who eats ice cream in winter," she said.

The nurse, who otherwise had been silent, said, "I'm sorry, no unauthorized food for a few days."

Delilah looked at Harrigan, and he frowned. Leaning over, she kissed him on the forehead, which somehow seemed more loving or caring than a kiss on the lips.

Collins and I said goodbye, and we all left. As we walked down the corridor, Doctor Ansell was coming toward us.

"Doc?"

"Brae," he said, nodding to me and smiling at Delilah. "Where's our friend?"

"Second to last room on the right."

Without a word, he scurried off. He always acted like he was late for something important. Despite his gruff exterior, he had a deep compassion and understanding of life that only someone who saw death every day could have. He wasn't very close with Harrigan, so I knew he was visiting him for me.

We took the elevator down and continued through the lobby. When we walked out, I shivered in the cold. After a long winter, everything looked gray. But in the air, I could detect the faint smell of spring and something like hope.

......

COLINS and I had been parked in the lot of Howard Johnson's Motor Lodge for almost two hours. Across from us, the black Buick shined under a single streetlight like a trap or temptation.

While surveillance always seemed like easy overtime, it wore down my nerves and tormented me with boredom. Worst of all, for all its sacrifices, there were never any guarantees. For all we knew, the three men had been picked up by someone or were in the motel lounge. Maybe I was getting soft, but I couldn't stand sitting around in a dingy parking lot while Ruth and Nessie were home alone.

"Lieutenant?" Collins said.

I leaned forward in a drowsy stupor and saw the three men get into the Buick. The headlights came on, and I squinted, hoping they didn't notice us. I waited a few seconds after they pulled out, then I started the car and followed them.

They turned right out of the lot and headed towards Dorchester. I kept a close eye on them, staying a few car lengths behind. One benefit of the Valiant was that it didn't resemble an unmarked cruiser.

As I followed them down Dorchester Avenue, I noticed they slowed each time they passed a barroom.

"They're definitely looking for someone."

"I knew it," Collins said, confidently but with no bluster.

"Can't we just pull them over?" he went on, "shake the fuckin' truth outta them?"

"No," I said with a chuckle.

Like any young cop, he was impulsive, but I liked his style. In my early days on the job, if we thought someone did or had information on a crime, we would browbeat them until we knew. Back then, *civil liberties* was still an academic term, and until the Miranda Act in '66, we didn't even have to tell suspects why they were being arrested. While it no doubt encouraged abuse, it also made solving cases easier. Everything about the legal system was a tradeoff.

In Fields Corner, the men double parked, and one got out. He went into the Blarney Stone for just a few minutes, then got back in the car.

Next, they stopped at a pub in Adams Corner, then another in Lower Mills. I thought they were going to the South Shore as they headed into suburban Milton, but they got on the expressway instead.

We followed them seven miles back into the city, and they exited in Southie. At Andrew Square, they went right, and I turned left.

"What're you doing?!" Collins exclaimed.

"Let's call it a night."

While he looked disappointed, he didn't argue. Neither of us doubted the men were looking for the suspect, but we couldn't follow them all night. Even in war, every patrol had its limits.

"What if they find him now?"

"Then maybe they'll take care of him for us."

"You think they wanna kill him?"

I raised my eyes, sighing. At this point, nothing would have surprised me.

"This is nuts," Collins said.

"Ain't it?"

CHAPTER 26

WHEN I ENTERED EGERSHEIM'S OFFICE THE NEXT MORNING, I WAS shocked to see the State Police colonel sitting across from him. He wore a tightly fitted cap and a gray and blue suit with pins and ribbons. Even at his rank, it seemed too formal, but their uniforms were always fancier than ours. Beside him was a thirtysomething trooper with buzzed hair and sideburns, an unusual combination. Collins was there too, but with no chairs, he had to lean against the wall. I walked over to join him, struggling to hide my resentment. It was the first time I had ever been forced to stand.

"Brae," Egersheim said. "This is Colonel Murgia."

The colonel glanced up, his expression stern but not unfriendly.

"This is Captain Flaherty," he said.

I forced a smile, and we all shook hands.

"We've got the killer narrowed down to two possible suspects," the colonel said.

He looked at the captain, who had a folder open on his lap. With his back arched, Flaherty acted more serious than Murgia. Already I knew he would be leading their side of the investigation.

"The first just got released from Walpole State prison," he said, "after serving twenty years—"

"Why him?" I blurted.

I could tell he didn't like being interrupted.

"In '54, he was convicted of killing a woman in Dorchester. He was suspected of killing two more."

"How?"

Flaherty frowned.

"How what?"

"How were they killed?"

He scanned his report and looked up.

"Brunt force trauma. The second victim was strangled in Ronan Park. A couple weeks apart."

"So you think a guy gets out of prison after two decades and goes on a killing spree?"

"It wouldn't be the first time," Egersheim said, a giddy nervousness in his voice.

"Who's the second?" I asked.

"His name's Gerald Devaney," Murgia said. "Four years ago, he was seen leaving a bar in Somerville with a young lady who was later found dead."

"How was she killed?" I asked, and he looked at Flaherty.

"Stabbing. Multiple times," the captain said.

"Annmarie Darrow," I said, and they all seemed impressed I knew. They may have been more refined, but they weren't going to outsmart me on local crimes. "They thought it was her ex-boyfriend. He had just gotten back from 'Nam."

"Maybe, but a month later, he left a bar in Charlestown with a young woman. She was found dead a week later."

"We know Devaney has been renting a room in Dorchester," Flaherty said, "the same place all the homicides have occurred."

"*Jane Doe I* was found in Dorchester Heights," I said, "which is South Boston, not Dorchester."

He looked more confused than Murgia, but that didn't mean they both didn't know. As members of the State Police, they were from towns across Massachusetts. Only someone born and raised in the city could understand the subtleties of its geography.

"*Jane Doe III* was killed in Roxbury," I added. "Just outside Dudley Square."

"Same general area," the colonel said.

While technically it wasn't true, I didn't argue. Already I could feel tension between me and Flaherty, and hostility was no way to start a collaboration, even one I was opposed to.

"Irregardless," he said, which sounded like he was trying too hard, "we expect him to strike again. We've got extra patrols on around the clock. We're going to have our forensic lab take a second look at some of the blood and hair samples. If you boys could keep asking around on the streets, it'd be a big help."

The word *boys* was demeaning enough that I wanted to snap back. And I could have. Even if they had more prestige, the State Police had no authority or jurisdiction over us. But I held back, knowing there was no reason to make enemies with other law enforcement agencies.

Colonel Murgia stood up, and everyone else did the same.

"I'll need a copy of the case notes sent over ASAP," he said. "1010 Commonwealth Ave, 5th floor. Attention to me."

Egersheim scribbled it down, his fingers shaking.

"Looking forward to working together, Colonel," he said, which was a lie.

As they walked out, Flaherty nodded, more out of professional obligation because I knew he didn't like me.

The door closed, leaving us in stunned silence. For all their pomp and confidence, the men had only named some random criminals, a few unsolved murders. They gave nothing close to a motive or a theory, and in some ways I was glad. If they wanted to waste time searching for a couple of ex-cons with violent pasts, it would at least keep them busy while we looked for the real killer.

The captain looked over and motioned for us to sit. Collins and I took our chairs. The fact that mine was still warm from the colonel was an added slight.

At least the case was still ours, the one thing the State Police couldn't take from us. But now that they had been called in to help, we were in the awkward position of having to prove our worth and competence. Rather than dwell on it, I focused on the case.

"We tailed the Buick last night," I said.

"They drove through Southie and Dorchester for hours," Collins added. "They stopped at a dozen bars."

I liked that he wasn't afraid to speak up.

"We also went by the house of the woman from my daughter's daycare yesterday—"

"Cecily Mullen?" Egersheim asked.

"Madden," I corrected. "The owner said a man came by to see her the day she went missing."

"The killer?"

"I don't think so. She said he had on a bomber jacket. A short leather coat."

"Suspects change their clothes," Egersheim said.

I couldn't tell if it was sarcasm.

"This guy was big. She said over six feet. I'm sure it was one of the men we cornered at the parade."

Glancing up, the captain gave me a sharp look. The incident at the park was still a sore subject. I was sure the department had gotten complaints.

"Maybe they're not after the killer," Egersheim said. "Maybe they *are* the killers."

"My gut says no."

"My brother only saw one guy the night of the first murder," Collins said.

"Same with the guy we interviewed in the Southie projects."

As the captain sat thinking, my heart raced, and my face felt hot. I didn't know if it was from anxiety, anticipation, or excitement, but somehow, I enjoyed the feeling.

"Why didn't you pull them over? Ask them what they were doing?"

It was an odd remark from someone who always lectured me on *probable cause.*

"If they know who the killer is, we're better off following them than getting in their way."

Egersheim rubbed his chin. He was jittery, almost confused.

"I know you're not happy the chief brought in the State Police," he said.

"Are you?"

He shook his head.

"Not particularly."

As one of the most revered law enforcement agencies, the State Police had an arrogance that bordered on megalomania. They had more money, influence, and jurisdiction than any local department, and yet they bungled investigations all the time. The summer before, their crime lab lost evidence for an illegal gambling ring whose suspects included a TV reporter, a restaurant chain owner, and the son of a judge. I didn't hate the department —— they had a lot of good officers. But it was no substitute for the instincts and wisdom of local cops.

"So, what do you suggest?"

I was flattered he asked, but we were all in over our heads. For all the murderous brutes I had ever apprehended, I had never gone after a serial killer.

"Let them chase around those ex-cons for a few days," I said.

"You heard the colonel. He wants the case notes."

"Hold him off, just until the weekend."

As Egersheim sat thinking, his brow was tense, his bald head gleaming. He never liked to stray from protocol or do anything that felt even remotely underhanded. But with the public in a panic and the chief upset, his job was more at risk than ours. At least we had union protection.

"Well," he said, finally. "There's only one thing to do."

Collins and I both looked up.

"And what's that?"

"Help you with the search."

......

IF COLLINS and I learned anything that night, it was that even vigilantes took breaks. We had been sitting in the parking lot since four o'clock and the Buick hadn't moved. I was tempted to go in and look for the three guys, maybe even knock on their door. But if our hunch was right, and they were after the killer, we had to believe they knew more about him than we did.

I had invited Egersheim to join us, but he insisted on driving alone. I couldn't tell if it was some symbolic gesture to the separation of rank or because he preferred the cruiser.

He was parked across from us, only four spaces away from the Buick. At his request, we took walkie-talkies, which I hadn't used in years. The static hurt my ears, the upper range of my hearing damaged from artillery blasts in the war. Either way, Harrigan and I were never far enough away from each other that we needed them.

It was the end of March, and the nights were still cold. We kept our engines off, staying warm with cigarettes and coffee. With smoke rising from our cracked windows, I imagined our cars looking like teepees on a winter prairie.

"What time is it?" Collins asked.

I glanced at my watch.

"Almost ten."

"What time we gonna stay 'til?"

"Why? You'll get paid until midnight."

"If we got out early, I was gonna go see my girl."

"Now?"

"She works downtown until late."

"Where?"

"Sagansky's."

I smiled, remembering the diner Ruth and I used to go to when we were dating. Open until 2 a.m., it was a hangout for late-shift workers and people leaving the bars and lounges in Park Square.

"You know it?" Collins asked but I had already reached for the walkie-talkie.

"Thunder," I called, unable to hold back the sarcasm in my voice.

In picking call names, Egersheim had suggested *Thunder* and *Flash*, the same ones used by American troops on D-day. Like a lot of men who hadn't served, he had a peculiar fascination with war and its practices.

"Flash."

I glanced at Collins, and we chuckled.

"It's getting cold. I think we're gonna call it a night," I said.

When the captain hesitated, I figured he was groping for the button. It would have been quicker if he rolled down his window and called over.

"Roger," he said, finally.

I started the Valiant and turned up the heat. Driving out, I waved to Egersheim, but we couldn't see him in the darkness.

We headed downtown, the streets busy on a Thursday night. When two cruisers flew by with their lights on, I immediately turned up the two-way. I kept expecting another call for a homicide. The only chatter I heard was about a car accident on Boylston Street and a domestic dispute in Back Bay.

At this point, I was feeling torn about the investigation. We all wanted to get the killer before the State Police did, and in some sense, the competition was good. But with Ruth expecting and Harrigan sick, my exhaustion was starting to overcome my determination. I would have accepted an arrest by either party, even at the expense of my own professional pride. I would never say it out loud. There was nothing worse for morale than doubts or indifference. And I had to be considerate of Collins. I didn't want his first case to be one where the lieutenant got frustrated and gave up.

There was always the possibility that none of us would find Carmody, which would have been a draw between departments but a travesty for the victims and their families. Law enforcement agencies were constrained by laws and jurisdiction; criminals could roam free. If his work was done, whether the killings had been a hit, vendetta, or random bloodlust, he could have easily fled the state.

I pulled up to Sagansky's, its old neon sign as iconic as any historical landmark in the city. As Collins reached for the door, I said, "Don't be out too late."

He turned, giving me a curious look.

"Sure thing, Lieutenant."

I watched as he walked over and went inside. Through the glass windows, I could see at least three waitresses. They were all young and pretty, so I wasn't sure which was his girlfriend. I looked for familiar faces too, cops or maybe some guys I grew up with. But most of the officers I knew from the local precinct had retired. One had even been killed on the job.

I drove away and sped through the night. I wasn't in a rush, but I was tired after a long day and wanted to get home. When I pulled into the driveway, the living room, hallway, and kitchen lights were on. I opened the door quietly, but it was obvious Ruth was up.

"Hi."

I looked in to see her lying on the couch in a bathrobe, the TV on low. Hearing the National Anthem, I knew it was midnight. Time for the broadcast signoff.

"Hey," I said, looking over while I hung up my coat. "Everything alright?"

"I couldn't sleep."

Her hair was long and wild.

"How'd it go?" she asked, sitting up.

"Nothing of note."

Even as I said it, I knew I sounded like a supervisor or a bureaucrat. As hard as I tried, I could never keep my private and professional lives separate. Ruth had been interested in law enforcement since high school, and we had met when she was working at headquarters. I was relieved when she later went into nursing, but it didn't stop her fascination with crime.

"There hasn't been a murder in almost a week," she said.

Our eyes locked, and I got a sickening feeling.

"Yeah?"

"Since last Saturday."

The days had been going by so fast, I couldn't keep up. I had worked on cases that took a month and some that took years. In the frenzy of an investigation, time became muddled and meaningless.

"I didn't know you were keeping track," I said, sitting down beside her.

"They said it on the news tonight."

"Momma!"

Hearing Nessie's voice, I went to stand up but Ruth stopped me.

"Don't," she said. "It'll only get her riled up."

It sounded like criticism, but I wasn't offended. I loved that Nessie was always excited to see me.

Ruth got up instead. I watched as she walked up the stairs, her feminine strut altered by the weight of pregnancy. I never liked that Nessie's bedroom was the first one at the top, worried that she would be more exposed if anyone broke in. It was more the idea that bothered me because I knew I could always protect her. Even when I did sleep, I would startle at the slightest sound, the creak of the trees in the wind, the distant rumble of a car. I could have blamed it on the war, but my vigilance had started long before then.

Moments later, Ruth came down, holding the banister like she was dizzy.

"Everything alright?"

"Just a nightmare," she said.

"I mean with you?"

She walked over to the couch with her arm around her abdomen. In her expression, I saw a hint of strain.

"Something's going on," she said.

As I helped her sit, I got a quiet panic.

"Is it?—"

"No," she said, pausing to catch her breath. "Could you get me some water?"

I ran into the kitchen, poured her a glass, and came back out. While her face was flushed, she didn't seem in distress.

"I think the baby might have dropped."

"Dropped?!"

"It's okay. It's normal. It just means she's getting closer."

"Like tonight?"

Ruth smiled tenderly.

"Not tonight," she said.

I was relieved but also embarrassed. I even felt a little helpless. For all my experiences in life, my training as a cop and as a soldier, I knew nothing about childbirth.

"It usually happens a couple of weeks before," she added.

I nodded, thinking about the calendar hanging on the door in the kitchen. Her due date was April 4th, less than two weeks away, and, ironically, the same day the black Buick was due back at the rental agency. So many things were coming together at once that my head was spinning.

"You're shaking," she said.

"Too much coffee."

She took my hand and placed it on her stomach. Something about the warmth of her body, the sound of her breathing, lulled me into a gentle calm. I put my head on her shoulder, my eyes half-closed, and enjoyed those few precious moments of peace and solitude.

CHAPTER 27

THE PHONE RANG LOUDER THAN A CHAINSAW IN THE QUIET ROOM. Jumping up, I realized Ruth and I had dozed off on the couch again.

With my crazy schedule, it happened a lot. I would come home so tired that once I sat, it was hard to get up. Ruth liked the firm cushions, saying they were better for her back. There was something poignant about it too, reminding me of our first apartment. On the third floor of an old and drafty triple-decker, the back bedroom sometimes got so cold in the winter that we slept in the living room.

"Who's that?" she said, yawning.

"Don't know."

I got up and went into the kitchen. Reaching for the phone, I hesitated before answering.

"Hello?"

"Lieutenant?!"

When I heard Egersheim's voice, I knew it was urgent. He never called me at home.

"Captain?"

"I just talked with Collins. One of the witnesses reported seeing the suspect."

He sounded nervous, almost panicked.

"When?"

"A half hour ago."

I looked at the clock. It was one thirty in the morning.

"Which witness?"

"Um," he said, and I could hear him flipping through his case notes. "William Trainor. 245 D Street, South Boston."

"Billy?"

"Wasn't he the guy who saw *Jane Doe I* at the Quiet Man Pub the night she was found dead?"

"He didn't just see her. He identified her."

"Right," the captain said.

He sounded embarrassed, and I didn't blame him. It wasn't our only case, although it was our most important one. He wasn't on the streets with us every day, so I didn't expect him to remember all the details.

"Where?" I asked.

"The Irish Rover. Dorchester."

"On my way."

As I went to hang up, he blurted, "Should I call for backup?"

I held out the receiver, looking at it with astonishment. Egersheim never asked my advice, especially with an investigation so critical.

"I wouldn't," I said. "We have nothing to hold him on. And we don't wanna spook him."

I hung up, impressed by my restraint. In the past, I saw law, procedure, and policy as obstacles, things to be ignored when possible. If I thought someone was a suspect, I would pursue him with all the blind determination of a linebacker chasing a ball.

When I walked back into the living room, Ruth was sitting up. Although groggy, she was awake enough that I was sure she had heard the conversation.

"Everything alright?" she asked.

"I gotta go."

She pressed her lips together, but I knew she was more worried than disappointed.

I leaned over, and we hugged. Putting on my coat, I adjusted my holster and smoothed out my shirt. Wool suits were surprisingly comfortable to sleep in.

"Be safe."

......

OUTSIDE IT WAS POURING. Even with the streets so quiet, I didn't dare speed. Ice was dangerous, but wet ice was treacherous. Still, I got to Fields Corner in fifteen minutes. It was almost 2 a.m., and the bars were starting to close. As I passed the Blarney Stone, I saw the bartender Pat under the awning, waving to patrons as they scurried to their cars. Rain hadn't been in the forecast, but the weather in Boston was always unpredictable.

I continued for another couple of blocks until I saw the sign for *The Irish Rover*, a storefront bar with glass block windows and a brick façade.

The call from Egersheim had been so quick that I forgot to ask if he was going to meet me there. But when I pulled over, I saw his unmarked cruiser across the street. I got out and walked toward the bar where I noticed two people in the doorway.

The captain wore a hat and long trench coat, his hands in his pockets. Beside him was Billy, the man Collins and I had questioned in the South Boston projects.

"Capt.," I said, and then I looked at Billy. "You saw the suspect?"

"He was in here about a half hour ago," he said, slurring.

His lips were chapped, his face red. In his Army jacket and torn jeans, he looked like a cross between a hobo and a hippie.

"Who was he with?"

"Alone. He didn't stay long."

"You sure it was him?"

"Sure as shit."

"What'd he have on?"

"The same," the captain said. "Long leather coat."

I looked up and down Dorchester Avenue, the rain pelting my face. It was quiet for a Friday night, and not just because of the weather. With a killer on the streets, people were wary of going out, especially women.

Headlights came toward us, and we all turned. A green Chevy Chevelle drove up and stopped, its V-8 rumbling. Whether it was from the darkness or the circumstances, I got an eerie chill. I never overreacted in tense situations, but I moved my hand closer to my gun.

Seconds later, a passenger got out, opened an umbrella, and rushed toward us as the Chevy rumbled away. I didn't realize it was Collins until I heard his voice.

"Hey, ya, Capt.," he said, then he looked at me. "Lieutenant."

"Juanito," Billy said.

When Collins smiled, I knew it was a nickname, not an insult.

"Thanks for the tip," he said to Billy.

"I would've grabbed the bastard. By the time I got back from the pay phone, he was gone."

"Any idea which way he went?" I asked.

He turned toward the street, waving like he was beckoning to the entire city, maybe the whole world. The shops were all closed, their grates down. Behind them, the flat roofs of the endless triple-deckers loomed in the darkness.

"Somewhere out there," he said.

The remark was as profound as it was sarcastic.

"You need a lift home, Billy?" Collins asked.

For someone without a car, he was being very generous. But I wouldn't have to drive because as if on cue, a rusted Dodge Dart rolled up.

"It's my lady," Billy said.

He gave Collins a clumsy hug and then nodded to me and Egersheim.

"Good luck, boys," he said.

With a quick salute, he stumbled over and got in. We watched as they drove away, and I was sure we were all thinking the same thing. If he had seen the killer, this could be our last chance to get him before the State Police did.

"Okay," Egersheim said, not wasting any time. "Let's canvas the area."

"Starting where?"

As he adjusted his hat, he gave me a stern look. I knew I sounded defeated, and now wasn't the time for pessimism.

"Starting here," he said, pointing down. "I'll take the backstreets. You two take the main roads. We'll head toward South Boston..."

I had never worked in the field with him and doubted he had ever been on a real investigation. So I was surprised that it was a strategy I would have used, as desperate as it was. Scouring the streets for a suspect was like searching for a needle in a haystack. But any movement or effort was better than nothing.

"Keep your radio on," the captain added.

"Will do."

While we didn't cheer, we concluded with all the enthusiasm and camaraderie we could muster. Egersheim crossed the street, and Collins followed me over to the Valiant.

"Did Billy call you?" I asked as we got in.

"He called my cousin Robbie. Robbie called my uncle. My uncle called me."

At one time, I'd hated the clannishness of blue-collar Boston where everyone was related. Raised in an orphanage, I never had that sense of community, those deep connections. But I had come to realize that, while a lot of things in life could be compensated for, family wasn't one of them.

"It's good to know people," I said, but he didn't respond.

We drove down Dorchester Avenue, Collins scanning one side of the road while I watched the other. I didn't know if the rain was a blessing or a curse. While it kept people off the streets, it also made it hard to see. It seemed unlikely the suspect would still be roaming around. At least we knew he was still in the area. My biggest fear was that he had completed his work and fled.

After half a mile, I started to get skeptical. The only lead we had was a sighting in a bar. Billy seemed honest, and he had helped us before. But he was half-drunk and, like many veterans, probably a little demented. Even if he had seen the suspect, almost an hour had passed, enough time for the man to disappear.

Beyond that, my eyesight was terrible at night. I was so tired I couldn't think straight. We would get paid overtime, but chasing a phantom suspect wasn't worth the aggravation. I decided we'd go as far as South Boston. Then I would call the captain and ask him to be relieved.

Stopped at a light, I reached for a cigarette on the dash. As I lit it, something caught my eye. Squinting, I noticed a woman running down the sidewalk on the other side of the street. The hair on the back of my neck stood up when I realized who it was.

"Hey," Collins said. "Is that—?"

Before he could finish, I cut the wheel and spun around.

"Cecily Madden," I said.

"Ain't she missing?"

I sped to the next corner to head her off. As she approached, I rolled down my window.

"Cecily!" I shouted.

She stopped short, her arms flailing, her dress soaked. She was so panicked I wasn't sure she recognized me.

"He wants to kill me!" she shrieked.

When she glanced back, I looked down the sidewalk but saw no one.

"Who?"

I was just about to get out when Collins said, "Lieutenant?!"

When he turned his head, I looked in the rearview and saw a car speed by. There were lots of black Buicks, but I had no doubt it was the three Irish guys.

"Stay with her!" I yelled, and Collins got out.

I backed out onto Dorchester Avenue and sped after them. With the windows fogged up, I struggled to see. Reaching for the radio, I called for Egersheim, and he answered. I gave him my status but didn't say *in pursuit*. Still not sure what was happening, I didn't want a dozen patrol cars to show up.

When the car blew a red light at Columbia Road, I slowed down. I would risk property, but I was no longer willing to risk my own life. I continued through the intersection and into the "Polish Triangle," a dense ethnic neighborhood between the expressway and the industrial areas of South Cove.

The Buick stopped suddenly, and I hit the brakes and slid. Watching the bumper come at me, I gripped the wheel, but there was enough room that we didn't collide. If they didn't know I had been tailing them before, they did now.

The black car idled in the middle of the road. I was about to get out when I saw movement on the sidewalk. I looked closer and noticed a long leather coat. For a split second, time seemed to stop, that strange interlude between calm and chaos. It was something I remembered from the war, more a sensation than an experience.

Two of the men jumped out, one from the passenger's side and another from the back. I knew then it was a chase.

The suspect bolted and went around the corner. I pulled over and slammed the shifter into park. Getting out, I ran after them, down a side street of rundown houses and commercial buildings. In the darkness, I saw only shadows. They were clear enough to follow, but not to know who was who. Ruth had been telling me for months to get glasses, and I wished I had listened.

At the bottom of the road, the men turned down a narrow lane. The asphalt was cracked, covered in ruts and potholes. I ran harder, gasping for breath, desperate to close the gap.

In the distance, I saw a fence and knew it was a dead end. I heard shouting and saw someone start to climb it, the chain link rattling. In one last burst, I sprinted ahead, reaching for my gun.

"Police! Freeze!"

Instantly, two sets of hands went up. I walked over, my pistol pointed and my arm steady. The glow from a nearby security light was just bright enough that I could see. Just as I expected, it was two of the three men from the Blarney Stone. I didn't know if the driver was still waiting on Dorchester Avenue or if he had taken off. But it didn't matter because I finally had them cornered.

"We meet again," I said.

"You let him get away."

Whoever they were chasing was gone, over the fence and into the shadows.

"Who're you after?!" I shouted.

"Who do you think?"

I stepped forward and put my gun against the big guy's forehead.

"Don't fuckin' move," I said, and he snickered.

Leaning forward, I gave him a quick pat down. It wasn't thorough, but it was enough to let them know I was serious.

"You," I said, looking at the other man. "You got any weapons?"

"No."

I wanted to frisk him, but I didn't trust his partner, who seemed too calm. Suspects who were the most compliant were also the most unpredictable.

Headlights flashed across the road. When I glanced back, I was relieved to see the captain's cruiser. He rolled up, splashing through the puddles, and came to a dramatic stop. Opening the door, he got out.

"Brae!?"

"Call for backup," I said.

"You don't need to do that," the big guy said. "We can help each other."

As Egersheim walked over, I was surprised to see Collins get out from the passenger's side.

"Where is she?" I asked him, and he pointed to the back seat. "We need her to make an identification!"

"Who've you got in there?" the man asked.

"None of your business."

"We ain't who you're looking for."

"We'll see about that."

I continued to hold out my pistol, but my arm was getting tired.

"We ain't," his partner said. "We're after the same fella. We can help each other."

"You need to tell me who the hell you are and what you're doing here."

"I will. Just let me get my wallet."

I nodded, and he put down his arms. Reaching into his coat, he took something out and held it up. Squinting in the dim light, I realized it was a badge. As my eyes adjusted, a chill went up my back when across the top I saw the words *United Kingdom* followed by *Security Service*.

CHAPTER 28

I DROVE TO HOWARD JOHNSON'S MOTOR LODGE WITH EGERSHEIM. THE ride was short, but we were silent, and not because we didn't have a lot to discuss. While I had wanted to arrest the men, he had decided to hear them out, canceling our request for backup.

If they were with MI5, the British intelligence agency, they had no jurisdiction in America. I wasn't even sure it was legal for them to be here. But the captain saw it as a chance to get information on the murders which, with an investigation that had been basically co-opted by the State Police, I could understand. I didn't agree, but I also didn't want to oppose him. More than ever, we needed unity.

Collins had taken the cruiser to bring Cecily to the Charles Street jail. Although the facility was grim, it had a special section for women who were at risk. She knew something about the killer, so we had every reason to keep her in protective custody.

By the time we pulled into the parking lot, the rain had turned to a sprinkle. We parked and walked to the entrance where one of the men was waiting for us.

Inside, we passed the reception desk, and I saw the same young brunette who was working the day we came in to investigate.

We followed the guy down the hallway, and he knocked on a door. The moment it opened, I smelled cigar smoke and body odor.

"Gentlemen."

The big guy waved us in.

"Sorry I didn't have time to clean up," he joked, looking at the scattered clothes and takeout food cartons.

His badge had said Martin Rowe, the same name from the rental car registration. For a foreign agent, it was strange that he hadn't used an alias. But he insisted they weren't trying to hide or fool anyone.

He was big and energetic, and he ended every sentence with a laugh. If he told me he had played professional rugby, I wouldn't have been surprised. Every group had a leader, whether it was a platoon, sports team, or street gang, and I knew he was theirs. The other two men just sat quietly on the bed.

"Wanna have a seat?" Rowe asked.

I looked around, and the only other chair was in the corner.

"We'll stand," Egersheim said.

"Right, then."

"You said you could help us."

"I said *we can help each other*. Who was the woman in the car?"

The captain gave me a sharp look, which was insulting. I had been a detective long enough to know what to say and what to keep secret. Either way, I would let him do all the talking. Everything about the meeting was shady, outside the bounds of any policy or protocol I knew of.

"She thought someone was trying to kill her," the captain said.

"And you'd be spot on."

The admission sent a shiver up my spine.

"What's her name?"

"How about you tell us the killer's name?"

Rowe reached for a cigar in the ashtray and lit it, his nostrils flaring.

"Derrick Carmody. Ring a bell?"

"No."

"Of course, it wouldn't. You Yanks got your own troubles, right?"

He flicked his ash and sat on the edge of the bed, the mattress sinking under his weight.

"He was a British soldier," he went on. "1st Battalion, Parachute Regiment. He served in Borneo from 63'-66'. Fought in Aden during the riots in '67. Received the *Distinguished Service Cross*."

"So he's English?" I asked.

"Depends on your perspective. He was born in Belfast. If you're Protestant, he's a loyal servant of the British Empire. If you're a Catholic, he's an Irishman and a treacherous one at that."

"We believe all the victims are Irish," Egersheim said.

Rowe peered up, a slight mischief in his eyes.

"Yeah? And why is that?"

"One of the girls had a driver's license from Northern Ireland," I said.

"Another had Irish money," the captain added.

Rowe nodded, but I couldn't tell if it was confirmation or just an acknowledgment.

"Carmody was discharged in late '68," he said. "He went back home to Belfast just as the political situation was heating up. He joined the UVF. Ever hear of it?"

While he wasn't taunting us outright, he seemed amused by our ignorance about Irish affairs.

We shook our heads, and he said, "*Ulster Volunteer Force*. Paramilitary organization, violently committed to keeping Northern Ireland British."

"No friends of the IRA, I assume," I said.

The other two men laughed. Rowe was so absorbing I had almost forgotten they were there.

"Sworn enemies," he said. "Carmody was one of their most radical soldiers, a real brute. No heart, no conscience. He was a butcher by trade…"

It explained not only the killer's method but also why he was so good at it.

"They'd send him out to do their worst bidding, assassinations mostly, threats sometimes. He was extra cruel, which is useful in times of war, but bad for public perception."

"A real saint," I joked.

"In November of '69, he kidnapped a member of the local town council in Fermanagh. He was only meant to scare the fella. Instead, he tortured him in a farmhouse, threw his mutilated corpse in a trough with the pig slop."

Although I winced, nothing shocked me anymore.

"A Catholic?" I asked.

"Good question. But no. Protestant. The man had been a little too…how would you say?…conciliatory with the local Catholic population. After that, the UVF realized Carmody was a psychopath. They tried to rein him in, but it was too late."

"Too late?"

"Aye. Once a man like that gets the taste of blood, there's no stopping him. They're like animals that way. He's slick, cunning. Skills he got in the jungle."

"He isn't good at camouflage," the captain said.

"We identified him by his long leather coat," I explained.

"I didn't say the man wasn't arrogant. He probably gets off on it. Sneaking around, stalking his prey like a feckin' cheetah. No one knows him around here."

"This town is loaded with Irish," I said.

"But not from Belfast."

"What about you?"

Rowe stopped, and I noticed his associates look over.

"Good with accents, are ye?" he said. "I was born in Portadown, Northern Ireland. Left when I was eighteen—"

"What's his motive?" Egersheim blurted, and I could tell he was getting impatient.

"Two years ago, Carmody planted a bomb in a hair salon on Grosvenor Road in Belfast. The RUC got a tip, evacuated the whole block, but they couldn't detonate it in time. Blew the building to smithereens. An old woman got hit by debris two streets away. She later died in hospital. Carmody fled. They caught him at a border crossing in Armagh. The girls from the salon were set to testify against him."

"They saw him plant it?" the captain asked.

"I don't know if they saw the bomb, but they saw *him*. He posed as a plumber. The owner had been having problems with the pipes for months. One of the employees recognized him."

"Why a hair salon?"

"Investigators think he might've gotten help. They've no proof, but he came in though a utility door behind the building. Normally, it was locked. The owner happened to be out that day."

"An inside job," I said.

"Maybe the owner?" the captain added.

"Ha, hardly a chance. A dyed-in-the-wool Republican she is. Her father was in the IRA. But she was no less committed to peace. The girls that worked there were a mix of Catholics and Protestants. A hair salon is no place for politics. Probably why they named it *Trinity*, a bit of doctrine that both faiths agree upon."

"What happened to Derek Carmody?"

"In January, they were moving him to a facility in Londonderry. The prisons are bursting at the seams now with all the trouble. Carmody got loose in the back of the lorry. He had forged a knife from one of the bench mounts. Cut the throats of the driver and guard."

He looked up with a grim stare. It felt like a long confession, and I knew he was done when he grabbed a glass of water off the table.

"So why are you here?"

"In February," he said, taking a sip and wiping his mouth, "we were contacted by the RUC. Royal Ulster Constabulary. They're the police in Northern Ireland—

"Yes, we know," Egersheim said.

"They had information that Carmody was in Boston. Our orders were to come here and verify it. We've been tailing him for weeks."

"Since March 4th," I said.

Rowe smiled.

"You've done your homework, Detective."

"We're trying to catch a murderer."

"We never expected him to go on a rampage. After he escaped, we think the witnesses were advised to leave Northern Ireland, probably by the IRA. Carmody somehow found out they'd come here."

"And he wanted to silence them?" I asked.

"Or get revenge."

"So why weren't we alerted about this?" Egersheim asked.

"Your FBI was. As was your CIA."

I looked at Egersheim. If anyone had been notified about such an arrangement, it would have been him and the chief, not me.

"We were never told," he said.

"Your higher-ups were. It was more a courtesy than anything else. We ain't acting in an official capacity. We're just sniffing around. Think of us as tourists."

"Foreign intelligence agents operating here isn't tourism," the captain said.

While it sounded clever, I knew he was stumped. I was too. Even if our department was the largest in the state, we were still municipal cops. We worked with federal authorities all the time, but mostly for gambling, drugs, and organized crime. We had been trained on Interpol, the global police network. But the closest I ever got to working with a foreign agency was when Polish officers came to arrest an anti-Communist activist who was wanted for killing a politician in Kraków. Even then, their arrival was all over the news.

"Look," Rowe said. "We've been upfront with you gentlemen. We're on the same side. We can help each other out."

Egersheim gazed at him, his expression cold. For all his bumbling, it was the calmest and most professional I had ever seen him.

"What do you propose?" he asked.

"Let us find him. We know his moves, his patterns."

"The State Police are involved now."

"And best of luck to them. But Carmody is no ordinary criminal, mate."

"Why haven't you found him?"

"We've come close. We would've had him at the parade, but your men got in the way," Rowe said, looking at me. "No offense."

"None taken."

"Several employees in the salon saw Carmody that day. That's why I asked about the girl in your car tonight."

"What makes you think it was a girl?"

Rowe looked at me.

"Because you said *she*. What's her name?" he asked for the second time.

"How about you give us the names of the witnesses so we can identify them?"

"That's the problem. According to the official record, there were four. The prosecutor thinks there might have been one more."

"And what? She didn't come forward?"

"These are mad times. You have no idea. The girl was probably afraid to testify. If we can find out who it is, maybe it'll lead us to Carmody."

He stopped, and the room went silent. As he stood waiting for an answer, it felt like a standoff. With no time to consult with Egersheim, I had to hope he would say the right thing. And he did.

"What do we get out of it?"

"You get Carmody. Once we find him, you make the arrest."

"You expect me to believe you're just here to help?"

"I don't expect anything," Rowe said. "We're here to do a job. If we can locate Carmody, that job is done. To be honest, I don't care if he gets hanged or walks free. We answer to a higher authority too. We're not bloody volunteers."

Of all that he had said, it was the first thing I could relate to. A few people went into law enforcement out of idealism, but most just wanted a steady job and pension. The way to rise up the bureaucratic ladder was to satisfy your superiors and stay out of trouble. As much as I hated to admit it, we were all just trying to satisfy our bosses.

"I'll see what I can find out," the captain said. "Until then, if you do find Carmody, you may detain him only, nothing more. You're to call headquarters immediately!"

The power in his voice was undermined by his small size and meek demeanor. Egersheim always had trouble projecting authority. But Rowe didn't balk, responding with a respectful nod.

I didn't know if it was an agreement or a mutual understanding, but it didn't feel right. I had made backroom deals before, but it was always with criminals in the pursuit of other criminals, never with other government agents. And the fact that they were foreign only made it riskier.

"If word got out that you tried to make an arrest on American soil," Egersheim added, "it'd be a diplomatic scandal."

Rowe smiled with a wink.

"Just a few good Samaritans."

......

BY EARLY MORNING, the rain had stopped. As I drove home, the sun was coming up, its yellow glow shining through the trees along the parkway. I hadn't been out so late in years. Even the toughest cases rarely required working overnight.

The dawn was peaceful, a part of the day I loved but never experienced. The streets were empty, and the homes were quiet, giving the impression of a world frozen in time. With the window cracked, I could hear the sounds of the birds —— a small consolation for all my stress and fatigue.

As I pulled into the driveway, I felt a slight shame. I hated being out for so long, although I knew Ruth would understand. Walking up the front path, I reached for the doorknob. It was damp from the morning dew. Creeping in, I got as far as the foyer before I heard footsteps and stopped.

"Jody?"

I looked up to see Ruth at the top of the stairs in her slippers and nightgown.

"Is Nessie up yet?"

She shook her head and tiptoed down.

"I want to let her sleep," she whispered.

"Won't Nadia be here soon?"

"It's only six thirty. Besides, it's Saturday."

I had left the hotel without checking the time and forgot to wind my watch. So much was happening at once that the days blended. I could handle the stress, but I didn't want to take it home. With a difficult pregnancy and a four-year-old, Ruth had enough to worry about.

"Anything new?" she asked.

"Someone saw the suspect."

"Where?"

"A bar in Dorchester."

"So he's been identified?"

With each question, she got more curious, her eyes widening. I never lied to her, but I couldn't always tell her the truth. Everyone around us knew I was a detective. If anything I said got out to Esther next door, the whole neighborhood would find out. I understood why people wanted to know. It wasn't just about gossip. But even the smallest breach could jeopardize the investigation.

"We're getting closer. That's all I can say."

Her expression changed, a look of mild disappointment. I put my arm around her, and we walked into the living room. I didn't so much sit on the couch as I collapsed on it. Every muscle in my body ached. Gazing out the window, I saw the streetlamps go off in the misty light of dawn, reminding me that I had been up all night.

"You've got circles," she said, rubbing my cheeks with her fingers.

"Must be all the coffee."

We snuggled close, and her warmth felt like a gentle cocoon. When she leaned forward and kissed me, I could tell my lips were dry.

"What time do you have to be in?"

I shrugged my shoulders.

"Don't know."

"Then go to bed," she said, her voice soft and caring. "I'll wake you up in a couple of hours."

I hesitated and then looked at her.

"Okay," I said.

When I stood up, I got dizzy.

"Daddy?"

Nessie came scurrying down the stairs in her pajamas, her hair still in a clip from the night before. Seeing her smiling face was rejuvenating. My exhaustion didn't fade, but somehow it felt less daunting. I glanced at Ruth, and she just smiled. We both knew I wouldn't sleep now.

"I'll go make breakfast," she said.

CHAPTER 29

As Egersheim talked, I squirmed in the chair, my back sore. Whenever I worked too much, those pains and twinges from years of abuse came back. I knew I was getting old, but the signs were more obvious when I was exhausted. The captain must have been tired too. Like us, he had been working around the clock. In four years, I had never seen him in on a Saturday. But this case was different. None of us could stop working until the killer was found.

I had gotten to see Nessie that morning, which always sustained me in tough times. Sitting on the rug, we watched *Sesame Street* and *Sabrina, the Teenage Witch*. Ruth never allowed food in the living room, but she made an exception, bringing us pancakes and sausages on paper plates. Nessie was more excited than I had seen her in weeks, laughing at everything I said. For a few hours, I was able to forget about the investigation, although I knew it wouldn't last.

"I still think we should've brought them in for questioning," I said to Egersheim. "At least let the chief know."

Collins nodded as if he agreed, but so far, he had been silent. I couldn't blame him. This was a cruel induction to Homicide.

"They weren't armed," the captain said. "And they haven't broken any laws that I'm aware of—"

"How about operating illegally on foreign soil?"

"Are they?"

"You said it yourself!"

When I raised my voice, he put his finger to his lips. It was the first time we ever had to be careful in the privacy of his office.

"We need to work with them. It's been three weeks."

"Two, Sir," Collins said, finally speaking up. "The first murder was on the 7th."

"Two and a half. Nevertheless, we've got no hard evidence. If they can help us nab Carmody, I don't see a downside."

"I don't trust them," I said.

As someone who didn't hesitate to bend the rules, it felt strange arguing with a man who never did.

"Look," the captain said, sighing. "They know the suspect. They're onto him. They probably would have gotten him if it weren't for—"

He stopped short of saying *you*, which would have been insulting. Collins and I couldn't have known that by chasing them, the suspect would get away.

"We've got four dead girls. None have been identified."

"Doris Hearn has."

"*Tentatively*," he said with emphasis.

I didn't argue because he was technically correct. The RUC had only confirmed Doris Hearn's license was valid. It would take more than that to get a death certificate. The autopsy photos and legal documents had all been sent to the authorities in Ireland, but we hadn't heard back. Transatlantic mail was slow, even first class. Although we could have sent them by telecopier, we still needed an affidavit to make it official. It would have been quicker if the woman's sister had flown to the States to claim the body.

There was a knock at the door. A secretary peeked in, her hair up, her lipstick dark.

"This just came in…"

She handed him a document and left. As he scanned it, he raised his eyes, building my anticipation. Then I saw a smile creep from the corner of his mouth and knew it was good news.

"We might have confirmation on *Jane Doe II's* identity," he said.

"Janice O'Brien?"

"This is from the RUC. A *Janice O'Brien* from Lurgan was reported missing last week by her mother. They're requesting autopsy photos."

We all smiled at one other, a moment of restrained celebration.

"Only two more to go," Collins said.

The giddiness in his voice reminded me of my early years on the force when every lead or break in a case felt like a triumph.

"I'll get this mailed out ASAP."

Under Captain Jackson, I always knew when our meetings were over because he would grab a pen or the phone and start working. Egersheim would just go silent. I was sure it was awkward for Collins, but by now I was used to it.

As we got up, I felt a slight dread, knowing now what we were dealing with. It was more out of laziness than fear. After years on the job, I no longer got the thrill from chasing murderers that used to make it worthwhile.

"Oh, Collins," Egersheim said like an afterthought. "Your hunch was right about those guys."

"Sir?"

"They were after the suspect too. Good work."

I didn't know what impressed me more, Collins' instincts or the captain's praise. For all my doubts about either of them, I finally felt like we were a team.

"Thank you, Sir."

······

We drove down Cambridge Street in morning traffic. As we passed City Hall, there was a crowd out front, people holding signs and chanting. The outrage over Vietnam had been waning for over a year, so I assumed it was about abortion or school desegregation. Like most cops, I no longer cared about protests or agitation.

Even after three cups of coffee, I was still exhausted, and my nerves were on edge. When a taxi swerved into my lane, I hit the brakes, and Collins flinched.

"You okay, Lieutenant?"

"Just tired. Maybe you should drive," I joked.

"Sure, but I ain't got a license."

"What? You took the captain's car last night."

He grinned guiltily.

"Orders is orders."

"What did you do before?"

"I walked the beat. The North End mostly, sometimes East Boston."

"All the Italians."

"That's right. People thought I was too."

In a city so tribal, everyone had to side with some group. With his olive skin, he could have passed for a dozen ethnicities.

"Did you tell them you were half Puerto Rican?"

"Why would I?"

We turned into the parking lot of the Charles Street Jail. Situated on a rotary between Beacon Hill and the West End, the prison seemed out of place amid all the newer hospital buildings. Its granite façade gave it the appearance of a dungeon; its barbed wire fence looked menacing. From above, it was shaped like a cross, ironic for a place with so little redemption.

"What's your take on Rowe and the others?" I asked.

As inexperienced as Collins was, I needed another opinion. Without Harrigan, I had no one else to talk to.

"They seemed straight up. I just don't get what they were gonna do once they found the guy."

"That makes two of us."

We got out and headed toward a private entrance behind the building, reserved for cops, lawyers, probation officers, and other officials.

"Did Cecily say anything?"

"No, she was pretty upset. I didn't want to push her," he said. "I just brought her here and went home."

I opened the large steel door, and we walked into a room that looked like a bomb shelter. The high cement walls were bare and cracked; there were no windows. Beside a desk, a skinny guard sat slumped in a wooden chair. I thought he was asleep until he looked up and said, "Morning, boys."

We showed him our badges, mostly out of habit since he recognized us.

"We got someone in custody up on three."

"The *ladies' floor*," he said with a flair.

"Cecily Madden."

He reached for his radio and made a call. A couple of minutes later, another guard came out. Overweight and bald, he had the vacant look of someone worn down by boredom and idleness. I never envied their jobs. The stability and salary could never make up for working around so much despair.

He waved, and we followed him inside, down a long corridor. I tried to make small talk, but he just nodded and grunted. At the end, we turned into a stairwell and walked up three flights.

When we came out on the female floor, the walls were bright, and the cells had normal doors —— there were no bars. It even smelled different. While some women were serving time for small offenses, the unit was mostly for protective custody.

We got to Cecily's room, and the guard unlocked the door. I knocked once as a courtesy and opened it. Peering in, I saw her sitting on the bed reading a book.

"Hello."

"Mr. Brae," she said, standing up.

"It's Jody. This is Detective Collins."

Behind her, the sun came through the barred window, casting a long shadow on the floor.

"Are you okay?" I asked.

"As good as could be, I suppose."

"We need to talk about what happened."

While she was calmer than the previous night, she still seemed troubled.

"Sure," she said.

I looked at Collins, and he closed the door.

"So where do we start?" she asked.

"First, why'd you leave *Sunnyside*?"

"I found another job."

"Why didn't you tell Delilah?"

"I meant to."

Her answers were short and snippy. We hadn't come to interrogate her, but she acted like a defiant suspect.

"You left the place you were staying at."

After a short pause, she said, "How'd you know that?"

"We went by the house. The landlord said you hadn't been home in a few days."

"I needed to clear my head."

I glanced around the small room which, although prettier than a cell, was no less confining.

"Is this what you had in mind?"

She frowned.

"Look, Cecily," I said. "We're only here to help."

I stepped closer, testing her trust. But she stayed by the bed and didn't move.

"We've got four dead girls," I went on, "and a killer on the loose—"

"And you wanna know who it is?"

"We know about Derek Carmody," I said.

Hearing the name, her expression changed.

"Then why'd you come here?"

Considering we had found her running hysterically in the rain, the question was odd. But traumatized people were never rational.

"For one, last night you said someone was trying to kill you."

"He was."

Our eyes locked.

"We need to know why."

While everything Rowe had told us made sense, we couldn't be sure that Cecily was the 5th witness he'd described.

She crossed her arms, looking sideways, her face racked with emotion.

"Derek was my boyfriend," she said.

"When?"

"I've known him all me life, really. We started dating in secondary school."

"Was he violent?"

"As kids?" she asked, frowning. "Hardly. He was just a quiet fella. After secondary school, he joined the Army. He was gone almost six years."

"Was he ever in combat?"

"Aye, Borneo, in Indonesia. Some bloody conflict no one's ever heard of. When he came back, he was different."

"How so?"

"More intense about things, like. More political. He hated the IRA."

"Did you two get back together?"

She wiped a tear from her eye.

"We talked about it. But by then the troubles had started, riots, shootings, bombs. Everyone thought there was gonna be a civil war. I suppose it helped that we were on the same side."

"So, you're Protestant?"

She paused.

"Yes. I mean…in spirit. I haven't seen the inside of a church in ages. But it doesn't matter over there. It's more about politics than religion."

I glanced at Collins, who listened but looked confused. Between her and Rowe, it was like a fast lesson in Irish history and politics.

"What do you know about the bombing of the Trinity Salon in Belfast?" I asked.

I could tell by the way she shifted the question made her uncomfortable.

"I remember it, of course."

"You worked there, right?"

"I did, but I had nothing to do with it."

"I didn't say you did. Were you asked to testify against him?"

"No, no. I didn't see anything. I wasn't working that day. They said a man came in posing as a plumber. He said the landlord had called him. The other girls saw him."

"Do you believe it was Derek Carmody?"

"I honestly don't know. I moved to Boston before the trial started."

"Why?"

"To start a new life, I suppose. To get away from all the madness in Belfast. My friend had a cousin in Dorchester. I stayed with her a few months and then found me own place."

As she spoke, her voice was jittery. She fumbled with her hands. But so far, her story aligned with Rowe's, so I had to keep pushing.

"Has Carmody been in touch with you?" I asked.

"Not really."

"What do you mean by *not really*?"

"It's silly. When he was in the Army, the Special Forces, he wrote to me, but he could never say much, where he was or what he was doing. It was all very secretive. So he'd send me song lyrics instead…"

She got suddenly sentimental, smiling for the first time.

"He wasn't much of a romantic, but he had his moments. About a month ago, I got a letter. There was no return address. I knew it was sent from the States. It had no Customs stamp."

"And what'd it say?"

"Nothing. That's how I knew it was Derek. It was just the words to a song by *The Who*, our favorite band.

"Just words?"

"The seeds are bursting, The spring's a-seeping, Lay down, my darling, Love ain't for keeping."

"Yeah," Collins said with a grin. "Good album."

"Not as good as *Tommy*."

I looked at Collins and then back to her. When it came to the tastes and trends of youth, I was like an old man. But we weren't there to talk about pop culture.

"So what?" I asked. "Was it some kind of threat?"

"Just a sentiment, that's all."

"Then why'd you say he was trying to kill you?"

"Maybe I overreacted."

"I hate to break it to you, Ms. Madden, but your old boyfriend is a serial killer."

Friends and loved ones of suspects always denied their guilt. So I was surprised when she dropped her head, nodding in agreement.

"When I heard about Doris Hearn—"

"That hasn't been released."

"News travels fast, Mr. Brae," she said coldly. "I got nervous, so I left my place. I was staying with a friend in Savin Hill. We were out at a bar last night. Everyone's talking about the murders now. It was late. I had a few too many. I went to the loo, and when I came out, I saw Derek beside the jukebox."

"Was he alone?"

"Yes. For a second, our eyes met. I was near the door. He saw me, and I ran out."

Someone knocked, and I looked back to see the guard. I held up my finger, and he grumbled something and walked off. There were no time limits on police visits, so I assumed it was a shift change.

"Did you ever work at the Blarney Stone?"

"In Dorchester? No, never."

"One of the victims was a waitress there. She used your name."

Reaching into my coat, I got my notepad and flipped through it.

"Cecily Madden," I said, my writing so bad that even I couldn't read it. "Belfast, Northern Ireland. Date of Birth, 2/12/48."

"That's not my birthday. I'm February 21st."

"It's close. Same year?"

"Yes."

"Is that a coincidence?"

"I'm sure it's someone I know. We all use fake names. She probably knew I had a green card."

"Could it be one of the girls from the salon?"

"I don't know."

I closed the notepad and put it away. She had told us more than I expected, and I knew when to stop. Too much information was often as bad as too little, complicating the facts and creating false leads. Captain Jackson had taught me that when it came to a crime, the simplest scenario was always the most likely.

"One last thing," I said. "I'm gonna need you to try to identify the victim."

Her arms fell to her side, her face turning to dread.

"Like, see the body?"

"I'm afraid so."

"What if I refuse?"

Our eyes locked. Knowing her from the day care, I sympathized with her more than some random witness. But we were also after a murderer. Even if she was frightened and distressed, I didn't have time to be gentle.

"You'll be charged with obstructing an investigation," I said, which was a lot easier to threaten someone with than to prove. "Your green card could be revoked. If that happens, you'll be deported."

CHAPTER 30

IT WAS JUST AFTER DARK WHEN WE PULLED UP IN FRONT OF SAGANSKY'S Diner. Inside, I could see that the tables were all full, people laughing, eating, and smoking. The plates of food reminded me I was hungry. The last thing I had was pancakes and sausages for breakfast.

"There she is," Collins said.

Through the glass, I saw a young waitress pouring coffee for some men in a booth. Just like Collins had described her, she had a slim figure but big breasts. Her dark hair was tied back, her red lipstick bright. If I didn't know she was half-Greek, I would have thought she was Italian.

"Wanna come in and meet her?"

"Maybe another time," I said.

Collins looked at me and back, but she was no longer in the window. As cool and streetwise as he was, he had a boyish excitement in his voice. I knew how he felt, the anticipation of young romance. I only hoped it would last.

"Thanks for the lift," he said, getting out.

"Pick you up in the morning?"

"Sounds good."

He shut the door, and I pulled away. As much as I complained about driving him, I had to admit I liked the kid. I wondered what would happen when Harrigan returned, whether Egersheim would keep him on or send him back down to patrol. It seemed cruel to give a young officer a chance at detective and then take it away. *Homicide* was no place for temps, interns, or apprentices.

Stopped at an intersection in the South End, I struggled to decide whether to go left or right. I was torn by my obligations and felt like I was letting everyone down.

I hadn't visited Harrigan since Thursday. While I had played with Nessie for a couple of hours that morning, I hadn't spent any time with Ruth in a week. Our marriage could take the strain, but I worried about her. Her due date was approaching, and she was on more medication than I could keep track of. It was only one more reason to find the killer fast.

When the light changed, I didn't notice. A car behind me beeped, giving me the nudge I needed to make a choice. Either would have left me feeling guilty, so I cut the wheel and headed to City Hospital.

I got there in minutes and parked out front. The lobby was quiet, that short respite between the daytime bustle and evening rush. When it came to medical emergencies, no one could predict where and when they would happen.

I exited the elevator and went down the corridor, returning nurses' smiles as I passed. By now, many of them recognized me. When I got to the door, I knocked once and opened it. Delilah was sitting on the chair beside the bed.

"Jody?" she said, and as she went to stand, I motioned not to. "You found Cecily?"

"We did."

"Is she okay?"

"Yes."

"Lieutenant," Harrigan said.

"Detective," I responded sarcastically.

We had been through so much together that formalities seemed like a joke.

"You look knackered," he went on.

"A long day."

His voice was strong, his eyes clear. He still had IVs and a heart monitor, but I could tell he was improving.

"I'm told things have taken a turn," he said.

I glanced at Delilah, who sat with her legs crossed, her feet bare. Under the chair, I saw a pair of red platform shoes.

"Yeah," I said hesitantly.

As much as I liked her, I still wasn't comfortable discussing cases around civilians.

"The captain told me. He came by earlier."

"How're you feeling?"

He looked at Delilah, and she smiled.

"They say I could be released as early as Wednesday."

In that instant, I felt a rush of relief and elation.

"That's great," I said, holding my breath to steady my voice. "Now maybe you can help with the investigation."

"The victims are all Irish?"

"We know at least two of them are. Did Egersheim tell you?"

"It was on the news."

"I'm not surprised," I said.

The murders had happened so fast that, at first, we had a head start on the panic. Now the State Police were involved, and everyone knew. I hadn't been back to headquarters since morning, but I was sure it was mobbed with reporters.

"Cecily knows the suspect?" Harrigan asked.

I gave him a sharp look.

"You didn't hear that on TV."

"That was from the captain."

"Where is she, if I may ask?" Delilah asked.

I looked at Harrigan, and he nodded as if giving me permission.

"In protective custody at the moment."

"Where?"

"The Charles Street Jail."

"Does she need to be there?"

"She was staying with a friend. But she can't go back. It's not safe."

Delilah's eyes widened.

"She could stay with me at BU. I have the dorm until May. It's discreet...and safe. There's a doorman."

"I don't—"

"Is she under arrest?"

"Technically, no."

As always, she was polite, but her tone was firm, insistent. In some ways, I admired her, acting out her beliefs about kindness and social justice in a way that many activists didn't. She wasn't the type to not help someone who was alone or suffering. I knew she wouldn't take no for an answer.

"Let me check with the captain," I said.

CHAPTER 31

Sunday morning, Collins and I waited in the parking lot of City Hospital, Cecily sitting in the back seat. She was so quiet that, for minutes at a time, I forgot she was even there. Whether her silence was from fear or despair, I didn't know, but at least she looked better. Delilah had given her some clean clothes, a flowered blouse and faded jeans. I was surprised they fit because their figures were so different.

Ansell's car finally pulled in, turning into a spot beside the dumpster. We got out and went over to meet him. He didn't look back as he hobbled toward the rear door, but I could tell he had seen us.

"Doctor," I said, hurrying to catch up. "This is Cecily."

He raised his hat with a sour smile.

"My pleasure," he said, then he looked at me. "You know I don't work Sundays."

"I appreciate it."

"You should," he said, fumbling through his keys.

He opened the door, and we went down into the basement like we were entering a cavern. With the lights off, the hallway was dark, but he knew where to step. I stayed close behind, and Collins and Cecily followed me.

When we walked into the office, he reached for the lights; the glare of the white neon made us all squint. The room was the same temperature as outside, but somehow the dank air felt colder.

The doctor puffed his cigar and put it in an overfilled ashtray. Walking over to the crypt, he opened the heavy steel door. When he waved for us to enter, I got a reluctance that bordered on terror. I was losing my tolerance for corpses, something Harrigan had noticed the night of the first murder. Coincidentally, it was the same body we were there to identify.

Leaning over, Ansell read off the numbers of the compartments in a way that was methodical but not dehumanizing. When he found it, he opened the hatch and rolled out the tray.

She was the oldest victim, deceased now for almost three weeks. I knew the morgue was built to preserve, but I worried about the condition of the body.

Ansell looked up and then pulled the white sheet back.

"Oh my God," Cecily exclaimed, putting her hands to her mouth.

It was the same young woman except her skin was paler, almost translucent. Her auburn hair was brittle too, no longer full and shiny. As I stared, I felt myself choking up, but it didn't last. I could always rein in my emotions when I had to.

"You recognize her?"

Although it was obvious, I had to ask. Cecily nodded, and tears flew from her eyes.

"She worked at Trinity Salon," she said.

"What's her name?"

"Trudy…Gertrude. Gertrude Haslett."

I looked at Ansell, and he slid the body back inside. When I put my arm around Cecily, she was trembling. I didn't usually console witnesses, but I was compelled to by some feeling of sympathy or duty.

Collins held open the door, and I escorted her back to the office. She would have to sign an affidavit, but with her condition, we all knew it could wait.

I thanked the doctor, and we left. Although it was cold and gray outside, anywhere was better than the mortuary. I always wondered how someone could work around so much death. Ansell seemed to enjoy it or at least, he was good at it, which was often the same thing.

"Are you taking me back?" Cecily asked.

I opened the door, and she got in.

"It's the best place for now."

Legally, we couldn't hold her unless we got an order from a judge, which we had no time to do. But I wasn't going to tell her.

"I wanna go home," she moaned.

"You can't. He knows where you are."

"I mean *home* home. Ireland."

"Once Carmody is apprehended, you will."

I tried to shut the door, but she held it open.

"I can't go back to that jail. It's like a prison," she said, so upset she didn't see the irony.

"I might be able to find you a place to stay."

"Really?"

"You need to help us first. Who was at Trinity Salon that day?"

She crossed her arms, looking away.

"I told you I was off," she said coldly.

"But don't you know who else was there?"

"I've no idea. Ask the RUC."

With each question, she got more defiant, squirming in the seat like she couldn't get comfortable.

"We did, but we won't know anything until tomorrow. We think there might've been another witness, maybe someone who didn't wanna testify."

"And you think it was me?"

"I didn't say that."

I had done enough interrogations to know when someone was hiding something. Human body language was revealing. Even if she wasn't lying, I knew she was avoiding the truth.

"Any idea who it might be?" I asked.

"I ain't a snitch."

All at once, it made sense. Rowe had been right. If someone was working that day and didn't come forward, it was probably intentional. As in any war, loyalties were complicated, and sometimes civilians didn't want to get involved.

"You're not a snitch, but we need your help…"

She crossed her arms with a bitter pout.

"Please!"

When I tried to make eye contact, she looked away. Until then, I had sympathized with her. But with Carmody on the loose, I didn't have time to deal with a stubborn witness.

"Fine. Back to Charles Street Jail then," I said, and I slammed the door shut.

……

WE DROVE over the Congress Street bridge into the seaport district, a vast stretch of vacant buildings and crumbling roads. It was once a center of manufacturing. Now all that was left were the fisheries on the wharves, and a few businesses still clinging to life in the aftermath of the city's industrial decline.

Since the sixties, some squatters had moved in —— bohemian artists and hippies. But at night it was desolate. Like any neglected place, it was dangerous and had become a dumping ground for the fallout of crime, from stolen cars to dead bodies.

We turned down A Street and went by an abandoned lot along Fort Point Channel. In the distance, between a fence and a stack of abandoned cement barriers, I saw the black Buick.

"What time is it?" I asked.

"3:55."

I didn't see Egersheim's cruiser, so I knew he hadn't arrived yet. We could have stopped, but I didn't want Rowe and his men to think we were eager. We already had the State Police, and now with British agents involved, my pride was hurt.

By the time we had gone to West Broadway Street and turned around, the captain was approaching the lot. I followed him in, and we parked. Like a choreographed dance, we got out and walked toward Rowe and his men, and they came toward us. The sky was overcast, but they all had on sunglasses.

"Gentlemen," Rowe said.

He wore a scaly cap and gloves, his leather bomber jacket zipped to the top. When he extended his hand to me first, I could tell Egersheim was annoyed. We shook, and his grip was weaker than I had expected for his size.

"What've you got for us?" Egersheim asked.

"What have we got? We know Carmody is either in Dorchester or South Boston."

"You're a regular sleuth," I joked.

"We've been closer to catching him than you boys," he said, giving me a sideways glance.

Conversations with him were a tug-of-war of irony, sarcasm, and innuendo. I couldn't tell if it was a cultural thing —— I hadn't talked with the other two men enough to know.

"Any updates on his location?" the captain asked.

"He was staying at a flat in Savin Hill. But we checked. He's gone."

"Could he have skipped town?"

"He wouldn't get far," Rowe said.

"Maybe he went home."

"Doubt it. Your FBI has him on a watch list. He tries to get through an airport, and he's done for."

"Does he know anyone else in the States?"

Rowe shrugged his shoulders, ignoring the captain's question. He reached into his coat and took out a pack of cigarettes, a brand I didn't recognize. When he offered us one, we all declined.

"Now," he said, lighting it. "Do we know if there were any other witnesses?"

Egersheim hesitated. I could see that he was thinking. He hadn't wanted to tell them about Cecily yet, the one thing I agreed with.

"I inquired with the *Public Prosecution Service* in Northern Ireland," the captain said. "They're gonna rush it, but I don't expect to hear anything until tomorrow."

"Tomorrow might be too late."

"Curious," I said to Rowe. "Wouldn't your department have the names of all the witnesses?"

He turned to me, his entire body pivoting.

"Only the ones the prosecutor had prepared for the trial. If anyone had seen Carmody and didn't want to testify against him, we'd have no way of knowing."

"They could've looked at the work schedule that day."

"The place was blown to bits," Rowe said, motioning with his hands. "Those little hair shops don't keep records."

"Still seems like sloppy police work," I said.

"Belfast is a sloppy place. If one of those girls was afraid to come forward, she probably had her reasons."

"Maybe she didn't see Carmody?"

"Or maybe she did."

"If there *is* another witness," the captain asked, "what makes you think she's in Boston?"

"Where else could she be?"

"Ireland," I said.

"Ah, I doubt it. It's obvious the girls were tipped off."

"Maybe by Carmody himself."

Rowe flicked his cigarette.

"Look, we could stand here speculating 'til the cows come home. But I've got a better idea."

"Go on," Egersheim said.

"You find out who that other witness is. She'll lead us to Carmody. I'm sure of it."

"Say we do, what then?"

"We'll find her."

"Or we will," the captain said.

"Don't be so sure," Rowe said, "You boys hadn't had a clue until you ran into us. Carmody had been running around this city for a week. And I know your chief has asked the State Police for help."

The remark was harsh, some indictment on our skills as detectives. I knew it hurt Egersheim the most. As the head of Homicide, his reputation was on the line. We hadn't done anything wrong. No evidence had been tainted, no witnesses strongarmed. If we were guilty of anything it was of having bad luck. Carmody's spree had been so sudden and so furious no one could have expected it. Even the State Police had been stumped, looking into old cases to find a suspect.

Finally, the captain looked up.

"I should know more by tomorrow."

CHAPTER 32

WHEN WE WALKED INTO THE OFFICE, EGERSHEIM WAS SITTING WITH Colonel Murgia. They were both drinking coffee, and on the desk was a box of donuts. If I didn't know better, I would have thought they were two old friends catching up over breakfast.

"Brae," Egersheim said. "You remember Colonel Murgia?"

"Good to see you, Colonel," I said, which wasn't true.

"And this is Detective Collins."

"Right," Murgia said, turning in his chair. "Filling in for an injured brother?"

Just the word *brother* seemed to lessen my bitterness. It was both a compliment and a show of solidarity for the risks we all shared. I couldn't blame the colonel for his department's participation in the case. He hadn't asked for it.

"Harrigan," Egersheim said. "He was shot in an incident two summers ago. He got an infection from it, but he seems to have pulled through."

While the truth was much more complicated, the explanation was good enough.

"The captain just updated me on what you found out," the colonel said.

I didn't know what he had told Murgia, which put me in an awkward position. I was about to say *about what?* until the colonel saved me the humiliation by asking, "Derek Carmody?"

"He seems like a good match."

I did my best to be vague without sounding evasive.

"Did you check with customs? Immigration? If he came into the country, he's gotta be on a flight manifest."

"Not yet. We just found out."

"How'd you discover all this?"

A quiet tension filled the room, or maybe it was my own apprehension. Facing us, the colonel couldn't see Egersheim, but we could, and he looked panicked.

"There's a girl,' I said, "a young woman who worked at my daughter's daycare. She told us about the bombing. She used to date Carmody."

"A nice coincidence. And she believes he's the killer?"

"Yes."

"Why?"

"She saw him in a bar Friday night. Yesterday we took her to the mortuary. She identified the body of Gertrude Haslett, one of the girls from the salon."

"And you think you've spotted Carmody?"

"Twice. Last Saturday we were leaving the scene of the murder in Dudley Square. We were going down Columbia Road and Collins saw someone who fit the description—"

"Which is what exactly?"

"A long leather jacket."

"We're gonna need more than that, Lieutenant. That's half the city."

It sounded like a reprimand until he smiled.

"The guy's short, wiry. We got out to ask him a few questions, and he ran. Then we saw him the next day at the parade."

The colonel looked at Egersheim.

"That was the incident you were telling me about?" he asked.

"It was a misunderstanding."

"It happens."

Not sure what Egersheim had told him, I was careful not to say too much. Either way, Murgia seemed satisfied. I knew there would be more questions, but it wasn't a formal meeting. Collins and I were still standing.

"Everything is in the case file," the captain said. "I was up 'til midnight pulling it all together."

"Good. My men will review it today. Now how about a donut?"

When the colonel looked at us, I declined, and Collins grabbed one.

"A cause for celebration," Egersheim said. "The colonel is retiring."

"Congratulations," I said. "When?"

"Next month."

I couldn't tell his age, but he wasn't much older than me.

"You look too young," I joked.

"Mandatory at fifty for us. How about you?"

"I've got a ways to go."

"The captain tells me you're a vet."

"Korea," I said. "Marines, 1st Division, 3rd Battalion."

"I was in the big war," he said, but it wasn't an insult. "407th Anti-aircraft Gun Battalion."

The small talk relaxed me enough that I changed my mind about the donut. Reaching over the colonel, I grabbed a chocolate-frosted one.

"With your military time you could get out early," he said.

I took a bite and looked up.

"Now you sound like my wife."

We all laughed, Egersheim the loudest. We resented that the State Police had joined our investigation, and Murgia probably knew it. But if we had to work with them, socializing was better than sulking.

"Sit down," the captain said.

With only one chair free, I didn't want to leave Collins standing. But I didn't have time to reply because someone knocked. I glanced back, and a secretary looked in, the same brunette from before.

"Lieutenant Brae," she said, her voice soft and feminine. "A call for you."

In an instant, I stopped chewing. My heart began to pound. My first thought was it was either about Harrigan or Ruth. Maybe it was all the horrors I had seen and experienced, but I always expected the worst.

"Shall I put it through to your office?" she asked.

"I'll head down now."

CHAPTER 33

IT HAD BEEN LESS THAN TWENTY-FOUR HOURS, AND CECILY HAD decided to talk. I had never wanted to be tough with her, but we needed her help. As Derek Carmody's former lover, she knew more about him than anyone. The only reason she had agreed to identify Trudy Haslett was that she didn't have a choice. The woman had been using her name.

There hadn't been a murder in almost two weeks, which was no consolation to the families of the victims or the public. But the pressure was still on with daily articles in the tabloids and editorials in the *Boston Globe*. Sometimes the quiet aftermath of a tragedy was as jarring as the tragedy itself. At least it seemed like Carmody's work was done. The risk now was that he would flee.

We raced into the lot of the Charles Street Jail, the tires chirping as we came to a stop. When we burst in the back door, a fat guard looked up, a newspaper spread out before him.

"We're here for Cecily Madden," I said.

"Cecily? Ain't that a girl's name?"

"She's in protective custody."

Stretching his arm, he reached for the phone on the wall, too lazy to stand. He made a call and hung up, and we stood waiting. When two minutes passed and no one came out, I asked, "Can you try again?"

The guy frowned.

"They'll be down when they come down."

I didn't argue, knowing it would only make things worse. As employees of the legal system, we were all supposed to be working together. But in the petty hierarchy of status between government agencies, prison guards were at the bottom. They didn't like getting pushed about by cops.

Finally, the steel door opened, and a young black guard peered out. He waved to us, and we followed him inside.

We came down the corridor and stopped at a different room, which wasn't unusual. Inmates were moved all the time. When I opened the door, Cecily looked up from her bed where she was reading *Rolling Stone* magazine. I knew it was old because Jim Morrison was on the cover, and he had died the year before.

"Mr. Brae," she said, standing.

She wore a long dress, and her hair was in braids like on the day I'd met her. On the windowsill was a vase with some dandelions; women could liven up the dreariest places.

"We heard you wanted to talk," I said.

"I'm sorry about yesterday."

"No need to apologize."

She looked at the door, and I nodded at Collins to shut it.

"I didn't want any part in all this. I came to America to get away."

"I understand. We know who three of the girls are. We need help with the fourth."

She bit her lip, looking around.

"Sure. I'll try."

I called for the guard, and he escorted us back. First, we stopped at the release desk so Cecily could get her things. She hadn't brought much, just a pocketbook, some hair clips, and the clothes she had changed out of. The fact that she had fled her rented room without anything was a measure of her panic.

The attendant put everything in a canvas bag, and we continued to the rear door. As we passed, the guard glanced up. I wanted to give him a hard stare but didn't, knowing I would probably have to deal with him again in the future. It was never wise to make enemies when you didn't have to.

As we pulled out of the prison, I had the urge to speed but didn't. Knowing what she had been through, I didn't want to make her uneasy.

......

WE GOT to City Hospital during a shift change, and nurses were streaming out the front doors. Some women got into cars, their boyfriends or husbands picking them up, while others walked down the hill. The South End was never safe, especially at night. With the rash of killings, the hospital had placed security guards at the bus stops on Mass Ave.

We drove around back and found a spot. One of the advantages of going to the morgue was that there was always plenty of parking.

Walking down through the decrepit basement, I realized I had gone there more in the past two weeks than in the previous three months. I missed the winter lull when the murder rate was low.

"Brae?"

Standing at the door, Doctor Ansell had on a white lab coat, some implements in his hands. I could tell we were interrupting him. Much like Egersheim, he only called me *Brae* when he was aggravated.

"We need to ID a body," I said.

He peered up, his glasses hanging at the tip of his nose. While visits technically required an appointment, we had known each other long enough that he always overlooked it. Now I worried I had pushed my luck.

"It'll have to be quick."

I smiled gratefully, and we followed him inside.

"When was the death?" he asked, opening the door.

"The 18th"

As we entered the morgue, he glanced back, and I knew why. He was old-fashioned enough that he thought in terms of days and not dates.

"Two Saturdays ago," I said.

He looked up squinting. I could always tell when he was thinking because his eyes pulsated. While his method for organizing bodies was a mystery, he seemed to know them all personally. It was both eerie and oddly touching.

He walked over to one of the chambers, undid the latch, and opened it. I brought Cecily closer, and she didn't look as upset as before. Ansell rolled out the bed and quickly pulled back the sheet. I hesitated before looking down, more from revulsion than dread. I was getting tired of seeing dead bodies.

At first, I was surprised that she had no sutures on her neck. Then I remembered that, like Doris Hearn, she had been stabbed. This was Carmody's fourth kill, and he was getting sloppy. She had more knife wounds than any of the other victims, all on her chest and abdomen. We had to assume she'd put up a fight, or maybe he'd just panicked. It was hard for an Irish guy to slip away in a black neighborhood like Roxbury.

I'd barely caught a glimpse of the victim on the night she'd been found. Now, standing inches from her corpse, I was able to see her. Her hair was dark, her face pretty, but otherwise, I had noticed nothing distinctive. As cold as it sounded, all these Irish girls were starting to look the same.

"I know her," Cecily said.

"What's her name?"

"Eleanor Reese. She worked at the salon. I didn't know her well. She worked different days."

When I looked up, the doctor was staring back. I could tell he was getting impatient.

"Thanks," I said, and he nodded.

He put the sheet back, slid the body in, and shut the door. Before we left, I thanked Ansel, but he just grumbled something and went into the lab.

We walked out and back down the corridor.

"Will her parents be notified?" Cecily asked.

"I'm sure they know."

If it wasn't true now, I knew it would be. The murders had happened so fast that we were only just starting to communicate with the authorities in Northern Ireland. So far, we had worked with them to identify Janice O'Brien and Doris Hearn. Gertrude Haslet would be next.

A verbal confirmation wasn't official and was mainly for the sake of the investigation and the relatives of the victims. Because the women were all foreign nationals, it would take weeks if not months to get death certificates.

Cecily tripped on our way out of the building, but Collins was there to catch her. Everywhere we went, he was alert and ready. Lots of young officers were sharp, but his instincts were beyond what any training could teach. While I wanted to think it was my influence, two weeks on *Homicide* was enough to bring out the best or worst in anyone.

Collins opened the door for Cecily, and she slid into the backseat. We got in, and I turned the key, the engine sputtering a few times. The Valiant was old but reliable. I never worried about it starting up.

"Where're we going?" Cecily asked.

Since picking her up, I could tell she was overwhelmed. All her youthful sparkle was gone; her voice was sullen.

"I've got a place you can stay," I said. "It's safe."

She sighed.

"Thank you."

I looked in the rearview mirror, and our eyes met.

"But we need more help from you."

I didn't know much about her past, but she had an edge, a quality that only a tough childhood could produce. I knew it because I had lived it. In the slums of blue-collar Boston, people wore their cynicism like a badge of honor.

I had always sensed Cecily knew more than she let on. If she was hiding anything, now was our best chance of getting her to talk. She was alone and weak. While it may have seemed cruel, detective work was always an ethical balance.

"Was there anyone else at the salon that day?" I asked. "Maybe someone who didn't come forward to the police? Someone who was afraid to testify?"

"I wasn't working—"

"Tell me, Goddammit!"

She flinched. Collins turned back, and we stared at her. It took a moment, but she finally glanced up.

"Yes. There was someone else."

CHAPTER 34

HER NAME WAS JILL SLATTERY. COLLINS SAID IT SOUNDED LIKE A PINUP model, but I thought it was more like a starlet. Like all the other young women, she was in her early twenties. Cecily knew her from school, and later they'd worked together at Trinity Salon. She had long blonde hair and high cheekbones, which was about as specific as Carmody's *mustache* and *long leather coat*. But I was used to vague descriptions. Short of a tattoo, scar, or other unique characteristic, most people generally looked the same until you got to know them.

The two girls had reconnected when Cecily met her in a bar downtown two years before. They had gone out a few times and then lost touch. Cecily still had her address, and I wasn't surprised it was in Dorchester. I could have pressed her for more, but after two nights in custody, she was tired and irritable.

We pulled over at 610 Beacon Street, a nine-story brick building outside Kenmore Square. With BU and all the other colleges around, the area was filled with dive bars, rock clubs, and record shops. The elegant brownstones that were once residences were now apartments and dormitories.

With the mild temperature, the sun seemed to wipe away the grayness of winter. The snow was melting, the gutters filled with murky water. If I wasn't in the middle of a murder investigation, I would have said it was a beautiful day.

As we got out, two young men walked by singing a folk song, and Collins frowned. Students got away with behavior that, in other parts of town, they would have been ridiculed for.

We escorted Cecily into the foyer where a black security officer was sitting behind a desk. When I gave him our names, he called up and then nodded for us to proceed. We took the elevator to the seventh floor and went down a long hallway that had a faint smell of cigarettes and perfume. I stopped at the last door and knocked.

"You made it!"

Delilah burst out and wrapped her arms around Cecily. She wore a purple turtleneck sweater and polyester pants, shiny hoops dangling from her ears.

"Hello, Ms. Reynolds."

Pulling away, Delilah gave her a warm, sympathetic smile.

"It's Mrs. Harrigan," she said. "But no more formalities."

Considering Harrigan had collapsed at their wedding, I always wondered if their marriage was official.

"Come on in."

We followed her into a room with a bed, a small couch, and a desk. Aside from some artwork on the walls, it was sparse. But it was tidier than other dorms I had seen, probably because, as a graduate student, she was older.

Delilah had been living there since coming to Boston to study political science at BU. When Harrigan met her, she'd had a roommate from New York, something I was sure made intimacy difficult. That roommate was now in Africa with the Peace Corps, so he stayed over a couple of nights a week, impressive for a guy who had lived with his mother most of his adulthood.

Delilah took Cecily's coat and bag and hung them on a hook beside the door.

"Now, the couch is a pull-out. It's got clean sheets. Pillows are in the cabinet beside the sink..."

For someone who used to talk about Marx and Derrida, she sounded remarkably conventional.

"Down the hall is the rec room," she went on. "There're cold drinks in the fridge. We'll get something to eat when I get back."

"You're leaving?" I asked.

"I've gotta go over to the daycare."

"We can give you a lift."

"Would you mind?"

"Of course not."

She got her coat and hat, fixing her makeup in the mirror above the desk. It was always fascinating to watch a woman get ready.

"If you need to leave, there's another key beside the lamp. Just make sure you lock up."

"I will. Thanks a million."

Delilah smiled, and we left the room. It felt strange leaving Cecily behind. With security at the entrance, I knew she would be safe. If Carmody had wanted to kill her, he would have done so already.

As we walked down the hallway, some girls were in the doorway of a room. Collins smiled, but I ignored them. I still wasn't comfortable around college students, even when they didn't know we were cops. The sixties had destroyed the trust between the police and young people, and I wasn't sure if it had recovered.

"You sure you're okay with this?" I asked.

Delilah glanced around. As sophisticated as she was, she had grown up in Cleveland, so I knew she was street-smart.

"She's gotta stay somewhere."

The elevator arrived, and we got on. As we went down, Delilah stood quietly with her hands clasped. I didn't know how much she knew about the case. If Harrigan was as discreet in private as he was on the job, he hadn't told her much.

"Is Harrigan getting out tomorrow?"

"Wednesday."

"We should celebrate, maybe have a little party or something?"

When the doors opened, we stepped out to the lobby, and she turned to me.

"Once this is all over, we will."

......

WHEN I GOT HOME, Ruth was at the door. Her eyes were red, her face puffy like she had been napping. With her due date nine days away, I knew she could go into labor at any moment. Her blood pressure had been stable, but she still had headaches and blurred vision. While she never complained, I could tell she was miserable. The doctors told us the only thing that would cure the symptoms of pre-eclampsia was having the baby.

Sometimes I wished she had been admitted to the hospital, at least for these last few weeks. But we had no one to take care of Nessie. As helpful as Nadia was, she was elderly and could only work a few hours a day. I had no parents and Ruth's lived far away. The misfortune of having no family around was never more apparent than when you needed them.

"How'd it go?" she asked, helping me take my coat off.

"We're getting close."

As the weeks went by, her questions had gone from specific to general to almost indifferent. For all her interest in my field, I got the sense she didn't care anymore. She just wanted the investigation to be over. I couldn't agree more.

"Daddy!"

Nessie ran in, her dress splattered with chocolate. When I picked her up, she felt heavier, or maybe I was just tired.

"Nadia and Nessie are making a cake for Jezebel," Ruth said, wiping frosting off Nessie's cheek.

"Jezebel?"

"Jezebel, formerly Lara."

I raised my eyes. Not only did Nessie have a dozen dolls, but she changed their names all the time.

When Nadia called from the kitchen, Nessie ran back in. She craved my attention but never seemed to expect it, probably because I was always in a hurry. The guilt I felt was eased only by knowing that I was doing it for them.

"Delilah called," Ruth said. "She said Harrigan is getting out Wednesday."

When we kissed, her lips were tense.

"I know. Maybe now he can help with the case."

She frowned, and we walked into the living room. She sat on the couch, but I remained standing. With only a half hour until I had to meet Egersheim, I didn't want to get too comfortable. I had considered not coming home at all. Even Collins had decided to wait at headquarters. But with the dangers of the job, I never missed a chance to see them.

"Won't you sit?"

"I can't stay long," I said.

On her face, I saw a mix of sadness and understanding.

"Won't you at least have something to eat?"

"Maybe when I get home," I said.

"I'll be waiting up."

"I'd rather you went to bed."

"You can't make me," she teased.

I appreciated her playfulness, especially in tense times. I didn't know if it helped her loneliness, but it soothed my guilt.

I went upstairs and washed up, putting on a clean shirt. Freshening up between shifts always made me feel better.

When I came back down, the evening news was on. Even with the volume low, I could tell it was about Northern Ireland. In Belfast, thousands of people were marching in the streets. Next, there were images of British soldiers throwing young men into the back of a police wagon.

"Those poor people," Ruth said.

I watched for another few seconds and then turned to her.

"I gotta go."

She stood up and came over, her stomach so big she had to lean back to stay upright.

"Okay," she said, peering up, her lashes fluttering.

"Don't wait up."

"I will."

I wanted to frown but didn't. When it came to how she dealt with my long hours, it was none of my business.

I was about to go into the kitchen to see Nessie when she started to sing. It was an old Polish song Nadia had taught her, the words transcribed to English in a way that didn't quite fit. Hearing her voice, all the joy and innocence, was bittersweet. I wanted to say goodnight, but I couldn't bear to see her disappointed.

"Kiss her goodnight for me," I said.

CHAPTER 35

THE WAITRESS LED US TO A BOOTH AT THE BACK OF VICTORIA'S DINER. With the lights low, it was dark and private enough that we could talk without being overheard. While I was sure we were all hungry, Egersheim and I just got coffee. Collins was the only one who ordered food: meatloaf with mashed potatoes. Even nerves and tension couldn't suppress a young appetite.

Once the waitress left, we all leaned in. The nearest customer was four tables away, but we still whispered.

"*Jane Doe I* has been confirmed," the captain said. "I got a message today. Her aunt reported her missing on the 10th. She had no idea she was in Boston."

At a time when the culprit was still at large, each new identification felt like progress.

"Cecily Madden identified the last body today," I said.

"*Jane Doe IV?*"

It was strange that, while we now had the names of all the victims, he still referred to them anonymously.

"Her name is Eleanor Reese. She worked at the salon in Belfast."

"That's good news," the captain said. "I'll call over to Ireland in the morning."

"Does the colonel know about Rowe?"

He hesitated.

"Not really," he said.

I cringed, although I had suspected it. None of us had wanted to collaborate with the State Police, but he was still required to disclose to them everything about the case. The fact that he didn't could put all our careers at risk, whether it was an abuse of power, ethical violation, obstruction of justice, or something else.

"Shouldn't we tell him?"

He lit a cigarette and took a long drag.

"He can go to hell."

I wouldn't have been surprised if the colonel already knew about Rowe and his men and didn't say so. Collaboration between agencies had all the lies, treachery, and deceit of espionage. If Egersheim had acted friendly with Murgia, it was only because he had to.

"If the chief finds out," I said, "it won't look good."

Egersheim sat with his elbows on the table. I had never seen him so despondent.

"It doesn't look good anyway."

We were all disappointed that the case had been taken over, but he took it the worst. He had never experienced the ups and downs of investigations because Harrigan and I always did all the work. I knew it was going to be a tough conversation, which was why I saved some good news for last.

"We might know who that other girl was."

Egersheim looked up.

"The witness for the bombing trial?"

"She wasn't called as a witness," Collins chimed in.

"But she was working that day," I said.

The waitress came over, putting down two cups of coffee and Collins' food. Seeing the hot plate made me hungry.

"Maybe she didn't see Carmody," the captain said.

"If she didn't, something spooked her. She left Ireland shortly after."

He gave me a confused look.

"She's in Boston," I explained.

"And how do you know all this?"

Collins and I looked at each other.

"Cecily."

"And she's sure about this?"

"She gave us an address."

"Where?"

"Dorchester."

He nodded, almost smiling. For the first time in hours, maybe days, I saw hope in his eyes.

"We need to find her."

......

WE GOT to Jill Slattery's address just before nine o'clock, a rundown house on the outskirts of Fields Corner. The front had a rusted fence and overgrown bushes, the ground still wet and muddy from winter. Aside from a faint light on the second floor, it was dark.

I backed into a tight space, and we checked our weapons before getting out. It was the first new lead in a case that was stalled. I didn't think Cecily had lied, and I didn't expect a setup, but we had to be careful.

I knew it was late to stop by, but there was no time for politeness or courtesy. With Carmody still out there, another young woman's life was at risk.

As we walked up the steps, the floorboards creaked. The porch was covered with junk, old chairs, crates of empty milk bottles, and even a bird cage. The home wouldn't have looked out of place in Appalachia.

I pressed the button and, moments later, heard footsteps coming down the stairs. A light went on in the foyer, and through the glass, I saw an older woman. She wore a long bathrobe over a sweater; her gray hair was tied back. She reminded me of the lady we had questioned at the South Boston rooming house.

When she looked out, I showed her my badge. She unlocked the door and opened it.

"Yes?"

"Evening Ma'am," I said gently. "I'm Detective Brae. This is Detective Collins."

She nodded as I spoke like she was either nervous or impatient. Although only in her sixties, she looked older, her hair brittle and her teeth stained from tobacco.

"Sorry for coming by so late—"

"What do you want?" she blurted.

Her rudeness caught me off guard, but I couldn't begrudge an old woman. Not only was she poor, but she had probably lived through two world wars and a depression.

"We're looking for Jill Slattery. Does she live here?"

"Why're you looking for her?"

I never liked it when someone responded to a question with a question.

"We think she might be in danger."

"Well, she don't live here."

"Then why'd you ask?"

She frowned, her face wrinkling. As with bullies, the only way to handle a cranky person was to strike back.

"A long time ago," she said.

"How long?"

"A year anyway."

"Was she the homeowner?"

"Ha! Hardly. My grandfather built this house. I used to have roomers. Only girls. Not anymore."

"Have you seen her since?"

She shook her head, chewing her gums.

"Haven't seen her."

Her long pauses and short answers reminded me of difficult interrogations. Stubborn people, whether they were suspects or not, always got a thrill from being evasive.

"Ma'am, has anyone else come by looking for her?"

"No. She's been gone a long time."

Reaching for my wallet, I took out a card and handed it to her. She looked at it, but I wasn't convinced she could read.

"If someone stops by looking for her. Or if you happen to remember anything, please call me."

"Will do," she said.

She smiled curtly and slammed the door. I looked at Collins, who raised his eyes. We walked back down the steps and stopped on the sidewalk. The street was quiet, the only sound the faint hum of cars on Dorchester Avenue.

"What's your take on her," I said.

"I think she's lying through her teeth."

"Yeah, all three of them," I joked.

"Strange old bat. Sort of reminds me of my aunt."

Everyone we met he compared to a relative, the trappings of a working-class dynasty. He had a cousin who was a sergeant with the Boston Police, and another who was a patrolman in Watertown. One of his uncles was doing life for murder. Another was a talent scout in Hollywood, rumored to be gay. In the past three weeks, I had learned more about his family than about Harrigan's in our first two years working together.

As we headed to the car, I walked easily for the first time in days. I didn't know if it was exhaustion or discouragement, but I no longer had the urge to rush.

We could have cruised Dorchester Avenue for another hour, but I knew we wouldn't find Carmody. His skills of deception and evasion were superb, something that, as a former soldier, I had to respect. Even if he was still in the city, we wouldn't get him by scouring every street and barroom.

"Need a lift home?"

Collins looked at me surprised.

"We're calling it a night?"

"Yeah."

"Then yes, if you don't mind."

"Of course, I mind," I said, getting in the car. "But how the hell else are you gonna get there?"

CHAPTER 36

On Monday morning, I got up before dawn. I had set the alarm, which wasn't necessary because I didn't sleep. I made some coffee and toast, then took a quick shower and got dressed.

When I kissed Ruth on the forehead, she stirred but didn't wake up. Knowing Nadia would be there in a couple of hours made it easier to leave her. More than ever she couldn't be alone. On my way out, I peeked into Nessie's room where I saw her nestled under the blanket. Then I grabbed my coat and flew out the door.

When I got to Charlestown, it was still dark. I worried I wouldn't be able to find Collin's apartment. Public housing projects were a confusing maze of identical streets and buildings. But when I pulled in, I saw a shadow under a stoop and knew it was him. I tapped the horn, and he ran over. He had on a long coat, his collar upturned, walking with that swagger all young cops had.

"Hey, Lieutenant," he said, getting in.

He smelled like cologne and cigarettes.

"You go to a strip club last night?"

He grinned.

"I stayed over at my girlfriend's."

"Yeah? How do her parents like that?"

He grinned but didn't answer. I knew it sounded old-fashioned, but I was more curious than appalled. I remembered those early years of dating when the biggest barrier to romance was finding a place to screw.

"Did you hear about the gun?" he asked.

"Gun? What gun?"

"A lady brought a Glock into C6 yesterday. She said she found it in some bushes. It was the same street we chased Carmody down."

"You think it was his?"

"Or someone else's."

When our eyes locked, I knew what he meant.

"Rowe? I frisked him."

Then I remembered that I hadn't patted the other guy down.

"It was pretty dark. They could've tossed it when you weren't looking," Collins said.

I gritted my teeth, shaking my head. Rage was no substitution for frustration, but it helped to relieve it.

"Let's go find out."

I pulled out and sped through the empty streets. We got on the expressway, and the traffic was so light we got to Howard Johnson's Motor Lodge in ten minutes. As we walked toward the entrance, we looked for the black Buick but didn't see it.

In the lobby, a cleaning crew was mopping the floor, a young man standing behind the counter in a navy suit and glasses. We continued down the hallway, and I knocked on Rowe's door. We waited a minute, and when no one answered, I tried again.

"Think they're gone?" Collins asked.

"I don't know."

We rushed back to the lobby. The attendant looked up with a smile, but I couldn't take any chances. When it came to getting someone to cooperate, attitude was everything. I whipped out my badge and held it out.

"We need to know if someone has checked out!"

He stepped back, appearing more stunned than intimidated.

"Um...which room, sir?" he asked.

I was so flustered that I had forgotten to check.

"102," Collins said.

I was relieved when the young man looked down and flipped through the ledger.

"It seems that," he said, his voice shaky. "Yes. They checked out last night."

"Son of a bitch!"

I stormed out the front doors, Collins running to catch up. He called out to me, but I didn't look back. When we got to the Valiant, I was so furious I was out of breath.

"Lieutenant?" he ventured.

Opening the door, I looked across the car roof.

"This ain't good."

......

FOR THE WHOLE ride to headquarters, Collins was quiet, which I saw as a sign of both respect and good judgment. Just like Harrigan, he knew when to talk and when to be silent.

Two State Police cruisers were already in the parking lot, which wasn't unusual. They had been there every day. We still didn't know if they had any leads on Carmody. So far, they had asked for a lot of information but hadn't given much back in return.

I should have known it wouldn't be a collaboration. The only person who had used that word was Egersheim, not the chief. Although ranks between agencies were different, I got the feeling that Egersheim thought Murgia was above him. As a result, he didn't challenge him on anything.

We burst into the office. The captain was so startled he stood up.

"Rowe and his men are gone!" I said.

"Gone?"

"Gone. We just went by the hotel. They checked out."

"Why'd you go by there?" he asked, and it was the wrong question.

I looked at Collins.

"A gun was found on the street we chased them down, Sir," he said.

The captain adjusted his glasses, his eyes twitching. We were all under stress, but he showed it the most.

"I didn't know that."

He sounded ashamed, but it wasn't his fault. Communication between precincts was a big problem in the department. Sometimes it took days for some fact or clue to make its way up to headquarters. Weapons were found every day around the city, lost in alleyways or ditched by the roadside, the remnants of feuds and crimes. Even if the murders were big news, it wasn't the only case.

Beyond that, all the victims had been killed with a knife. After Rowe revealed that he was a foreign intelligence officer, the captain had chosen not to report it. I didn't agree with him, worried there would be no record of the incident. No one could have expected some young patrolman from C6 to make a connection between a stray gun and an investigation.

"I'll put an APB out on the car," Egersheim said. "Get me the plates."

"We don't even know if they still have it," Collins said.

"Check and let me know."

The captain paused and then sat down. Clearing his throat, he looked up.

"Please, take a seat," he said, and we did. "There's other news. The RUC put me in touch with a man from the Anti-terrorism unit in Northern Ireland yesterday – MI5. I've been trying to find out more about this *Jill Slattery*. Was she working at the salon the day of the bombing? Did she refuse to testify? Could she be in the U.S.? When I told him we had run into three of his agents, he was immediately suspicious…"

As he spoke, his voice got lower, more regretful. He couldn't look us in the eye.

"He called me twenty minutes ago," he went on, and I remembered Ireland was five hours ahead. "He said there's no agent by the name of Rowe operating in Boston."

The room went quiet. We all sat stunned. It was the biggest twist in the case so far, and it wasn't in our favor. Not only were we tracking a killer, but now we had to figure out who we had been dealing with.

"Maybe Rowe is a pseudonym," Collins said, the wrong word but a good try.

"Maybe the guy is mistaken," I said. "I'm sure MI5 is huge. One department can't know everything the others are doing, especially in field ops."

Egersheim gave a tight smile as if he appreciated the support. But I knew nothing about the British intelligence services. I was only going on my experience working with agencies like the FBI and DEA, who were notoriously guarded with their information.

"I guess it's possible," the captain said, "but the man looked into it. That's why he just now got back to me. He said they'd never send agents here to track a criminal, even in a civilian capacity."

"Even a terrorist?" I asked.

Egersheim shook his head.

"Unlikely. If they did, the chief would know. Remember the Polish officers who came here to arrest that guy a couple of years ago?"

"He assassinated a politician," I said.

"It was on TV, in the newspapers. There was even a press conference about it."

"That was a different situation."

I had no reason to side with Rowe and his men. I'd never trusted them to begin with. But I couldn't gloat about it. Two weeks into the case, we had made very little progress. The State Police joining the investigation was a humiliation, so I understood why the captain had been tempted to accept Rowe's help.

Egersheim stared down, his crown shining. His head was too big for his body, but it was more obvious now.

"I should've told the colonel," he said.

The admission was admirable, but it was also too late.

"It doesn't matter. They're gone," I said.

"What if they got Carmody?"

"You mean, like, killed him?" Collins asked.

Egersheim and I looked over at the same time. Like a lot of young people, he tended to speak before he thought. While it was often useless, sometimes it revealed things that more mature minds overlooked.

"No, I meant—"

"It would make sense if that's their plan," I said, cutting the captain off. "If they only came here to confirm Carmody is in Boston, why would they be chasing him around?"

"It would explain the gun that was found," Collins said.

The brainstorming gave us all a little boost. Egersheim sat thinking with his fist under his chin. In his eyes, I saw a glimmer of confidence, which gave me some hope too.

"Whatever the case," he said, finally, "we're looking for four people now."

"Not if Rowe and his men are gone."

He looked up, and our eyes met.

"Then we need to find out for sure."

CHAPTER 37

We flew out of the tunnel into East Boston, swerving around cars and taxis. Each time someone got in my way, I hit the horn and went around them.

"You ever use those?" he asked, pointing at the switch for the sirens.

"When I need to," I said, but the real answer was *no*.

I had installed them when I first made detective. No one on the force used their own vehicle, so I didn't know where I got the idea. I had bought the Valiant on a cold November morning twelve years before, the same day JFK got elected, and it had been with me ever since.

We pulled into the rental car shop and stopped. Collins and I jumped out and ran inside. The same clerk was behind the desk helping a customer who had an accent I couldn't quite place. Not wanting to scare the man's wife and two kids, Collins and I waited until they were done.

As the family left, I smiled and got the door for them.

"Can I help you?" I heard.

The clerk looked up, squinted, and his expression changed.

"Officers," he said.

I went up to the counter and looked him straight in the eye. I didn't have time to argue, and I had no cash to bribe him again.

"I need to know if a car has been returned."

"Right, the Buick."

He opened the rental book and quickly looked through it.

"This can't be right," he said, flustered. "Hang on a minute."

He walked over to his desk, grabbed the phone, and dialed. I tried to listen, but the man just nodded and hung up.

"That car was found abandoned yesterday."

"Abandoned?"

"In Roxbury. Someone set it on fire. Our insurance company has already filed the—"

I smacked my hands on the counter and stormed out the door. As I walked back to the car, I heard Collins trailing behind me, but he didn't say anything.

I leaned against the door, fuming and out of breath. In the distance, a jet was taking off at Logan Airport, the roar sending a tremble through the ground. In some ways, I would have been relieved if Rowe and his men had disappeared. I wouldn't care if they went to Dublin, or Belfast, or England. Anywhere but here. If it hadn't been for the victims, I would have wished the same for Carmody.

"Lieutenant?"

I looked up, and Collins was holding out a cigarette.

"Thanks," I said, and he lit it.

"What now?"

"Well, no use for an APB."

"You think they skipped town?"

I blew out the smoke and shook my head.

"I don't know."

In the past, it would have been hard to admit. But I liked Collins, and I was too tired to lie or pretend.

"Let's go see the car?"

We got into the Valiant and pulled out, circling the airport road and going back through the tunnel into the city.

When we got to the South End, we drove down Albany Street and turned into the BPD tow yard, a large lot between City Hospital and the expressway. Surrounded by barbed wire, it had everything from abandoned cars to vehicles impounded for parking and other violations.

I stopped at the gate and tapped my horn. A middle-aged guy in a gray coverall walked over. Like most men who worked around automobiles, his face was streaked with grease, his chin scruffy.

"Afternoon."

"Afternoon," I said, taking out my badge.

"We close in fifteen minutes."

"We'll only be ten. We're looking for a black Buick Skylark."

"Criminal or civilian?"

"Not sure. It was found abandoned. Someone burned it."

The man nodded and pointed.

"Anything evidence-related would be at the back."

"Do you happen to have the report?" I asked, and when he squinted, I added, "We just found out it was here."

"I've got a copy. I'll meet you over there."

"Thanks."

He lifted the barrier, and we drove in. Crossing the lot, we passed dozens of rows of cars of all ages, models, and conditions. There were Ford Thunderbirds and Chrysler 300s, a Mustang convertible and a sparkling red GTO. I even saw a milk van up on cinder blocks with no wheels.

When we reached the back, I saw the Buick, sitting among a half dozen other burned-out vehicles. While some could have been arson or insurance fraud, stealing cars and lighting them on fire had always been a pastime for young punks.

We got out and walked over, the smell of the ash still strong. The windows were blown out, the tires melted, but it hadn't been completely incinerated. When I grabbed the handle, the door opened easily, telling me it had never gotten hot enough for the parts to fuse.

I leaned in, careful not to get my suit dirty. There was nothing on the seats and floors, so I punched the glove compartment. It fell open to reveal some charred paperwork, an ice scraper, a bottle of aspirin, and an 8-track of *Van Morrison*.

As I stepped out, I saw the man walking over.

"You can look," he said, giving me a folder, "but I can't let you have it."

I nodded and opened it, skimming through. It was a typical police report with the time, location, and description. I wasn't surprised the car had been found in Roxbury. As a slum, it seemed like a dumping ground for all the city's unwanted people and things.

"It says the windows might've been shot out," I said as Collins looked over my shoulder.

"How the hell would they know?"

"Not sure. Maybe someone heard gunshots?"

I turned over the document, hoping for more notes, but the back was blank. It was sad to think a torched car that might have been shot at didn't even make the news.

"Should we go see *Forensics*?" Collins asked.

As I handed back the report, my eyes caught City Hospital, its brick towers higher than anything around it.

"Naw, let's go see someone else."

......

WHEN WE WALKED into the room, the bed was empty. I gasped until Harrigan came out of the bathroom. My mind was in a fog, and I was losing track of days. For a second, I panicked that he had already gone home.

"You're timing is impeccable, Lieutenant," he said.

"Ain't it always?"

While he still wore a hospital gown, he looked as healthy as ever. He didn't have a blood pressure cuff on, and his arms were clear of IVs. He had even put on weight.

"Hello, Detective," he said to Collins.

"How're you feeling?"

"Ready to go home."

He sat back on the bed; the mattress was propped up so he could sit upright.

"Any news on things?" he asked.

"News? Like what?" I joked.

"Celtics are in the playoffs."

"I don't follow basketball."

I walked closer, speaking quietly.

"Rowe's car was found burned in Roxbury. The report says the windows might've been shot out."

In his expression, I saw some glint of humor, sarcasm, or whimsy. Considering how reserved he was, I assumed it was the pain medication.

"Well, it seems like things are unfolding—with or without us."

I laughed because it was true. Some crimes just resolved themselves, like when feuding gangs killed each other off. We didn't mind those cases; the elimination of everyone involved saved us the hassle of trials and testimonies. But this one had innocent victims.

"Have you located the lost witness?" Harrigan asked.

"We went by her last known address. The owner said she hasn't seen her in months."

Someone knocked, and Collins and I turned. Delilah walked in, a bouquet in one arm, her pocketbook dangling from the other.

"Is this a gentlemen's powwow?"

"Not anymore."

"Hello Juan," she said to Collins.

She always showed him special attention. I assumed it was because he was young, but it could have been that they were both minorities.

"How's Cecily?" I asked.

Delilah put the flowers on the table beside an already crowded display, gifts from friends and colleagues.

"I took her into the daycare. We needed the help, and she needed to get out. My apartment is so damn cramped."

Apartment was a stretch for her tiny dorm.

"If you don't mind," I said, hesitantly, "just make sure she stays off the streets."

She glanced back, her smile friendly but pointed. It was only a reminder. I knew she understood the dangers.

"We're gonna take a taxi back."

"Good. I think that would be best."

CHAPTER 38

"We interviewed a woman on W 6th Street in South Boston."

"Charlotte," I said.

I sat in Egersheim's office with Colonel Murgia and Captain Flaherty. For the past hour, we had gone through every detail of the case. But it was hardly a group effort because Flaherty had done most of the talking, sometimes asking the same question twice. With his stylish glasses, he looked sophisticated for an officer and might have even had a college degree. The State Police always seemed to be from better backgrounds than city cops. Unlike Murgia, who was professional but friendly, Flaherty was arrogant. At times, he talked to us like subordinates, which bothered me more because he was younger than me.

"The woman told us *Victim A* had been living there," he said.

Victim A, *Jane Doe I*. All the technical jargon was starting to sound ridiculous, especially when we knew the victim's name.

"She was staying there," I said. "The lady takes tenants."

"Is she licensed?"

"It's a flophouse. What do you think?"

Flaherty looked up.

"I don't know, Lieutenant. That's why I'm asking you."

I knew the meeting would be tense, which was why I had told Collins to wait in my office. Our association with Rowe and his men put us all in jeopardy. Because we left them out of the report, we couldn't afford a single slipup. I omitted the Buick too, knowing they wouldn't make the connection.

The lies were starting to pile up. For the first time in my career, I felt corrupt, and I blamed Egersheim. If we got caught withholding information, I was sure we'd be reprimanded, possibly fired. I could handle the shame, but I didn't want Collins to go through it. The only thing that could save us now was finding Carmody.

"Can you read this?" Flaherty asked.

Squinting, I looked over to see a page of scribble and notes.

"Perfectly."

He frowned and flipped to the next page.

"And we've confirmed that these women were all witnesses at Derek Carmody's trial?"

"Three of them," Egersheim said. "We're still waiting on Eleanor Reese."

Flaherty looked at the colonel.

"I'll get this expedited," he said.

Murgia just nodded. So far, he had stayed neutral, at times sounding indifferent. I wanted to think it was out of sympathy, but it was probably because he was retiring in a few weeks.

"And who's Cecily Madden? What's her connection?"

"She worked at my daughter's daycare. She knew Derek Carmody."

"Is she credible?"

"I'd say so."

"And where is she?"

"Somewhere safe," I said.

If he asked where, I wasn't going to tell him. I was tired of feeling like we were under interrogation. They were assisting in the investigation, not running it.

"Is this the man you saw at the St. Patrick's Day parade?"

Flaherty held up a large photo of Carmody. It had arrived the day before, sent by the RUC along with a report. His arrest history and previous addresses weren't important. But it was good to finally get a clear look at him. In the picture, his hair was a little shorter, and he looked like he had a black eye. He stared at the camera with a scowl, his lips tightly pressed together. I wouldn't have guessed he was a killer, but I was sure he was a thug.

"That's him."

"Look the same?" Murgia asked.

"Probably a few pounds lighter now."

"We've put together a task force," Flaherty said. "Twelve undercover troopers. Dorchester and South Boston appear to be Carmody's hunting grounds. So we're gonna post them to all the barrooms."

"You'll need more than twelve," I joked.

Everyone chuckled except Flaherty.

"Is there anything else we should know?"

I glanced at Egersheim. His expression was blank, but I could tell he was nervous. Even if the meeting wasn't being recorded, I had to be careful. I couldn't say anything that could later prove we had lied or been misleading about the facts.

"Sounds like enough for now," I said.

I knew it was evasive, even flippant. As I waited for his response, my heart pounded.

"Good," Flaherty said, closing the folder and looking at Egersheim. "We'll keep you updated. I expect your department will do the same."

"Of course."

We all got up and shook hands. I worried my sweaty palms would be revealing, but I was able to avoid Captain Flaherty.

......

I LEFT the meeting with a feeling of temporary relief. I walked down the hallway and turned into the lavatory. Standing over the metal sink, I stared into the mirror. I looked so bad even I could see it.

I splashed some water on my face and adjusted my tie, noting that my collar was stained. With Ruth on bed rest, I hadn't asked her to wash my shirts, and I didn't have time to do it myself. I could have asked Nadia, but the last time she did our laundry, she used an old Polish technique that left everything smelling like lemon.

Walking out, I went straight to my office, not wanting to see anyone. The whole force knew the State Police were involved and that Carmody was still at large. Had it been a game, the score would have been nothing to nothing, which was some solace for all our aggravation.

The name of the killer was finally made public. That morning, the news had shown his face for the first time. The photo was different from the one Flaherty had. In it, Carmody looked more put together: his hair shorter, his cheekbones higher.

I didn't have a clear image of what he looked like anyway. Of the two times I'd seen him, once was at night and the other was through a crowd at the parade. He was good at hiding out in the open. I only hoped that I would recognize him again.

As I approached the door, I reached for my keys until I remembered Collins was inside. I opened it and stopped.

"Hey, Lieutenant."

When Collins stood up, I realized he was in my chair. But that wasn't why I was so stunned. Sitting beside the desk was a young woman with blonde hair. She still had her coat on, so I knew they couldn't have been there long. My office was always stifling.

"What's this about?"

Getting up, she walked over and held out her hand.

"Jill Sansone."

Her Irish accent didn't match her name.

"Sansone?"

"It was Slattery. Sansone is my married name."

"I was gonna bring her to the captain's office," Collins said, "but I knew you were in a meeting."

I gave him a look that implied *I'm glad you didn't*. After the debacle with Rowe, I didn't want to say anything more that could have been seen as deceitful or dishonest.

"Are you the Jill Slattery who worked at the Trinity Salon in Belfast?" I asked.

She nodded.

"Northern Ireland," she added.

With fourteen *Belfast's* in America, I understood why she was specific.

I walked over to my desk, motioning for her to sit. With her lean figure and sharp features, she was prettier than the other girls, although it was awful to compare someone to the dead.

"Did you know we were looking for you?"

The answer was obvious, but I had to ask.

"That's why I came. Mrs. Farrington called me yesterday."

"Mrs. Farrington?"

"The lady with all the junk on her porch," Collins said.

"I lived with her when I first came to this country," Sansone said. "She was good to me. We became friends of sorts…"

Thinking back to the rude encounter, I wasn't sure it was the same person.

"An older woman? Thin, white hair, spots?"

Sansone grinned.

"She can come off as a bit of a curmudgeon. But she's really lovely."

"I'll take your word for it," I said. "You said you knew we were looking for you. Any idea why?"

She sighed, clutching her pocketbook. But she looked more anxious than afraid.

"It's about Derek Carmody, I suppose."

"Who else saw you come in?"

"The front desk called," Collins said. "I answered it. I went out and got her."

"We believe Derek Carmody is responsible for the murders of four women between March 7th and March 18th."

I spoke slowly, pronouncing each word like a courtroom testimony. Everything I said now had to be careful and precise.

"I saw it on the news."

"Did you know they were all girls you had worked with?"

"Not at first. Not until I heard the name Janice O'Brien. Then Doris Hearn."

"When was the last time you saw Derek Carmody?"

"Saw him? I never met him. Or if I did, I don't remember. The salon was a busy place, people always coming and going."

"Is that why you didn't testify against him?"

"Testify? How could I?"

"You didn't see someone come in dressed as a plumber?"

Our eyes locked.

"Mr. Brae, I wasn't working the day of the bombing."

The room went silent. When I looked at Collins, it was hard to tell if he already knew.

Suddenly, the phone rang. Calls always came in at the worst possible times. Holding up my finger, I grabbed the receiver.

"Lieutenant Brae!" I barked.

"Jody?"

My heart sank when I heard Ruth's voice. The shift from work to family was always jarring, two worlds I still couldn't seem to reconcile.

"I think the baby's coming."

I stood up.

"Now?" I asked, more out of shock.

"Come get me…"

Her voice was shaky, breathless.

"Where's Nadia?"

"Here…ugh," she moaned. "Hurry…please!"

I stood paralyzed by panic. In those few seconds, I had to make a choice. I could have called an ambulance, but Nadia had to stay at home with Nessie. I wouldn't let Ruth go to the hospital alone.

The investigation wasn't over, but it was stable. There hadn't been a murder in almost two weeks, and the whole city knew who the suspect was. If anyone was still in danger, I would have sacrificed duty to my family for the safety of the public. The victims were worth it, but Carmody was not. We would get him one way or another.

"Give me fifteen minutes," I said.

"Okay."

"Tell Nadia to help you get your things together."

"Okay. Jody?"

"Yeah?"

"I love you."

With Collins and Jill watching, I just smiled. I didn't have the courage to say it back. After all I had been through, from combat to crime fighting, sentiment still seemed the hardest battle.

"See you soon," I said.

I hung up and looked at Collins.

"I gotta go."

His mouth dropped open, but he didn't argue or ask why. Jill sat with a hesitant smile. Even if she hadn't overheard, I was sure that, as a woman, she sensed what the call was about.

"Take over for now," I said.

Collins stiffened up like a soldier called to attention.

"Yes, Lieutenant."

CHAPTER 39

I raced home with the sirens on, the first time I had used them in years. Although the Valiant looked nothing like a cruiser, people turned their heads and drivers pulled over. I never gloated over the power of being a cop, but it felt good to have it when I needed it.

When I got to the house, I was so frantic I parked at the curb, not the driveway. The moment I stopped, the front door swung open. Ruth hobbled out, helped by Esther and another neighbor I didn't know.

I jumped out and ran over.

"She's ready," Esther said.

"Ugh," Ruth said, holding her stomach.

"Do you need anything?"

"Yeah, a long nap and a bath."

I smiled nervously, not sure what to do.

"Go, go," she said, struggling to speak, "Go say goodbye to Nessie. Tell her you'll be home in a little while."

I hurried up the walkway, and Nadia and Nessie met me at the door.

"My sister coming?" Nessie asked, wiping one of her eyes.

I picked her up and kissed her on the cheek, running my hand through her hair.

"We don't know that yet, love. It could be a brother."

Nadia stood holding the door open, a wide smile on her face.

"Jody! C'mon!"

I kissed Nessie again and put her down. When I got back to the Valiant, they had put Ruth in the backseat, probably so she could lie down if she had to.

"I'll come by the hospital later after Jim gets home," Esther promised, gently closing the door.

"Thank you," I said.

The women both waved. They were strangely calm for such an urgent situation, which I attributed to them being mothers. Going through something always made it less frightening.

I got into the car and turned around. As we pulled out onto the main road, I punched the gas until Ruth exclaimed, "Not so fast!"

"Sorry."

I slowed down but still went around other cars. I would have used the sirens too except I didn't want to make her uneasy. Watching her in the rearview mirror, she seemed more relaxed than she'd been at home. Maybe it was the motion. I didn't know much about birth, but it had some similarities to war: months of boredom followed by sudden chaos.

When we got to the hospital, I drove right to the front. I got out and called to the first orderly I saw, a woman in scrubs pushing an empty wheelchair.

"Jesus, Jody," Ruth said, getting out. "Don't make a scene."

I took her hand, and we walked toward the entrance. Two nurses rushed out, and, ironically, waved to the same woman with the wheelchair. Ruth got in it, and we all went inside.

As usual, the lobby was hectic. The noise of people mixed with calls over the intercom. At the front desk, a row of attendants sat answering the endless incoming calls. But when we reached the maternity ward, the mood was completely different. The lights were softer, the walls painted soothing colors. No one was rushing around. I even heard the faint sound of classical music.

Another nurse led us to a room, and Ruth got into a hospital gown. The woman helped her onto the bed and then put a blood pressure cuff around her arm.

As I waited, I glanced out the window. In the distance, I could see all of South Boston and Dorchester: the narrow streets, flat-roofed houses, and church spires. I didn't know where Carmody was, but I knew he was out there.

Even with Ruth finally settling in, I still couldn't relax. My heart raced, and I was sweating all over. I wanted a cigarette, but smoking wasn't allowed on the floor. All my life, I got ramped up in an instant, and it took me hours to wind down.

A few minutes later, a doctor walked in and closed the door. He wore a white smock over a gray suit, his silk tie held down with a gold clip. As distinguished as he looked, he was probably only in his late thirties. At first, I was intimidated until I realized most people were younger than me now.

"Good evening," he said, smiling at me and then looking at Ruth. "How're you feeling?"

"Tired."

"As you should be. Nine months is a long time. How're the headaches?"

"Awful."

He chuckled and wrote something on his clipboard.

"Let's have a look," he said.

I didn't know what he meant, but Ruth did. Leaning back, she opened her legs, a position that had always been erotic yet now seemed clinical. When the doctor crouched down, I turned away.

"Good," he said, and I knew it was over. "Almost five centimeters."

"That's close."

"Getting there. Any contractions?"

Ruth nodded.

"They come and go."

"Good. You just try to relax. I'll check on you in a little while.

As he went to leave, I said, "What do we do now?"

"What do we do now? We wait."

......

I HAD BEEN SITTING on the chair for four hours while Ruth read magazines. I hadn't eaten since breakfast, and I was craving a cigarette. I would have been satisfied by either, but I preferred to smoke.

When a nurse came in to check Ruth's vitals, I slipped out. I took the elevator down, crossed the lobby, and walked outside. Standing under the portico, I was about to light a cigarette when I saw Delilah and Harrigan's mother coming up the sidewalk.

"Jody!"

I hugged Mrs. Harrigan first because, while I loved them both the same, I had known her longer. They were dressed up, Delilah in red pants and a silk blouse, Mrs. Harrigan wearing a long dress and a church hat with a bow. If I hadn't seen them, I would have forgotten Harrigan was getting out.

"Ruth's in labor," I said before they could ask.

Their faces beamed.

"Congratulations, dear," Mrs. Harrigan said in her soft Caribbean accent.

"And why aren't you in there with her?"

"Actually, she's not in labor. Her water broke. She's close, I think."

"Spoken like a man," Delilah said, swatting me playfully.

"You here to pick him up?"

"Didn't they just fix my boy up fine," Mrs. Harrigan said with a proud and grateful smile.

"I'll come up to see him. I've got time."

I extended my arm, and they led the way. We used a different elevator bank than the one I had come down on. I had been going to the hospital all my life, and the layout was still confusing.

As we walked down the hallway, I got a nervous excitement. I didn't know if Harrigan's release was a happy ending or a new beginning. And I still wasn't sure what it meant for Collins. If the chief found out about Rowe, Harrigan might be the only one left employed.

When I turned into the room, he was sitting on the chair next to the bed, a newspaper open on his lap. He was freshly shaven and had on a clean suit. It looked like his shoes had been shined.

The moment he saw us, he got up and walked over. He hugged his mother and kissed his wife, a reunion so emotional even I got choked up.

"Ruth's in labor," Delilah said.

Harrigan looked at me.

"Now?"

It was the same reaction I'd had when Ruth called me at headquarters.

"She's had some contractions," I said.

"Then go back to her this instant!"

"Hey, I still give the orders."

Standing in a circle, our laughter was followed by a poignant silence. When Harrigan's condition was at its worst, I had never thought about the outcome. Sometimes the only way to cope with uncertainty was to ignore it. But seeing him healthy and alert, I considered his death for the first time, and it made me shudder.

"Shall we be off?" he asked.

"What about all the flowers—"

"Pardon me!?"

We all turned, and a young nurse burst into the room. Her eyes were wide, and she was out of breath.

"Are you a police officer?" she asked, looking at Harrigan.

"We both are," I said. "Why?"

"Could I speak with you?"

Harrigan told Delilah and his mother to wait, and we followed the woman out to the hallway.

"A man was admitted an hour ago," she said, her voice hushed but panicked. "He had a gunshot wound. Now he's gone!"

"Gone? Can you show me?" I asked.

She nodded, and I turned to Harrigan.

"How well are you?"

He smiled.

"Well enough, Lieutenant."

I waited with the nurse while he went back into the room. I didn't know what he said to his mother and Delilah, but seconds later, he came back out and said, "Let's go!"

We ran down the hallway and got on the elevator.

"Where was he hit?" I asked.

"In the thigh and calf, I believe."

"Can you describe him?"

"I didn't see him. One of the nurses called. She knew there was a detective on my floor. They said he was Irish, that's all I know."

Harrigan and I turned to each other.

We got off at the first floor and went down the corridor, quickening our pace. At the end, three nurses and a security officer were standing outside a room.

"Boston Police," I said.

"He skipped out," one of the women said. "He's still hemorrhaging badly."

When she pointed at the floor, I could see tiny drops of blood. Although scattered, they were clear enough to form a trail.

"Did you call BPD?" I asked, and everyone nodded.

"It just happened, not even ten minutes ago," the guard said.

Harrigan and I followed the blood to a stairwell and went down the bottom. Pushing on a utility door, we found ourselves outside of the building. In the shadowy evening light, the droplets were hard to see. I couldn't help but think how ironic it would be if they led to the mortuary, just a few yards away.

Instead, they went left, through the parking lot, and down to the road. Each time I lost them, Harrigan found more. I didn't know if they were from Carmody, but I was sure we would find a body at some point.

Soon we reached the intersection at Mass Ave. With the streetlamps now on, there was just enough snow that I could see the trail. I got a chill when I realized they went up the sidewalk toward the daycare.

"Do you have your gun?"

When I looked back, Harrigan was frowning.

"Are you serious?"

I grabbed my keys and tossed them to him.

"Then go get the car. It's parked at the front entrance. My Beretta is in the glove compartment."

"Where should I meet you?"

"*Sunnyside Nursery.*"

I could tell he was shocked, but he didn't ask any questions. With a quick nod, he turned around and went back to the hospital.

I shoved my hands in my pockets and continued walking. I kept one eye on the blood drops, which were getting smaller and more spread out. If I didn't know they were there, I wouldn't have noticed them.

Mass Ave was busy, car horns honking and buses roaring by. I passed an old black woman pushing a shopping cart and a group of homeless men outside a liquor store. When I was younger, I hated the filth and poverty of the city. After a few years of living in a tidy middle-class neighborhood, I realized that grit was part of me. I didn't know if I missed it, but it certainly felt familiar.

I approached the daycare, and the lights were off, which wasn't unusual because it was late. After weeks of confusion and dead ends, I finally had a theory about the murders. I didn't have the whole story, but I had enough chapters to understand it. The next few minutes would determine whether I was wrong or right.

I walked up the steps of the building, squinting to see a few last drops of blood. When I got to the top, I took out my gun and undid the safety. I turned the knob, opened the door, and went in.

The reception room was quiet and empty. On the wall, the St. Patrick's Day decorations had been replaced with cutouts of dolphins, whales, and other fish.

I walked over to the door that led to the classrooms. Looking through the glass, I saw only the dark corridor. But I heard something too, movement or even voices. My heart pounded, and my ears buzzed. In the intensity of the moment, it was hard to tell which sounds were real and which were imagined.

Finally, I opened the door. Stepping in, I cringed when the floor creaked. In the distance, I saw a faint glow. But I didn't have time to go any further because I heard a click and stopped.

"Evenin', Mr. Brae."

CHAPTER 40

I CONTINUED DOWN THE HALLWAY, MY HANDS UP AND A GUN AGAINST my back. It was too dark to tell which one of Rowe's men was behind me, but I could feel his breath on my neck.

When we turned the corner, I realized where the light had been coming from. It was Nessie's classroom.

"Go in Detective!"

"It's Lieutenant," I said, and he pressed the barrel into me a little harder.

I pushed the door open and froze.

"Lieutenant?!"

Seeing Rowe again was bittersweet, but at least he got my title right. Cecily sat cross-legged on the floor, streaks of black mascara on her cheeks. Her hands were tied behind her back, and there was something around her mouth.

In the corner, a man was lying on his side in a long leather jacket. I didn't have to see his face to know it was Carmody. I thought he was dead until I heard a groan. Rowe's other associate was leaning against the teacher's desk smoking. It looked like a torture scene.

"Let her go!" I said.

"We don't let murderers go!" Rowe barked. "Nor their accomplices!"

I winced in confusion.

"Accomplice?"

"Bloody right, she is. Who do you think helped him find all those girls?"

With her mouth bound, Cecily tried to speak, shaking her head wildly. It was beyond unbelievable, but at this point, nothing surprised me.

"Who the hell are you?" I asked.

Rowe laughed and stormed over, looking me in the eye.

"Us? We're your worst feckin' nightmare, especially if you're the Brits."

The relief I felt in finally realizing the truth was tempered by the regret of not having figured it out earlier. But even the most puzzling things were obvious looking back. The only comfort I got was in knowing that I had never trusted them all along.

"IRA," I said.

Rowe smiled, wagging his finger.

"I always figured you for a smart fella. Now, I've got a deal for you," he said, looking over at Carmody. "This bastard's got about five minutes left in him. Five minutes too long. I'd be just as happy to tie you up and then knock them both off..."

I gave him a cold stare. I never liked being threatened.

"But there's already been enough killing," he went on, "and I know you've got a baby on the way."

"You seem to know a lot."

"We rely on information. Otherwise, we'd be no match against our enemies."

"Then you know the penalty for espionage?"

He gave me a sharp look.

"Now don't test my kindness, mate. You're not exactly in the arrest-making position."

"The police are on the way."

"And we plan to be long gone."

"You won't get far on foot."

"Foot? Ah, right. The Buick. Lovely little racer. Blame that eejit for it. He figured out where we were staying and burned it. A case of the mouse chasing the cat, eh? But we know the cat always gets the mouse. We almost had him today in Dorchester. Actually, we did get him, there was just a delay. Sort of like the delay he put on them explosives in Belfast!"

Gritting his teeth, he kicked Carmody, but the man's body was limp. He was dead.

"Now, you just let us get on our way, and no one has to find out about our little rendezvous. I'm sure your chief wouldn't be happy to know you and your captain were conferring with the likes of us!"

"What do I tell them?"

I couldn't believe I was asking him for advice.

"Whatever you please. Carmody came here to get his last victim. You got to him first."

"We've got a thing called ballistics."

"Fair enough. I'll make it easy for you."

He nodded, and the man who caught me at the door tossed him my gun. With no hesitation, Rowe fired two rounds into Carmody's corpse, the noise echoing through the room. Then he opened the magazine, removed the last slugs, and gave me back the pistol.

"Now how's that for an airtight case," he said, and the other men laughed. "You say nothing, we say nothing. A gentlemen's agreement between soldiers, eh?"

When he held out his hand, I stared at it. It was the biggest ethical dilemma of my career. But I didn't have time to think, argue, or deliberate because I heard sirens in the distance. So I reached out, and we shook.

Waving to his associates, Rowe gave me a quick salute, and they left. Seconds later, I felt a cold breeze and knew they had gone out the back door.

I walked over to Cecily and took off her mouth bind, leaving her hands tied.

"Ah," she cried, gasping for air.

I knelt in front of her.

"You helped Carmody?"

"No—!"

"Don't fucking lie to me!" I shouted.

"No, I swear," she said, crying. "Derek did call me. We went out. I hadn't seen him in two years. He said he wanted to apologize to the girls at the salon for what he did. I knew where some of them lived. I had no idea what he was doing until I heard about Doris Hearn on the news."

It sounded more like a defense than a confession.

"So, you didn't have any contact with any of the victims?"

"No—"

"Why was Gertrude Haslett using your name?"

She stopped, her face trembling but her eyes steady.

"Okay, I called her for Derek. She agreed to meet with him, but she needed a favor. She wanted to use my name for a job."

"Why were you running down Dorchester Ave. in the rain? You said he was trying to kill you."

"We were at a bar together…"

Already, I knew she was lying. She told us she had bumped into him, not met him intentionally.

"I confronted him about the deaths," she went on. "He said if I said anything, I'd be next."

"Why didn't you tell us when you knew?"

All at once her expression changed. Her eyes got fierce, her mouth tense. It was like watching someone turn into a different person.

"Because I am not a snitch!"

I stood up, shaking my head in disgust. I had never hit a woman, but I got the urge to smack her. She was spared my outburst when I heard the front door open, the sounds of quick footsteps. Then Harrigan burst into the room with four patrolmen.

"Lieutenant!?" he yelled.

One of the cops went over to Carmody, crouching to feel his neck.

"He's dead, Sir," he said.

"What happened?" Harrigan asked.

When he looked down, I realized I was still holding my gun.

"That's Derek Carmody. He's responsible for the murder of four young women," I said, and then I looked at Cecily. "Almost five."

Two officers helped her up and untied her hands.

"Thank you, Mr. Brae," she said.

She stared with a sinister smile. I didn't know if she was traumatized, brainwashed, or just scared. In Northern Ireland, the scars of that ancient feud ran deep. Loyalties were fierce, and alliances were uncompromising. Even if I didn't understand it, I knew about war. Hatred did strange things to people.

Harrigan touched my shoulder, and I flinched.

"Lieutenant," he said.

When I turned, Egersheim and Collins were in the doorway. I had never been so glad to see them.

The captain walked in and looked around. On the walls were pictures of rainbows, soap bubbles, and stars. The chalkboard had a Mother Goose rhyme written in pink. When he raised his eyes, I knew what he was thinking. The innocence of childhood seemed shattered in a room with a dead body and the smell of gun smoke.

"Brae, your work here is done," he said. "Go get back to your wife."

CHAPTER 41

I SAT IN THE WAITING ROOM WITH COLLINS. ON THE EMPTY CHAIR beside him was a box of *Garcia y Vega's*, a gift from him and the captain. It was strange that, for someone who smoked, I detested cigars. But they wouldn't go to waste. In the last hour, Collins had already smoked one down to the bottom, creating such a cloud that a nurse asked him to go outside. He put it out until the air cleared and then lit it up again.

The maternity ward was quiet for Thursday night. Of the dozen people there when we had arrived, mostly men but relatives too, only two were left. Lots of fathers went into the delivery room now for the birth, but Ruth was too old-fashioned for that.

"Mr. Brae?"

I stood up, my heart pounding. A nurse came over smiling and took my hand. As we walked away, I looked back at Collins.

"I'll wait, Lieutenant."

We went through a set of double doors and down a long hallway, the neon making me squint. It was an area of the hospital I had never been to, and it looked newer, more modern. The ceilings had recessed lights and intercoms; staff pushed around portable diagnostics stations that looked like they were from Buck Rogers.

As we approached the room, I tensed up. The nurse must have noticed because she gave me a warm look. She held open the door, the only time I would let a woman do it, and I walked inside.

Laying in the bed, Ruth looked up smiling, as spry and alert as a weekday morning. In her arms was a heap of blankets. I didn't see the child's face until I got closer.

"It's a girl," she said, her eyes glassy.

I nodded as if I knew, but the truth was that all babies looked the same, especially after birth. Either way, Ruth had been right. I would never again doubt that women *had a sense about these things.*

A doctor walked into the room.

"You must be the happy father," he said, and we shook hands.

"Good guess," I said, and Ruth smirked.

"She did fabulously. Both of them did. Have you given any thoughts to a name?"

"A name?"

We were both stumped. It was something we had talked about but never decided on.

"How about Teresa," Ruth said.

"Teresa?"

"Like my grandmother."

For two people without much family, legacy wasn't important. I never knew my parents, and we hardly saw hers. Both our childhoods had been hard, although in different ways, and neither of us looked back. But you couldn't move into the future without acknowledging the past. I had never met her grandmother, who died of the Spanish Flu when Ruth's mother was nine. I was sure she would have been honored.

"Teresa," I said.

"Agreed?"

The doctor looked at Ruth, and she nodded.

"Then Teresa it is."

"Nessie and Tessie," I said.

Ruth laughed, and the man smiled.

"I'll have the birth certificate finalized in the morning," he said.

He congratulated us again and left the room. We sat together in silence, staring at our daughter, taking in her angelic face and pink lips. Watching her sent me into a quiet trance, more from exhaustion than bliss. I would have fallen asleep standing up if Ruth hadn't tapped my arm.

"You have to get home to Nessie," she said.

"Home?"

"Nadia is watching her. Esther is gonna drive her home."

"Okay," I said, still in a daze.

"See you in the morning."

A nurse walked in to take Ruth's vitals. It was the interruption I needed because I didn't want to go. I kissed Ruth on the forehead, took one last look at Tessie, and left.

......

As we pulled out of the parking lot, I leaned back in the car seat, my head throbbing. I'd drunk from the lobby water bubbler for five minutes straight and I was still thirsty.

"You alright Lieutenant?"

I looked over at Collins.

"Just keep your eyes on the road."

I only let him drive because I was tired and he needed the practice.

"It's been a long day."

I wanted to say more but waited until we were away from the hospital. It could have been superstition or paranoia, but I always felt safer talking in the anonymity of the streets.

"Cecily," I said, rubbing my temples. "Where is she?"

"Probably still at headquarters. She could be home by now."

"She doesn't have a home."

"I thought she was staying in Dorchester."

"Maybe. I don't trust anything that girl says."

"You ain't the only one."

"What does that mean?"

We stopped at a light, and he turned to me.

"After you left, I talked some more with Jill Slattery—"

"Sansone," I corrected.

"Right. Anyway, she said Cecily kept asking her to come down to Boston. She got a weird feeling about it."

"They were friends. What's so weird about it?"

"They weren't really. Jill hadn't seen her in years. She thought it might've had something to do with the bombing trial, so she was worried."

"Why would she worry? She wasn't working that day."

"That's the thing. She wasn't, but Cecily was."

It was news that even a week before would have left me speechless. But I was tired of being stunned, shocked, or dismayed.

"Is that what Jill said?" I asked calmly.

"Yeah. Why?"

I'd wanted to believe in Cecily's innocence; it was my greatest error. I always gave more credit to women. With one or two exceptions, all the criminals and killers I had ever known were men. When I was younger, I dated a few crazy girls, but Ruth was my model for what a female was.

"I'm gonna tell you something. You gotta keep it quiet," I said, and it was an order, not a question.

"I will—"

"No! I mean…quiet. Not a fuckin' word. Never. It could mean all our jobs."

His face dropped, but he kept his hands tight to the wheel.

"Of course, Lieutenant."

The fact that he said *Lieutenant* told me he understood.

"Cecily helped Carmody commit the murders. She called the girls, lured them out to bars. I don't think she stabbed anybody, but she made it happen."

"Sick bitch!"

As tense as the conversation was, I had to laugh.

"Then we gotta get her," he said.

"We can't. If we arrest her, she'll spill the beans about Rowe. Once that gets out, we're all screwed."

"Couldn't we say we thought they were a lead?"

"Not a chance. Foreign agents? Egersheim was a fool for believing it in the first place."

"I did," Collins said humbly.

Hearing his honesty made me ashamed of my own mistakes. I never trusted Rowe and his men, but I hadn't done anything to stop them.

"Withholding information like that is a crime. If it got out, we might not just get fired. We could get jail time."

His face went white. It was strange seeing such a tough city kid look so spooked.

I stared at him until he looked over.

"Not a word," I said.

"Never."

He made the sign of the cross, ironic for a pact that was anything but holy. But I was relieved the talk was over.

It was almost eleven when we pulled into the driveway, and the lights in the house were on. In all the turmoil, I hadn't even considered how Collins would get home, so I invited him in.

"Come meet the family," I joked.

We got out and walked up to the door. When I turned the knob, it was unlocked for the first time in weeks. With Carmody dead, I was sure housewives across the city would sleep a little easier.

We went inside, and Nadia and Esther rushed out of the kitchen.

"Nadia?!" Collins said.

"You two know each other?" I asked.

"Yeah, her nephew's girlfriend is my uncle's sister-in-law's kid."

I grinned, acknowledging the connection but not trying to understand it. In Boston's complex web friendships and intermarriages, everyone was related at some level.

We all hugged, and I looked at Nadia.

"Where's Nessie?"

She put her hands together, tilted her head, the universal sign of sleep.

"Oh," Esther said, "Captain Egersheim called twice. He said to call him the minute you got in."

I went into the kitchen where the counters were covered with trays of food, gifts from friends and neighbors. I reached for the phone and dialed. While I had hoped he'd called to congratulate me, I knew it was something else. He wasn't that considerate.

"Capt.," I said when he answered.

As he spoke, I felt the blood leave my face. Over in the doorway, Collins stood watching me. He must have read my expression because he looked worried. I nodded a few times, hung up, and looked over.

"It's Cecily," I said. "She's dead."

CHAPTER 42

WE GOT TO CITY HOSPITAL EARLY THE NEXT MORNING. COLLINS HAD stayed on my couch the night before, and it showed. His shirt was wrinkled, and his hair was sticking up in the front. Esther had driven Nadia back the night before, getting home after midnight. Now she was watching Nessie.

When we first moved in, I didn't talk to anyone. My entire adulthood, I lived in triple-deckers and apartment buildings, places where people didn't interact. Ruth was the first one to meet the neighbors, and I was glad she did. We wouldn't have been able to manage without them.

I parked in the back, and we got out. The sun was out, the temperature warm enough that I didn't need a coat. It was the last day of March, the harshest month. I always loved winter, but I was relieved every time it ended. It felt like I had survived, not just endured.

We walked into the rear entrance and went down the basement corridor. When we reached the end, I knocked once, and the door swung open.

"Brae!"

"Mornin', Doc," I said.

"Congratulations on your baby girl," Ansell said, waving us in. "Now let's go see the body. I gotta be somewhere in a half hour."

I chuckled. Only in our line of work did the subjects of birth and death mix so easily.

He opened the door to the morgue, and I felt a cold draft. We followed him inside where he unlocked one of the compartments and rolled out the tray. He looked at me first, and this time I didn't cringe, freeze, or brace myself. Somehow, I had gotten my mettle back. To be a detective, callousness was necessary, but it was never something I was proud of.

He pulled back the sheet and, lying on the bed, head turned and eyes closed, was Cecily. I didn't see any injuries other than small abrasions on her cheeks. They could have been from the bind Rowe had on her.

"Suicide?" I asked.

"She kissed the front of a truck. What do you think?"

I gazed at her, remembering the first day we talked at the daycare. If I hadn't known what she'd done, I would have felt pity.

"Maybe it was an accident," I said.

"Check the witness accounts. What I heard is she ran deliberately out into the street. But I'll let you decide."

With that, he slid the body back inside. The door closed with a loud clank, bringing some finality to the entire horrific episode.

I thanked the doctor, even shaking his hand. As grumpy as he was, I enjoyed his company, and I appreciated his help. With spring coming, I knew we'd be seeing each other again soon.

Collins and I left the building and got back into the car. As we drove past the main entrance, I was tempted to go inside. It was hard to leave knowing my wife and child were in there. But I was sure Ruth was resting, and I would be back in a few hours. The case was nearing the end, but it wasn't over. We still had work to do.

When we got to the front gate, I stopped to light a cigarette.

"Does this put us in the clear?" Collins asked, his first words since leaving the morgue.

"Yeah. I think so," I said, relieved but not proud.

"I'm glad that's over."

I looked over, and our eyes met.

"Now you ready for round two?"

......

WE SAT at a long table in the conference room at headquarters. It was strange that Harrigan, who had been hospitalized for most of the investigation, was there, and Collins was not. Egersheim said he needed someone to mind the phone, but I knew he was worried Collins would slip up.

Across from us sat Chief McNamara, Captain Flaherty, and an older female stenographer named O'Driscoll. Considering the suspect and victims had all been Irish, the lineup couldn't have been more fitting.

Murgia was absent, which was unfortunate because I had grown to like him. As someone with only weeks until retirement, he was probably done with murders and their consequences.

Egersheim sitting with us almost seemed like a snub. As a captain, he should have been on the other side with the chief. But the arrangement wasn't intentional and had nothing to do with rank. We all chose our seats.

"How'd you know Derek Carmody was at the hospital?" Flaherty asked.

"I told you. My wife was in labor. A nurse ran in and said a patient had fled."

Like the first time we met, I had to repeat everything. I couldn't tell if he was trying to be clever or thorough, but he sounded stupid.

"And you knew he'd been shot?"

"The nurse told me. That's why I followed the blood trail," I said.

"Any idea who shot him…before you did?"

I shook my head but didn't answer *no*. With the meeting being recorded, I didn't want to say too much.

"What happened when you walked into the classroom?"

"I saw the girl tied up, Carmody standing over her."

"He was holding a knife?"

"Yes."

In forty-five minutes, it was the first time I lied. I was surprised I had made it that long.

"Did it look like he was going to kill her?"

"It didn't look like they were gonna kiss," I said, and everyone laughed.

"Then you opened fire?"

"Twice."

It wasn't an interrogation, but it was starting to feel like one. Nothing he asked had revealed anything new. I could tell even the chief was getting impatient.

"Thank you, Captain," he said, cutting Flaherty off mid-sentence. "We get the idea."

He cleared his throat, loosened his tie. As a former football player and veteran, he could at times look fierce. But he was friendly and fair, and we all liked him. If he had brought the State Police on, it was probably because the mayor or governor had asked him to.

"Any evidence of accomplices?" he asked.

"We don't believe so," Egersheim said. They were all killed with the same knife. And Carmody had a motive."

It was the hardest question so far, but Egersheim answered it with ease.

"That's what I thought," the chief said, and then he looked at me. "Did you identify Cecily Madden?"

"This morning."

"That should be adequate for now. We'll get the autopsy photos over to Ireland."

He wrote something down and then peered up.

"As you know," he went on, "she was brought in for questioning yesterday after the incident. Right after she was released, she ran into Beacon Street and killed herself. Any idea why?"

"They were in love once. I think she couldn't handle knowing what Carmody did," I said, which in some ways was true.

The chief just raised his eyes. No one was interested in romantic endings.

"I've already spoken with the DA. I expect him to dismiss the case by Friday."

Egersheim, Harrigan, and I turned to each other, smiling somberly. The fact that the killer and victims were all dead brought some closure to the case, but it wasn't a cause to celebrate.

"If there's nothing else, I think we're done," the chief said, and everyone started to get up. "Good work gentlemen. I don't know if justice was served, but perhaps we prevented any more victims."

As we headed out, I saw Captain Flaherty coming toward me. Whether he wanted to shake hands or had more to say, I didn't know. But I darted out the doors before I could find out.

We continued down the corridor with intense relief. An investigation that could have ended all our careers was finally over.

At first, I had resented Egersheim for trusting Rowe. I'd assumed he'd done it out of selfishness —— we all wanted to get Carmody before the State Police did. But when we found out the truth, he acted more ashamed than guilty. That told me that at least some of his intentions were noble. Like in war, crime-fighting was always a balance between ethical choices. No one could do everything by the book all the time.

We walked into the captain's office to find Collins on the phone. He slammed the receiver and stood up.

"Who's that?" Egersheim asked.

Collins hesitated.

"My girl," he said.

"While on duty?"

"I ain't seen her in a while."

When the captain went over to his desk, Collins quickly got out of the way.

"You'll be seeing more of her now," he said.

Collins froze. His position had been temporary, a fill-in while Harrigan was out. I wanted him to stay on, but that was between the captain and chief.

"How do you mean, Sir?"

"Take a few days off, that's an order. Be back in my office by Wednesday morning."

Harrigan and I chuckled, but it was a tender moment. The excitement on Collins' face reminded me of my early years on the force when every promotion, praise, or attaboy meant the world. While those things still mattered, they would never be as important as family. When it came time for Collins to have his own, I only hoped he would realize it.

"Not sure what you two are laughing at," Egersheim said. "That goes for you, too. Effective immediately. Now everybody outta here!"

Sign up for Jonathan Cullen's newsletter to stay up to date on new releases.
https://liquidmind.media/j-cullen-newsletter-sign-up-1/

I'd love to hear your feedback! Consider leaving a review by following the link below and scrolling down to the review section.
www.amazon.com/B0BGQHSZ58

JONATHAN CULLEN

ALSO BY JONATHAN CULLEN

The Days of War Series

The Last Happy Summer

Nighttime Passes, Morning Comes

Onward to Eden (Coming Soon)

Shadows of Our Time Collection

The Storm Beyond the Tides

Sunsets Never Wait

Bermuda Blue

The Jody Brae Mystery Series

Whiskey Point

City of Small Kingdoms

The Polish Triangle

Love Ain't For Keeping

Sign up for Jonathan's newsletter for updates on deals and new releases!

https://liquidmind.media/j-cullen-newsletter-sign-up-1/

ABOUT THE AUTHOR

Jonathan Cullen grew up in Boston and attended public schools. After a brief career as a bicycle messenger, he attended Boston College and graduated with a B.A. in English Literature (1995). During his twenties, he wrote two unpublished novels, taught high school in Ireland, lived in Mexico, worked as a prison librarian, and spent a month in Kenya, Africa before finally settling down three blocks from where he grew up.

He currently lives in Boston (West Roxbury) with his wife Heidi and daughter Maeve.

facebook.com/jonathancullenbooks